WHITE HEAVEN WOMEN

JESSIE B. TYSON

WHITE HEAVEN WOMEN

http://jessiebtyson.blogspot.com

FIRST EDITION trade paperback

Imajin Books

August 30, 2012

ISBN: 978-1-926997-79-7

Cover designed by Ryan Doan: www.ryandoan.com and Sapphire Designs: designs.sapphiredreams.org

Praise for WHITE HEAVEN WOMEN

"Jessie Tyson evokes the sights, smells, accents and atmosphere of early 20th century northern England to give us a tale of reincarnation that marches past even our present times; a novel of hope and of the multiple chances that reincarnation provides the soul in search of enlightenment."—Shane Joseph, author of *The Ulysses Man*

"A terrifying tale of reincarnation, demons and protective blue ghosts. Debut author Jessie B. Tyson paints a literary landscape of bygone days so skillfully the main characters leap off the pages into our hearts."—Betty Dravis, best-selling co-author of *Six-Pack of Blood*

"Jessie has written a fast paced book with vivid characters. The sense of place is thoroughly described and puts the reader firmly in the scene—I could imagine everything clearly. Her main character is likeable and you will find yourself wanting to know what happens next. A great book to get lost in on a rainy day."—Dionne Lister, author of *Shadows of the Realm*

"Nobody knows how to entwine a novel together better than Jessie B. Tyson, as she draws us into a life with Beth, a young lady who seems to have the most complicated life and survival. Beth's path is paved with horror, suspense, the paranormal, life, death, love and hate all woven together with such powerfulness, so real, so fragile, yet gripping enough to keep you on the edge to know more. I fell in love with Beth and her sharp mind, fragile body, and her warm heart and you will too."—Peggy Grigowski, author of *A Glimpse of What If*

Acknowledgements

To my father, who showed me how to see a universe inside of a raindrop, and to know anything in life is possible if we believe and hold on to our dreams.

Blessings to my lifelong friend Judith Thompson for her loving friendship and hundreds of encouraging phone calls. If I could pick another sister, then she is the woman I'd choose.

A special thank you goes to Cheryl Kaye Tardif for her patient support until this story was completed.

The hymn, "I Sing a Song of the Saints of God," written by Lesbia Scott, first published in 1928 and found in the public domain.

"It is Christmas Day in the Workhouse," written by George R. Sims (1847-1922) in 1879 and found in public domain.

CHAPTER ONE

Whitehaven, Cumbria, England, 2000

Sally Witherspane spied screaming women racing from a thick fog, their blood-soaked skirts trailing on the muddy road. A ghoulish creature with cruel red eyes slithered into the walls of an old building. Sally glanced at her feet and saw a stiff blue skirt touching the top of beautifully beaded shoes.

Horse's hooves clip-clopped down a cobbled street. The stench of fresh horse manure floated in the damp night air and exploded in her nostrils. She couldn't escape the smell.

A woman's voice called out, "Lady Sarah, it's late. You'll catch a chill. Come inside. You don't want the red-eyed devil to find you and steal you away."

Sally frowned. "Where is this place?"

No answer from the woman, just the sound of a weighty door slamming, echoed by a roll of thunder and the patter of heavy rainfall.

Sally shivered in her drenched clothes.

A door appeared in front of her as she struggled to get away from the rain. "Help," she screamed. "This door is locked!"

Still yelling, Sally woke up in a lather of sweat. "Oh God, that dream was so real this time." She was clammy and her nightie was drenched. "And hell, all those screams. What do they mean?"

She showered, anxious to rid herself of the clammy feel of her sweat. As she dressed, the unstoppable north English sun surged like a search beacon across the mountaintops and entered through her window. She bathed in its warmth and made an early breakfast to eat while reading her favourite book, *Wuthering Heights*.

She'd read the book a thousand times and her attention wandered. She skipped the pages she knew well, waiting until a respectable hour to call Mrs. Harris, a local psychic she knew.

"I must know what my dreams mean," she muttered, her fingers dialling the number.

Mrs. Harris's answering machine picked up and an outgoing message belted into Sally's ears.

"Damn." She wanted to talk to the psychic in person and hated leaving messages.

When she finished speaking, she hung up and thought more about the dreams. She knew something supernatural had yanked her back to her birthplace in West Cumbria, a place she'd vowed never to return to. Yet there she was. She'd lived close to Lancaster University for the best part of five years. That was home until she reeled in a job as a columnist for West Cumbria's largest newspaper, the *White Heaven Weekly*.

Her new life was off to a good start.

The first week at the newspaper office flew by. Her boss, Dennis Baker, was known for his foul moods after his booze binges, but she received a lot of help from her co-worker, Peter Flannigan. Peter was a tall man, in his forties, with brown hair and remarkable grey patches at each temple. He had that handsome, middle-aged look and the animal magnetism that most single women of Sally's age sought. She was no exception.

Peter approached Sally on the afternoon break. "I know Dennis asked you to cover the past-life meeting on the weekend. I'm fascinated by anything paranormal and want to learn more about the psyche. Would you like a ride to the meeting?"

Before Sally could reply, he boldly leaned over and tenderly kissed her on the cheek. She twiddled her fingers through her hair, savouring the soft but masculine touch of his lips, and her thoughts flitted about like a pollinating honeybee. His lips felt so good. She wondered if she should let him pursue her now or wait until she'd written her novel.

Peter smiled. "Well, what do you say?"

"Oh, that's okay. I can get there on my own."

The frown on his face made his wrinkles appear more prominent.

Sally watched him as he returned to his desk. With a sigh she walked to the washroom, where she caught sight of her reflection in the mirror. For a split second, the reflecting image appeared blue and didn't look like her at all. Then it vanished.

"Must be my overactive imagination," Sally mumbled.

Sally walked home after work with thoughts of Peter preoccupying her. When she arrived at her cozy apartment, she poured a glass of brandy, flopped into a chair and flung her legs onto a leather footstool. She sipped the fiery nectar and contemplated the strange blue reflection. She drained her glass and checked her answering machine, hoping to hear some news from the psychic.

Nothing.

When it was time for sleep, she lay in bed and gazed at the moon through the skylight. It slipped behind wispy clouds.

All of a sudden, a heavenly floral aroma filled the air.

Hmm...the Wiccan elders taught me such Spirit scents are a good sign, so I'll not have any bad dreams tonight.

Sally fell into a blissful sleep with help from the brandy.

As dawn broke the following day, Sally awoke to the sound of distant thunder rolling ever closer to her home. Her heart pounded with each echo.

"I was happier in Lancaster," she muttered. "So why did I return to this damn waterlogged hole?"

She had read once that certain people have been on earth before and that something in their psyche makes them return to places in which they had lived. Maybe it was true. What else could make her return to this place?

A brilliant light suddenly engulfed her room, followed by a clap of thunder that rattled the windows and vibrated through the floor.

She shrieked and raced to the window to see what it was. The scene on the horizon left her speechless. A vortex of forked lightening hurled long, demonic claws tirelessly at the fells. Trees instantly burst into flames.

"Jesus, Mary and Joseph," she said. "It looks like hell has risen over there."

Torrential rain bounced three feet off the ground and water gushed down the storm drains beneath the window. Within seconds, the wind changed course and launched a deluge at her apartment building. Rain hammered at her window as if the devil were outside aching to break in to possess her. The glass creaked, threatening to shatter.

Bridled with sweat and stricken with terror, she threw her curtains together. Thinking it might be safer away from the window, she retreated to the doorway on the other side of the room.

As she stood under the protective doorway, she remembered what had happened to her friend Josie years earlier. One morning when Josie had opened her back door, she'd discovered a gaping hole in her garden.

Smoke had belched from the fissure.

"Like an entrance to hell," Josie had said.

The phone rang and snapped Sally from her train of thought. She snatched up the receiver and instantly recognized the psychic's voice on the other end.

"Hello, this is Mrs. Harris."

"Hells bells," Sally answered. "I am s-so glad you called. This s-storm's a bloody doozie, isn't it?"

"The worst these parts have had for many a year. Sally, don't be scared. Even though flood water is battling down the mountains a barrel a minute, you're safe. Your route to the past-life meeting tonight is all right."

Sally released a pent-up breath. "I saw a few lightning fires on the fells earlier. Good th-thing the storm put them out, Mrs. Harris, or the unfortunate mountain sheep would have been f-fried. Can you imagine *that* stink permeating down into each village? You know, this could be the basis for the novel that I've always w-wanted to write. I mean, why did I move to Lancaster to st-study for a writing degree if I don't use it? I could write a book on w-what people suffer during the f-floods of Cumbria. I could even call it *The F-floods of Cumbria*."

"Sally, calm down. You've developed a bad stutter. The damn climate is *not* why I called you. There are more important matters for you to write about than the weather conditions in this seemingly godforsaken area."

"Sorry, Mrs. Harris. It's my n-nerves."

"Yes, I know. The reason I rang is to remind you of tonight's past-life meeting at seven."

"Mrs. Harris, I'm s-scared frigging s-stiff of storms."

"That's probably why you're stuttering. All the same, you asked me for help with your nightmares. You'll have to pull yourself together and be strong if you ever hope to make sense of your dreams."

"What must I do?"

"Well, for one, I'm happy you returned to Cumbria in time to call me."

"In t-time? In time for what?"

"In time for me to enlighten you about tonight's past-life meeting, silly. You must attend to discover the truth. I already know you will never get another chance because this small, scared community might not tolerate another get-together such as this. You know how some people here feel about spiritual matters. They're leery about the subject. Isn't that one of the reasons you left Whitehaven in the first place?"

Sally mumbled a wordless reply, remembering the local yokels always drop their "H's" and pronounce Whitehaven as White 'eaven—the reason the local news office called their rag The White Heaven Weekly.

"Knowledge of your past is more important than your future, Sally."

"You lost me there, Mrs. Harris."

"Yes, I thought as much by the vacant expression on your face."

Sally chuckled. "How do you know what my expression is like? I didn't think psychics could see through a phone."

"I just know."

"Crikey, you have me all curious now. Are the buses still running? I'd like to get there dry and in one piece."

"You do remember that Cumbria lacks public transport on Sunday nights, don't you?"

"Oh, I had forgotten. Yes, I remember what the stupid bus service is like around here. I guess I'll have to walk."

"Okay. Just be careful which footpath you choose. Stay away from the river edges, Sally. They've overflowed before and have taken many lives."

"Yes. I'll take care. I'm determined to know what those nightmarish dreams of mine mean. Maybe it's all been my vivid imagination and...Mrs. Harris, there's no such thing as demons or phantoms, right?"

"Some experiences are not our imagination, but don't worry. Stay calm and don't fret about devils or ghosts. To make you feel better I will tell you this. When I heard your phone message the other day, I shuffled the Tarot cards on your behalf and noticed something quite extraordinary. I know who you were. I mean, I *believe* I know who you were in one of your past lives."

"Y-you already know who I was? Please tell me."

"Sorry, Sally, you must go through this first part unaided. I can't explain anything until it's perfectly clear to me. Just pay great attention to a woman called Lillian Canterbury tonight. She has the most remarkable story. For *you*. You might even glean a bit in relation to the devils you've dreamt about, as well."

"That sounds a bit p-portentous, Mrs. Harris. My new employer, Dennis Baker, chose me to cover the meeting tonight. I might as well be paid to learn about past lives, right?" She giggled awkwardly while chewing her upper lip.

"Remember to let me know what happens tonight," the psychic said. "You have my phone number."

Sally took a deep breath. "Can you tell me anything about Peter Flannigan, the handsome co-worker I mentioned to you?"

"Oh, yes. Sorry. I almost forgot about him. I can tell you he is a good-hearted man and he's not as meek as he wants people to believe. I do not know if he is the man for you though. I'd have to do another Tarot interpretation."

"He is a good-hearted man, eh? This is wonderful news, Mrs. Harris. Thank you. Bye."

Throughout Sally's childhood her mother had drummed into her that believers in reincarnation were afraid of death, and this was the reason mischievous spirits and goblins gained control of people in dreams.

Is one snatching at me in my dreams?

She relaxed by listening to gentle tunes on her CD player. From the corner of her eye, she saw a blue wispy shape slip into her washroom.

What in the hell was that? She scuttled into the bathroom and found nothing moving or anything that would reflect any light. She shrugged her shoulders and looked at the clock. *I must leave for the meeting. It's now or never.*

As the squall outside made its presence known, she threw on a raincoat and Wellington boots, grabbed her umbrella and left her flat. A mighty gust of wind blew her backward, throwing her hard against the sandstone doorway. It knocked the breath from her and she dropped her purse. "Damn!" she said, watching it skid into a murky puddle.

When she caught her breath, she peered up and down the street. Every curtain in every house was drawn. Not one store was open. Except for a few chimneys belching black smoke from coal fires, the town was lifeless. The imagery made her want to choose the easier option—return indoors and snuggle under her duvet. But that would be cowardly.

The opportunity of a great writing career is ahead of me if I cover tonight's meeting. If I back out now I could lose Peter's attentions as well as a grand occupation.

Her courage strengthened when she thought of her reward. She sucked a long, deep breath into her lungs, grabbed her bag, heaved it over one arm and stepped onto the road.

Within minutes the wind changed course and howled like a gnashing banshee. Paranoia gripped her. She looked for the owner of the cries, totally convinced a demonic spirit was inside the squall. Her eyes darted everywhere as blood raced through her veins.

But she saw no spirit wailing in the wind.

True to north English climate, the blustery weather clawed at her umbrella. It blew inside out, leaving her with no defence from the driving elements. She flung the busted umbrella, which now looked like an upturned dead spider, into a trash can and raced down the sidewalk, ducking in and out of doorways to escape the blustery deluge. In one entryway she questioned whether her motives were worth the torture she now suffered. She glanced back and saw forked lightening demolish the trashcan she'd just passed. The same lightning bolt then danced up the street like it had won a West Cumbrian weather prize.

The flattened garbage can reminded her of the dream in which she'd seen herself crushed to death. She didn't understand any of her dreams, least of all that one.

Gripped with fear she leapt from the doorway and sprinted down King Street as if chased by the hounds of Hades. She stopped to catch her breath in the entryway of the old Glessal's shop. It was in grave disrepair. The timber door was decayed and flaking away. Cement from the keystone had fallen off, making a messy pile on the ground. When Sally peered through the window, she spied a surreal blue glow shaped like a person.

It moved.

CHAPTER TWO

Sally blinked and the blue glow vanished.

"Just a trick of the light," she said with a huff.

Through the curtain of rain, she noticed the town hall clock and then saw a vintage Rolls Royce parked outside the *White Heaven Weekly* employees' hall. She smiled, speculating a celebrity was inside the hall.

But who would want to visit this remote hellhole?

She galloped up the hall steps and fumbled to find the door handle.

Without warning the ground shook with a deafening rumble. She turned around and saw smoke soaring up from a massive hole close to the old car.

Crikey, that lovely car could've been destroyed. And I could've been killed too.

Sally flung the door open with a mighty push and bolted inside like a three-year-old filly in season. She ran down the hallway until she found the meeting room. It was dark inside, except for three diffused lights on the far side. When her eyes adjusted to the low lighting, she realised the room was jam packed with people.

"Hello and welcome," the doorman said. "Still stormy out, I see."

Sally answered with a mumble.

"There's one seat left in the front row miss, on the far end right beside the stage." The doorman pointed out the way.

"Thank you." She stuffed the soggy ticket into the man's hand.

She found her seat and sat down. No one seemed to notice she was soaked except for a wrinkled woman in a wheelchair on the end of the same row. She gave Sally a sympathetic smile. The old woman looked ancient, reminiscent of an Egyptian mummy. Sally cracked a grin in return, more relieved to be out of the wicked downpour than to be friendly.

Many of the attendees appeared keyed up as they fidgeted and mumbled to each other. This made Sally wonder all the more why they were there. She didn't know the locals believed in this sort of thing. Matter of fact, they used to be scared shitless of anything different.

A high-pitched bell rang. The sound scared Sally so much, she gasped and jumped up. A man behind her giggled at her skittish reaction. The meeting commenced before she could snap at him.

A middle-aged woman wearing a long, black-buttoned dress stood up. "Hello, everyone. My name is Agatha Jones. Thank you for coming in such shocking weather. Please introduce yourselves and tell us your tales. Let's start with the back row."

One by one, people took their turn at the podium. Most of their stories were either so boring or so farfetched that Sally wondered whether they'd been spending too much time at the pub. After forty minutes, she decided their stories were as dreary as the weather outside.

Until Mrs. Lillian Canterbury stood up.

Lillian addressed the group in a bold, high-pitched voice. "Ladies and gentlemen, please allow me to introduce Mrs. Beth Madeleine." She indicated the fragile elderly woman who had smiled at Sally earlier. "She is 101 years young."

The crowd whooped and cheered.

"Mrs. Madeleine was born a noblewoman at a remote French convent during a raging electrical storm in 1899. She was christened as Lady Elisa Witherspoon. Her twin sister, Lady Sarah, died when their mother, Lady Constance Witherspoon, was giving birth. Sarah was killed instantly when the roof caved in, crushing her tiny body."

The crowd sighed compassionately.

Lillian paused for a second. "Everyone, we have reason to believe Lady Sarah has already reincarnated and is with us in this very room."

The audience looked around in awe.

Sally couldn't take her eyes off Beth Madeleine.

Could it be me? Was I Lady Sarah?

A tempest had killed Sarah back in 1899. That would explain why Sally was so scared of storms.

Is this why Mrs. Harris wanted me to come here tonight?

She wished the psychic hadn't been so bloody vague. She had so many unanswered questions.

Lillian held up a small, leather-bound book. "This is Lady

Constance's diary." A murmur swept through the room as she pointed to a line in the journal. "Lady Constance wrote here, 'The storm that killed my daughter is a punishment from God because I am not married.'"

Sympathetic moans rose from the crowd.

Lillian took a deep breath. "Back in those days it was taboo to be a spinster with children. Mrs. Madeleine, or Beth as we fondly call her, was born with the palsy, which we now understand could be cerebral palsy. In 1899, the doctors didn't know much about the disease. Beth's disability has left her unable to walk or articulate coherently, hence the reason why I'm here talking to you today instead of her."

All eyes were on Beth as murmurs of concern swept through the room.

"You might be wondering how or why I know so much about Beth's life," Lillian said. "Well, ladies and gentlemen, I know a great deal about her from over fifty journals that her mother had written. Amongst a multitude of subjects, the diaries mention frequent, glowing apparitions that have hovered around Beth throughout her life. These ghostly blue lights have been seen by countless people."

The audience cooed in amazement. A few excited people jumped up and waved their arms in the air, desperate to ask questions. And then Sally noticed Peter Flannigan in the crowd.

Why is he here?

Lillian interrupted her thoughts. "Please, if you have questions, I ask you to kindly wait until I'm finished. Thank you."

People returned to their seats, mumbling their disappointment. Sally, however, was glad Lillian didn't waste time answering queries.

"On occasion," Lillian said, "I'd noticed these radiances myself. The first time I saw one was many years ago. It was so transparent I could see the wall behind it. To be honest, seeing my first one scared the living bejesus out of me."

The audience laughed.

"You're right to laugh. I realised later on there was no reason for alarm. Well, not as alarmed as the inmates of Ginns Workhouse were many decades ago." Lillian giggled nervously. "A few people who lived there saw a black demonic shape with glowing red eyes."

A chill slithered up Sally's spine. *Oh my God. That sounds like the demon in my dreams.*

"Would you like me to tell you more of that time?" Lillian asked.

An excited *yes* echoed throughout the hall.

"All right, here goes. This diary says a huge beast materialized inside the workhouse and devoured two women. In my personal opinion, this could have been the reason why Ginns Workhouse closed its doors. The creature repeatedly revisited the building, even after several exorcisms were supposed to have spiritually sterilized the place. To stop local residents from asking more questions, each time the beast showed up local tabloids stated that a runaway bear from a passing circus had entered the building. Readers believed the editorials."

Lilian paused for a moment. "Only the descendants of the people who escaped the creature's torments knew what had really happened. The bishop didn't want the media to know that dark forces were afoot, so the church silenced them with threats of slinging all the witnesses into the most inhumane asylums in the country. This was enough of a threat to keep most people's mouths shut...except Lady Constance, the headstrong writer of this diary."

Lillian's tale about the beast of Ginns stunned Sally. She began to sweat. The people in the room were unable to contain themselves, desperate to have their questions answered. Arms shot into the air as cameras flashed and rampant applause broke out.

Lillian ignored the din while Agatha rang the bell several times.

"Please, ladies and gentlemen," Agatha called out. "Be patient. There will be time for questions at the end of the meeting. Please be respectful and allow this woman to finish speaking. Thank you."

The room slowly hushed.

"Thank you, Agatha," Lillian said. "Now with everyone's kind permission I will begin reading again from another journal. You can believe what I am about to disclose to you or not."

She lifted up a small ragged diary and held it high for everyone to see. Then she placed it back on the podium, opened its old yellowed pages and began to read.

"This attention-grabbing account begins in the Whitehaven Township in 1899 with these words, 'Dear diary, my mother does not know what my father is doing to me each night. I am only fourteen years of age and he has made me with child.'"

The room fell into a tomb-like silence with neither a breath nor a murmur audible.

"'If I tell Mama, whatever will she say? What am I to do? People will shun me.'"

Half an hour into the reading Sally was positive she'd read the story in a newspaper or magazine because it seemed so familiar.

When Lillian finished speaking, she asked the audience if they had any questions. A hundred hands rose into the air. Peter gave Lillian a chair so that she could answer questions in comfort. Then he slipped into the chair beside Sally.

"How gallant of you," she whispered.

"Well, I couldn't allow the lady to stand any longer, although it was actually a ruse." He grinned.

"A ruse?"

"To sit beside you."

She didn't know what to say at first. "Still, I think it was an endearing thing to do. Are you always chivalrous?"

"Only when you're around, my dear."

She grew hot and flushed. *Had* he put on the courteous display just to impress her?

"We'd best stop talking, Peter, or we'll miss what Lillian's saying. We can talk during the interlude. Okay?"

His fingers slid from his knee to her hand. "Okay, lass, I can wait."

Once Lillian had answered everyone's queries, the group took refreshments and mingled, discussing the night's proceedings. There was a long lineup of people waiting to meet Beth. Many who'd spoken to Sally said it was remarkable that the woman survived an era when horrible atrocities occurred to disabled children.

Sally deemed three areas under discussion to be incredible. Firstly, the red-eyed demon of Ginns, because she connected it to her own nightmares. Secondly, that Beth had used a wheelchair for almost one hundred years. And thirdly, she was enthralled about the blue spectre and wanted to know more about that.

I saw something blue in Glessal's store on my way over here.

The clock struck ten and the meeting ended with a great deal of applause for Lillian's presentation of Beth's story.

While Sally gathered her belongings, Peter said, "Would you like to grab a coffee?"

Although she'd enjoyed his attentions, she shook her head. "I'm sorry but I must decline. I have to submit my report to Dennis in the morning. Perhaps another time?"

"Sure. Another time then."

She headed in the direction of the exit but Peter caught up with her.

"Would you like a ride home, Sally?"

"No, thank you. I want to walk and think about what Lillian shared."

The sparkle left Peter's eyes.

She patted his arm. "I must finish writing my book before I can...do anything else. I do hope you understand. It's my priority right now. Maybe I can join you for a coffee when it's completed. You can help me celebrate."

He smiled. "Fine then. I'll look forward to it."

Pleased, she moved toward the exit.

As she passed Beth Madeleine, the old woman peered deeply into Sally's eyes. With a shaky voice and a devilish wink she said, "Hello, Sally."

Sally froze for a second, stunned. *How does she know my name?*

Beth gave her a sunny smile that, although gummy, seemed to brighten the entire room. Sally acknowledged the frail woman with a friendly nod but said nothing.

When she finally reached the exit, she noticed the weather had calmed.

She sighed with relief. *Thank God the tempest is over.* Her clothes were still damp from the trip to the hall. Sally strode home paying no attention to the puddles, completely swamped with ideas for Dennis about the evening's events and with some ideas for her own book. She arrived home twenty minutes later, turned up the heat and called Mrs. Harris.

No answer.

"The meeting went well," she said when the psychic's answering machine kicked in, "though I didn't learn much more about myself, neither past nor future. But Lillian's tale about a demon sounds like the one from my dreams. I'll talk to you later."

After hanging up she decided a hot shower would warm her, so she tore off her soggy clothes, soaked under the showerhead for far too long and then threw on her favourite pink flannelette pyjamas.

Settling down to a steaming cup of hot cocoa at her desk, she mulled over the evening's strange events. And Beth's story. She hoped to produce a fantastic story for the newspaper.

"Something sensational," she murmured. "Something—"

An electrical buzz seared through her body. Her mind went blank, her body rigid.

Her fingers danced across the keyboard. But Sally's mind was elsewhere.

CHAPTER THREE

Next morning, bleary eyed, excited and a bit dazed, Sally entered her employer's office, her submission gripped tightly in her hand. She barely remembered typing it. In her mind she could see herself sitting at the computer. She could hear the clacking of the keys. But the story? Why couldn't she remember writing it? How—

"Sally! I need to see you."

As she approached Dennis, she became aware of his strong body odour. He stank of liquor. The scowl on his face told her he was in a foul mood.

"I've brought my story," she said.

He snatched the papers from her hand and chucked them onto a pile on the far side of his desk. "I've changed my mind, Sally."

"You've what?" She gritted her teeth.

Noticing her expression he added, "Don't start anything. No disrespect meant. I've just decided the story isn't suitable for our type of readers, so let that be an end to it." Sweat ran down his crimson face.

Furious, she scrunched her brows together and mulled over everything she wanted to say but couldn't. *What a bad-tempered butthead you are, Dennis. You're nothing but a stinking drunk. You've wasted my flipping time. I could have had a good sleep instead of busting my ass off all night for you.*

Judging by the foul mood he was in, it would be no surprise to her if he fired her on the spot. He would have done so immediately if she'd expressed her opinions of him aloud. But she bit her tongue.

Without a word, she darted from his office, tears pooling in her eyes. Dennis reminded her of her father. When her father drank, he was rarely pleasant to anyone. *If Dennis is anything like my father, he'll shred my work. The drunken swine!*

Resentment simmered. She almost felt ready to quit her job.

At the far end of the office Peter gave her a reassuring smile and waved her over. Like a child in a sulk, she trudged across the room, her feet dragging along the linoleum and her head bowed.

"Now then, lass, don't fret just because Dennis threw your story out."

"He behaved like an utter asshole," she snapped. "Where the frig does he get off treating people the way he does? I stayed awake all night to make sure it was a grand story. I told him I didn't want to attend that frigging meeting because of the rotten weather. But he still made me go."

"Ah, don't fret, Sally. Just remember Dennis is a big-time boozer. He's always ill tempered the day after a binge. Give it time. You'll get used to his ways. I bet he looks at your submission when his hangover subsides a bit. You'll see." Peter hesitated. "Let me take you for a coffee at lunchtime. It'll cheer you up."

I'm in no mood for frivolity over coffee.

She shrugged. "Not today, Peter, but thank you."

He returned to his side of the office, a dejected look on his face.

Sally chewed her bottom lip. *Poor Peter. I can't keep rejecting him.* She didn't want to put him off altogether, so she called across the room to him. "I'll go with you for coffee another time, perhaps tomorrow. I'm going to be busy these next few weeks, that's all."

Peter's face turned red, probably because half the office knew he was interested in her. He kept his head low and continued working, ignoring the taunting laughter from his co-workers.

Sally ignored them too but she couldn't help but feel sorry for him.

At twenty-nine years of age, she was the youngest employee at the *White Heaven Weekly*. Part of her job as the office lackey was to serve the senior workers coffee and snacks. She wasn't happy about that. Like many new columnists, she wanted nothing more than to escape into writing.

Today she cleaned the communal cupboards and the disgusting kitchen sink, a job she hated. As she wiped and sorted, she muttered choice words, calling Dennis a *bastard* and other choice expressions beginning with the letter *F*.

She saw Dennis pick up her work at the end of her gruelling day.

"Sally. Bring me a coffee!" Dennis barked.

She poured his coffee and scowled because she'd taken enough coffee around the office for one day. *What am I, his bloody servant?*

She stomped into Dennis's office and deliberately banged the mug hard onto the desk. A few drops splattered on the wooden surface.

Dennis was reading the last few lines of her submission. Without looking up he said, "Don't worry about a few accidental drops, lass."

She was gobsmacked that he didn't yell at her for making a mess. She left his office, annoyed, even though he was reading her work right there and then. She barged past her co-workers' desks on the way to the coat closet, shoved the other staff coats out of the way, flung on her jacket and headed toward the exit door.

Behind her, Dennis rushed from his office, whistling and hollering at full volume, like a rowdy fan at a football match. "Sally. Hold on a minute there, girl. Your story is great. I'm putting it on the front cover tomorrow morning."

She stopped dead in her tracks. "Really? On the front page? Wow!"

"This is a first-rate piece of writing." He waved the papers in the air. "Your teachers at Lancaster University knew what they were doing for you to bang out a story like this. You've made a brilliant start to your first week. Well done."

"Oh gee, thanks." She wore an ear-to-ear grin.

Peter moved to her side and lowered his voice. "I told you he'd come 'round when his head had cleared, didn't I? Congratulations."

"Thanks, Peter. See you tomorrow."

"Come on, you've just received fantastic news. You should celebrate."

"I'm too exhausted."

"Okay then, sweet dreams. You've earned it. See you tomorrow."

"Tomorrow," she repeated.

Vivid dreams about Beth and her deceased twin sister, Sarah, disturbed Sally that night. Even seeing her story on the front page of the newspaper the next morning did nothing to distract her from dark thoughts and glaring red demon eyes.

Every night for a week, terrible visions had assaulted her sleep. During the day, her mind had wandered constantly to Lillian's revelations at the past-life meeting. It left her incapable of completing the simplest of tasks. Myriads of memories rushed through her mind. Night after night she dreamed she was the reincarnation of Beth's twin sister, Sarah.

One night she had dreamed that a demon was outside her door, trying to get in. She'd awoke in utter panic, sweat leaching from her skin. She had jumped out of bed and paced the room, sick to death of her damn nightmares. Either she had been dragged into the hysteria of past lives or she was going mad.

Am I reborn?

If she wasn't, then why did she sense such a close connection to a wizened old woman, whom she'd never met before?

What strange phenomenon makes me dream like this?

"These are worse than the dreams I had in Lancaster," Sally muttered. "Did I really see the demon of Ginns?" She let out a huff. "I must be mad. I'm even talking to myself."

The next day countless recollections erupted in her mind and played like an old silent movie. Should she call Mrs. Harris again?

She caught her reflection in the closet mirror. "Mrs. Harris will think I'm off my bloody rocker." She sighed. "Maybe I am."

Sally took the rest of the week off work in an attempt to catch up on sleep. Her co-workers rang numerous times, leaving several phone messages. She refused to answer their calls.

Peter Flannigan called three times to enquire if she was sick. "Please, Sally, call me back," his last message implored. "Let me know how you are. I'm worried about you. By the way, after your article was on the front page, the newspaper sold thousands more copies than normal. Dennis is thrilled. He can't wait for you to return to work and write more magic."

Sally smiled at his words but didn't call him back.

Mrs. Harris, the psychic, also called. "Sally, you *are* the reincarnation of Lady Sarah Witherspoon. It's imperative you return my call as soon as possible so I can help you with the second stage of your spiritual development."

The woman's message ricocheted around in Sally's brain until she finally rang her.

"I'm glad you called me," Mrs. Harris said. "You didn't say much the night of the meeting. I've wondered how things have been for you since then. Your message said something about demons?"

"Well, yeah. I haven't been in good health."

"I'm sorry to hear that. Haven't your nightmares stopped?"

"Hell no! They're worse. I had to take time off work because I've lost so much sleep." She took a deep breath. "Mrs. Harris, what's the matter with me? I'm still dreaming about evil spirits. Why?"

"You need to understand that some people just *think* they're reborn, while others actually have been. Like you. If you're in denial, Sally, it could be the reason why you're still having nightmares."

"I'm not in denial. I just don't consider myself special, despite the fact that I'm sure I've seen that demonic fiend of Ginns Workhouse in my dreams. And I do seem to know a lot about the old woman's life, so—"

"Which old woman?"

"The woman who lives with Lillian Canterbury. Beth Madeleine."

What Mrs. Harris said next shocked Sally to the core.

"Old Beth *knows* you are her reincarnated twin sister."

"You know this for sure?"

"As a matter of fact, I know more than you realise. You see, everything unfurls when the universal time is right."

There was a long silence.

"Well?" Sally snapped, tired. "Aren't you going to tell me what you know?"

"I don't want to natter about it on the phone. Can I come over? I know you're tired, but it could help."

"Yes, come over. Although I should warn you, my home is a mess and I haven't eaten properly in days, so I probably don't look too good."

"Don't fret about it, Sally. I'll be there in ten minutes."

Sally drew a blanket around her shoulders and curled up in the recliner with a cup of chamomile tea. She was in deep contemplation when Mrs. Harris arrived.

"This must be so confusing and upsetting for you, dear." The woman paused to look around the room. "You *are* in a bit of a mess, aren't you? You must pull yourself together, lass, and look after yourself or you'll make yourself poorly. Let go of all your old fears that your mother has instilled in you."

"Oh, you're good," Sally said. "How do you know what my mother said about past lives?"

Mrs. Harris laughed. "I'm a psychic, silly. Look, Sally. This is nothing to be scared of. It just depends which way you look at things. You're one of a small number of people to be reborn in the last fifty years. It's a gift that you must use to your advantage. Expand upon it to help the world."

"Expand upon it? I don't know what the hell you mean."

Mrs. Harris gave her a stern look. "Stop denying your own reincarnation! Write the story the spirit world has given you. You called upon them to give you a subject to write about for your bestseller, didn't you?"

Sally glared but said nothing.

"The spirits have graced you with a fantastic story," Mrs. Harris said, softening her tone. "They want you to tell the world about reincarnation, let humanity know it isn't just the belief of a few cranks. It is *real*. People like you are here to change the way the world thinks about spirituality."

Sally's mouth hung open. "You mean that is all my nightmares have been about? I have to write a flipping story about reincarnation?"

"Yes. However, there's more to do later on. For now, just concentrate on the story that the spirits have given you. You'd hoped and prayed for this, remember? You still want to write a book, don't you?"

How did the woman know so much?

"Yes, of course I do, Mrs. Harris. I just...I don't know. But I think I believe you."

The woman patted her arm. "You know in your heart it's true. Who else do you know who dreams the same as you with so much clarity, as though they're actually there? The world has worn blinkers for far too long. I mean, look what they did with witches in days of old. They burned them alive." She glanced at her watch. "I must go, Sally."

Mrs. Harris headed toward the door, then glanced at Sally with intense black eyes. "Do not second guess yourself."

Then she was gone.

Sally let out a ragged sigh. It had been a long, emotional day.

She thought about her deepest desire, to become a bestselling author. She'd never told anyone. *Mrs. Harris is right. Something has been telling me things while I've been asleep and I didn't pay attention. My dreams are telling me I'm the reincarnation of Sarah Witherspoon.*

"Sarah Witherspoon." She tested the name.

I'm insane.

That night she sank into a restful, dreamless sleep.

The following morning, Sally felt completely rested for the first time in days. Whether Mrs. Harris was right or wrong, she swore to tell the world the chronicles of Beth's family and of her own dreams. If people considered her crazy, so be it. The story had to be told.

She stared at the empty computer screen for what seemed like an eternity. Not knowing how to begin, she made another cup of tea, took a swig and sighed. Her fingers hovered over the keys, waiting for inspiration.

Waiting...

Her fingers flipped into autopilot. Clickety-clack. She began to type a story that began a century earlier in 1899 at Whitehaven, Cumberland, north England...

CHAPTER FOUR

Lady Hannah Witherspoon was a controlling, calculating woman who considered herself far superior to anyone.

"You'll tie the knot with any available gentleman who'll have you," she told her daughter. "You'd better marry and give that baby of yours a name, Constance, or mark my words, I will have both you and that little bastard you're carrying dumped in a convent. Lord help me, I will."

"Mother." Constance said in a sharp tone.

Later, Constance thought about her mother's threats. *I'm her only daughter. She will never do it.*

Three months passed by with Hannah constantly nagging her strong-willed daughter to marry someone...*anyone*...or else. Most of the time, Constance laughed in her mother's face and walked away.

Sir Mathew Vermont had been Hannah's first choice all along, but Constance refused because he was more than twice her age.

Hannah prepared the local gentry. "My daughter will be going to visit an elderly aunt soon. She will not return for at least six months, possibly more."

Upper-class girls in Cumberland often went away for weeks or months on end to assist older relatives or to attend finishing school, so people thought nothing odd about Hannah's statement.

When it became obvious that Constance was with child, Hannah had her whisked away during the night and taken to the Sisters of Charity, a twelfth-century convent in the south of France. It sat on a gradual slope and looked more like a small bastion than a house of God, with its thick, strong walls and spire. The convent housed forty-three nuns, three novices and a dozen or so disadvantaged orphans.

The day Constance's labour pains began, a dreadful storm raged. Three lightning bolts that looked like an electrical tidal wave cracked the roof wide open. Large sections of roofing slate and timber slid to the ground, allowing heavy rain to gush through. The walls shook with each strike, but the stones held fast. Wild, electrical surges vibrated the windows, which shattered, sending long, colourful stilettos of stained glass everywhere. Several nuns broke their vow of silence and screamed as they raced down fifty steps into the crypt for safety.

Constance agonized with contractions. It was as though her babe did not want to come into this world. The nuns who didn't leave were afraid they would lose mother, child and their convent in the frightening tempest.

Hours later, at the exact moment the squall subsided and the skies calmed, the astonished nuns discovered that Constance was expecting twins. The first to be born was blue-eyed Sarah. The nuns laid her in a crib beside the birthing bed. Sarah's twin sister came into the world seconds afterward. Without warning the nuns heard a sudden rumble and large chunks from the severely damaged roof caved in on top of both babies. Sarah died instantly as huge stone slabs crushed her to death. Her sister, struck by dozens of smaller missiles, had blood oozing from her head. Her face was unmarked, though colorless and pale, without any sign of life.

The nuns dug out both newborns from beneath the rubble with their bare hands, thinking they were both dead...until a tiny dusty hand moved. The infant fought for life and survived.

The thankful young mother named her surviving newborn Lady Elisa after a kind, sympathetic grandparent. Her pet-name for Lady Elisa was Beth.

The nuns covered Sarah's broken body with a white sheet and placed her on what was left of the Altar.

Half a dozen villagers arrived the following day to fix the convent roof and windows. When they finished a few days later, the building looked as if the evil storm had never taken place.

The funeral for the lifeless babe was held the same day. As they interred Sarah inside her miniscule coffin, a dozen angelic looking orphans sang hymns. Directly afterward a small remembrance plaque was set in place. A simple etching on the plaque said, *Lady Sarah Witherspoon, 1899.* Before, during and after the funeral, Constance was unable to stop weeping. She asked if she could remain at the convent to convalesce. The nuns agreed.

When three weeks had passed by, to the joy of the nuns and the mother, Beth gurgled and wriggled energetically. To them, it was an outward sign of her good health and strength. She showed no signs of any injuries from the storm.

After two months Constance said to two nuns cooing around Beth's crib, "I feel like my old self again, Sisters. I'm much stronger and so is my baby. I'm completely over my initial disbelief of being with child and plan to return to Whitehaven. I will take my darling Beth with me."

One of Sister Francesca's eyebrows tilted downward showing she was troubled.

"You must do whatever you think is best, my child. However, we must tell you that your mother sent a message with your escort. Her instructions stated we must keep your fatherless child here. Those were her words, not ours."

"My mother said what? How dare she insist on this?"

Constance noticed the nun's disappointed face and stopped yelling. A long silence ensued before she spoke again.

"No, Sisters, I refuse to leave my Beth here. I do know you would take good care of her, except I'm her mother and I want to take full responsibility for her. I plan to masquerade my baby as a distant cousin's child until I locate the man I can love and marry."

"You are a feisty-willed teenager. I'll give you that," Sister Monica, the younger nun, said.

Sister Francesca interjected. "Even though your child is fatherless, I am pleased you have come to this conclusion. You have our blessing for wanting to keep your babe with you." Her eyes shone with loving approval.

"Will you return to visit us from time to time? You will, won't you? We'd love to see your baby grow."

"Very well. Although I cannot promise, I will make an effort to return when she is two years old. In the meantime, I will send you her painted likeness when she reaches six months old and again when she is one year old."

Young Sister Monica clapped her hands and spun around like a top. The nuns helped Constance pack. The following day, they said their goodbyes.

The trip home was gruelling, with brutal seas and waves lashing across the ship's deck. Constance and her babe were dry and somewhat safe in a cabin below decks.

When they arrived at the manor, the older servants scurried around to welcome her home. Constance informed Ingrid, her personal maid, that her baby was her cousin's child. Ingrid believed her. She prepared both Beth and mother for bed then returned to the servants' quarters, where high-spirited gossip began.

"Hey everyone, the wee baby Lady Constance returned home with is her cousin's bairn, the one whose husband died."

"Ah, then it must have been her cousin who was sick, not her aunt." The cook paused for breath, grinning from ear to ear. "Well, hasn't this been a nice turn of events, Ingrid. We have our bonnie Constance back, as well as a bubbly baby. With any luck, things will be happier 'round here."

"Yes, our young lady might be spoiled and wilful, but I enjoy having her around. You know, I have missed her. It's been rather quiet without her."

"It's not been exactly quiet, Ingrid. What about that old rat bag Hannah? She never shuts up complaining, does that one."

"Hush, Cook. She'll hear you, then you'll be for the high jump. And hey, I meant it's been quiet without our Constance being around. I didn't mean the old bag had been quiet."

"Just joshing you, Ingrid. You'd best be quiet now though. Someone might hear *you*."

The next morning, Lady Hannah was furious when she discovered Constance had returned home with her baby.

"Why did you bring the infernal thing home? I explicitly told the nuns not to allow you to return with it. Your baby is not welcome here and neither are you, if you do not marry."

"Mother, I've informed the house staff that Beth is my cousin's child. No one will ever know she's mine."

"Beth! You called it Beth. How dare you name her after a relative?"

"Well, my baby's name has already been registered as Lady Elisa Witherspoon, so it cannot be changed. Besides, mother, I do not want to marry any man that I don't love."

"Pah! Love indeed. I've told you before that love has nothing to do with your baby being a bastard, and it will remain one unless you marry. Constance, I will not have a bastard child in my house. When you marry, we will have to tell people that your husband died in France one week after the ceremony. No one will know any different."

Constance stuck her nose high into the air and left the room.

"Come back here this minute, child! How dare you walk away when I'm talking to you?"

Ingrid had been cleaning rugs in the hallway and heard the fracas. She ran to tell the staff in the scullery.

Cook was the first to realize the truth about the baby. "Oh my God,

Ingrid. It's the child's own baby she's came home with. We'll have to watch our backs now. Hannah will be beside herself for sure. She'll be on the warpath for anyone who gets in her way."

"I agree with you there, Cook. Nothing's as sure as she'll take it out on us lot. Never did I think Constance would have a baby out of wedlock. She didn't bother with men. Yes, she's fiery, and that's a fact, but she's too young to be a mother."

"I know, Ingrid. What I want to know is, when did she ever leave the manor to get pregnant in the first place?"

"Hey, you're right there! I don't think she ever stepped a foot further than the garden alone."

"Ingrid, I've just thought of something. You don't think it was the night when her father..." Her eyes widened.

"Hmm. You got a point there, Cook. We thought he just beat her, but it makes sense. What other man's been near the girl? The male staff here wouldn't lay a hand on her."

Word about Beth escaped out of the manor, and all hell broke loose as the community flurried with gossip. People called Constance a common harlot. Furious about the whole affair, Hannah snarled at her daughter, "If you had listened to me in the first place and got married, my girl, there would be nothing for them to gossip about."

"I don't care about their tittle-tattle, mother. We hardly ever see anyone, so why should I let gossip mar my joyful motherhood? Besides, they're just people from the common herd and not well-bred, as we are."

Hannah shrieked, "Well, I care what people say! Why in precious name did you bring your infernal child into this house, when I explicitly told you not to? I knew they would eventually discover the truth. Our family name has been blackened enough."

Constance flung her heavily embroidered shawl around her shoulders, tossed up her head as high as heaven and ran upstairs to see her daughter.

A couple of months later, against her mother's wishes, Constance took a trip to Whitehaven to buy lace for her daughter's cot cover. She had no trust in any servant to purchase the genuine product because only Nottingham lace would do. With her cape wrapped around her shoulders and Beth clutched to her bosom, she exited her carriage to walk to Glessal's store on King Street.

At the same time a rough-looking woman wearing threadbare clothes bellowed across the cobbled street while pointing her finger at Constance. "Hey, Fred, look over yonder. It's the Witherspoon harlot dressed in all 'er finery with that bastard baby of 'ers in tow. She thinks she's oh so special, she does, tossing 'er nose up as she passes by. Well now, look what airs and graces got 'er. A misbegotten baseborn. And folk say she's a lady? Lady, my foot. She's a bleeding tramp."

The woman's jeers ended with high-pitched cackles and frenzied laughter.

Another woman added, "No man other than the father of it will have Constance now. I heard somebody say the father of her little bastard is the devil himself. To be honest, I believe even that evil fiend doesn't want it. Hell, have you good people seen it? The wretched thing can't stop thrashing around."

Constance's face dropped in sheer astonishment. How could they talk about a baby in such a way? Furious, she turned to face the woman, who glared fiercely back. Constance was rendered speechless for the first time in her short life. The wild, vicious expression on the woman's face had frightened Constance. She wanted to say that she had no doubt they had done worse things against the divinity, but at that moment another passerby threw a rock at her. She ducked in time to avoid it. As the stone soared past Constance's head, it hit the carriage and left a deep gouge on the beautifully carved redwood frame. Constance hoisted her skirt up, spun around and climbed back on board the coach. She placed Beth on the seat and pulled down the brown leather window blind. The frightened teenager held her tear-covered face in her hands and screamed at the driver, "Aren't you going to say something to these...these ruffians?"

The driver didn't utter a sound.

Realising he wasn't about to defend her honour, Constance snarled at him, "Driver, take us home. Now!"

"Righty-ho, milady," he said with a wide, scornful grin, as if he hated her. He flicked the reigns and used them like a whip on the horses' backs.

When the carriage turned the first corner, a man joined in the fray, yelling his two pennies worth. "Oye, Constance. You are such a high and mighty cow. You should've drowned your devil child at birth. All deformed people are evil spirits walking the earth. You must be in league with the devil to give birth to a bairn like yours."

A woman leaning out of a second-floor window threw dirty water at the carriage, frightening the horses. One horse reared up on its hind legs and fell over, landing onto the back of the second horse and pummelling it with its hooves.

Another woman shouted, "Look! That wicked spirit child 'as even got the poor horses afraid."

"Demons. I agree with you," said a woman wearing a large feathered hat. "They're trying to bring on Armageddon, I tell you. Before long, there'll not be enough churches left for good people like us to take refuge in. And if those damn devils 'ave their way, they'll burn our churches to the ground. Evil they are."

The carriage driver smirked and muttered under his breath, "She asked for all she gets, the young tramp."

Constance arrived home panic stricken.

"I should have listened to mother," she cried while racing to her quarters to find her personal maid.

After she told Ingrid what had happened, her maid paused for a moment and then muttered sheepishly, "Begging your pardon, milady. The mocking won't stop 'til you wed your baby's father."

Of course Constance knew this was impossible and bellowed, "Oh, do be quiet, Ingrid. You've no idea what you're talking about. Go away, you stupid woman!"

Her mother seemed enraged at the town's gossipers and again tried to force Constance to marry Sir Mathew Vermont, in spite of knowing who the real father was.

"Mother, you've said this before. You know I can't stand the Vermont family. They're terribly unfriendly and utterly snobbish."

"Constance, if you do not marry Mathew Vermont and give that damned bastard baby of yours a name, then I will have no other choice but to commit you to Garlands Asylum."

"Mother! I can't believe this. How can you threaten your own daughter with that?"

"Child, our family honour must be protected, at any cost. And if that means putting you in there, then this is what I'll do. Then people would understand your behaviour." Hannah glared at her daughter as if her eyes were going to burst from their sockets.

"Oh, sweet angels above. I can see it in your face. You'd do it, wouldn't you? You would put me in there."

Her mother had finally gotten through to her. She narrowed her eyes as if daring Constance to make her carry out her threat.

Constance changed her voice to one of gentle pleading. "Mother, please. Mathew might be tall, but he's far from handsome and besides, I'm much too young for him."

"Child, Mathew is just one of a mere handful of single men in this area with a respectable background and enough money to keep a wife. Constance, he is the only one left. You've refused all the others."

"But mother, he is ugly and so old."

"Poppycock! Looks or age has nothing to do with this, Constance. Your child needs a father."

"Mother, Mathew is old enough to be my father."

Her face turned ashen at the mention of Constance's father and her voice sharpened, "You silly, foolish child. Mathew has money. You need money to survive."

"Mother, I flatly refuse!" Constance tossed her head high into the air, picked up her skirt and whooshed into the library for peace, slamming the door. The thud shook the painting beside the door, sending it crashing to the floor, breaking its frame.

Her mother had seemed furious as well as nervous. Constance thought there must be a part of her that didn't want to commit her only daughter. She was well aware of Constance's tornado-like temper, so hopefully she would leave her alone to reflect for a while.

Constance paced in the library with growing feelings of animosity toward her mother. Her chest heaved as she breathed fast, as if her lungs would rupture if she didn't calm down. She grabbed a few books and threw them out of the open window. They landed with a thud in the garden beneath. Constance's heart was breaking. She dashed to her bed in tears. Exhausted with crying so hard, she dropped off to sleep.

When she awoke an hour later, she glanced at the painting of Aunt Betsy on the bedroom wall. She smiled. *Yes, that's it. Aunt Betsy will help me. But how can I tell her what mother plans to do with me if I do not follow her wishes? Auntie doesn't know it was me who was pregnant. She'll surely be ashamed of me.*

CHAPTER FIVE

For the first time since Sally Witherspane began typing, she moved her aching eyes away from her computer screen, worn out, her mind a vacuum. She edged across to her bed as if her legs were gangly and weak. The second her head hit the pillow, the ancient historical name for Whitehaven echoed rhythmically inside her mind's eye. *Whittengomotte... Whittengomotte... Whittengomotte...*

Although Sally had acknowledged that she *could* be Lady Sarah reborn, she fidgeted around on her bed, wondering if it were true. *If not, then how is it possible for me to write as much as I have about the lives of women I do not know?*

She hadn't studied any notes from the past-life meeting since writing the first chapter and it began to trouble her.

All of a sudden, a strange pulsating blue light manifested at the foot of her bed and a humming voice resonated throughout her room.

"Speak to Lillian. Speak to Lillian Canterbury." The voice reverberated, pinging off each wall like a rubber power ball.

Sally sprung up into a sitting position on the edge of her bed and her wide eyes searched every nook and cranny.

The voice returned with a significant sighing tone.

"Don't be afraid," the echo uttered. "It is I, Constance Witherspoon." It whooshed around, ricocheting up and down each wall, gaining quicker momentum with each bounce.

In a cold sweat, Sally lunged off her bed and hurled herself toward the door.

"Sally, stop. Wait! Please do not be afraid. I'm here to help you remember." The voice echoed around her room once again and spun into her closet.

The sound suddenly stopped.

Sally placed her hands on either side of her face. Her skin felt cold and bloodless.

The deafening silence continued. Her eyes searched every corner and cubbyhole to find the owner of the voice. She mulled over the events and decided if she didn't discover who had been speaking then she'd go to her doctor to tell him she was hearing voices and needed psychological help.

She glimpsed a cornflower blue light radiating from inside her closet. It grew intensely luminous, akin to the beacons at cliff shores to guide ships past treacherous rocks.

"My dear child, you are not mad." The echo hummed and reverberated, pulsating to the rhythm of the voice.

Sally didn't know whether to listen or make a run for the exit.

"Dear Sally, there is so much in the universe you do not understand," the voice whispered.

"Whoever you are, this is not funny," Sally said, panic stricken and sweaty.

"Child, do not be afraid. I really am the spirit of Lady Constance. I'm here to help you put pen to paper, to complete the novel you want to write. Please go to the manor and speak to Mrs. Lillian Canterbury. She will give you my journals. They will help you finish our story." The pulsating voice slowed and then stopped.

Sally gasped, as if she were taking her last breath, and froze. Then she heard a different, softer voice.

"Come along, Mother. Let's leave Sarah alone for a while. She is tired. And she is frightened. I don't like her feeling frightened."

Sally giggled uneasily. "What in God's name is going on in here? Why did you call me Sarah?"

"Because you are...because you are...because you are..."

"All right," Sally screamed. "I'll admit I've mulled it over. Mrs. Harris told me I was Lady Sarah Witherspoon in another life, okay. But do you really expect me to believe the spirit of Lady Constance spoke the words I just heard a moment ago? C'mon now, whoever you are. Ghosts don't exist." Sally heard nothing but silence. "Answer me, damn you!"

Still no sound. Just the wind whistling through a small crack in her skylight window.

"You're probably some dipstick who lives in my building and is playing a prank on me." She paused, waiting for a nonexistent reply.

"And who does the other voice belong to? It's that damn awful Mrs. McKinney on the top floor, isn't it? You're such a bitter woman, McKinney. You never did like me. Damn it, which one of you is shining that frigging blue light in my face. Turn the bloody thing off!"

Gentle female laughter echoed. "Calm yourself, Sally. Rest assured this is not a hoax. Please just do as I ask. You will receive solid proof of everything very soon. Now, my dear, go to Forsythe Manor to collect my journals from Lillian Canterbury. Before long, everything will be made clear to you. Just do this one thing first. I promise you will never regret it...regret it...regret it..." the voice echoed, repeating over and over, until the light shrunk in size and slipped into a tiny gap in the closet wall. The echo stopped and appeared to follow the glow and it seemed like the crevice sucked the light into it.

The room fell dark and silent. Sally panicked. *What the...what just happened?*

She leaped up to turn on a light and raced into her bathroom. She doused her face with cold water, feeling altogether shaken at what had taken place. As she dried her face, she gazed at her reflection in the mirror and pointed her forefinger toward her own reflection. "You, my girl, have gone flipping barmy. You're talking to yourself. And there's no such thing as ghosts."

She flung her head 'round and returned to lie on her bed, leaving the light on all night. Before she fell asleep, more visions careered around her mind. She saw so many that she bounced out of bed and paced her room, lathered in sweat.

"For pity's sake. All right, all right! I will visit Mrs. Canterbury to resolve these stupid visions of mine once and for all, for peace. I cannot continue like this. I'm bloody knackered."

She pulled a bus schedule from inside her bedside drawer. *Hmm, a bus is due at nine tomorrow morning. Great. I can board a bus on the next street and be home by early afternoon.*

Now it was the small hours and she had no idea if she would get rest that night or not. Sally made herself a cup of hot cocoa and then showered to wash off the night's perspiration. When she felt clean, she threw on her favourite pink cotton pyjamas and set her alarm for seven thirty. She climbed back into bed and was in deep REM slumber in minutes.

The following morning Sally's digital alarm startled her. It buzzed like a gigantic bee was stuck inside the clock's mechanism. With half-closed eyes she leapt from her bed to silence the irritating hum and threw the clock into her laundry hamper. When she fully opened her eyes, she noticed the sun streaming through the small stained-glass window opposite her bed. Its colourful rays cascaded over everything in her room.

"Hey, no blue light," she said giggling. As she headed for her bathroom, she banged her knee on her bed's footboard. "Frigging shit! You stupid frigging bed. I hate you."

She hopped the rest of the way on one leg, muttering profanities under her breath. By the time she finished her shower, the throbbing in her knee had subsided, despite the fact that she had an enormous bruise. When she finished the rest of her morning ablutions, she grabbed her green summer coat and left her home.

While Sally waited at the bus stop, a fat-breasted robin chirruped on a branch high above the bus shelter. Other birds joined in its song as though welcoming the sunshine, which continued to grow hotter. Her bus arrived and the driver dropped her off a mere five minutes' walk from Forsythe manor.

As she approached the huge red sandstone building, Sally tried to imagine what it had been like for Beth when she was still young and lived in the old building. Her imagination ran amok with pictures of what the interior of the historical building would look like. The outside looked wraith-like and menacing, even beneath the warm rays of the sun. She continued walking with uncertainty toward the arched entranceway of the gatehouse. Its carved finials looked like eyes, watching, waiting, sending a chill up her spine. She shuddered as she scurried through.

A little further up the dirt lane, Sally marvelled at the appearance of the half-mile-long boulevard with its rows of multi-coloured rhododendron bushes and different breeds of rabbits bobbing about beneath them. As she paused to enjoy their innocence, she spied three red deer grazing in a thick copse nearby and a sheepdog resting in the shade. On the opposite side of the thicket, a sandstone seat baked in the sunshine. She paused in the dappled sunlight for a few moments to stare back at the archway and wondered why she had felt so nervous of its carvings.

The temperature rose dramatically, so she wandered around and under trees and bushes to find shade for the rest of her walk. When she reached the manor's grand entrance door, she shivered at the sight of even more ghoulish carvings on the huge stone doorframe.

She didn't know what she would find inside, but she needed some answers. Inhaling deeply, she held her breath to the count of three and grabbed the massive doorknocker.

CHAPTER SIX

Sally stood there for what seemed like an eternity.

Finally, an elderly gentleman dressed like an old-world butler in a black and white penguin suit opened the massive carved door. He looked directly into her eyes. "Hello, milady. I am John, the doorman. We've been expecting you."

The old man beckoned her to cross the threshold and go inside. As he opened the door wider, it creaked louder and louder. Sally imagined it was a huge mouth opening to swallow her whole and froze, glued to the spot. Her legs trembled like jelly. *Oh cripes. This is as scary as a horror movie, but I've come too far to turn back now. Just a minute, how in the world did he know I was visiting today? And why did he call me milady?*

John silently raised his right arm and pointed with his index finger at a huge double door on the far end of the hallway. With the old man hobbling beside her, she walked along the hallway, her feet heavy as if she had lead in the soles of her shoes. As soon as they reached the open door, Sally noticed Mrs. Lillian Canterbury sprawled on a velvet chaise longue beside a huge bay window, gazing into nothingness. It looked like she was in a trance. John coughed as he presented her visitor.

"Excuse me, Mrs. Canterbury. Your young lady is here."

The woman shook her head as if to escape her trance-like state and shakily stood up.

"Thank you, John. That will be all."

Mrs. Canterbury reached to shake Sally's hand. "Hello, dear. Thank you for coming. Please, do take a seat."

"Thank you, Mrs. Canterbury."

Sally sat on the front edge of the chair closest to the door in case she needed a quick exit. The bookcase to her right brimmed with books bound in black leather that had gilding. To its right was a desk and on its surface, a dark-blue quill pen stood proudly beside a vintage typewriter. Sally turned her head to look out the bay window and saw a beautiful view of a lush green glade overflowing with wildflowers, complete with a miniature brown-and-white piebald pony grazing in among a few sheep.

Mrs. Canterbury sighed contentedly.

"Isn't this a lovely room, Sally? I much prefer this morning room to any other room in the manor. It's the blue. I just love blue. It's so clean and fresh, although the music room is nice and cheery too. It's been painted a warm sunny yellow, with hints of green and purple."

"Yes, Mrs. Canterbury, it is a lovely room. Sorry for changing the subject, but I'm curious how you knew I was coming here today?"

"It is not important. What is important, is you. And please, do call me Lillian."

"I'm important, Lillian?"

"Yes, my dear lady, you are important." Lillian paused.

To fill the silent void, Sally told Lillian what had transpired in her bedsit the previous night.

"Lillian, you may think I'm insane when I speak of this. You see, last night I saw a pulsating blue light in my bedroom and then a ghostly female voice said it was the spirit of Lady Constance Witherspoon. The voice told me to visit you to collect some journals. I guess they're the ones you read at the past-life meeting?"

Sally paused when she saw Lillian staring as if she was looking right through her. Her expression sent a chill up Sally's spine.

"Well, that strange voice instructed me to obtain some journals from you, Lillian, to help me write a story about the people who used to live here. And then I heard another voice much different than the first one. Faint and almost childlike. It said I was..."

Sally stopped talking when she realised tears were cascading from Lillian's eyes. "Beth," Lillian muttered excitedly, "it was Beth."

"What?" Sally said. "How could Beth..."

She paused again when Lillian abruptly sat up and reached across to a side table. She grabbed a dozen journals from inside the table drawer and offered them to Sally.

"These inscriptions are just on loan. A funeral will take place at the manor tomorrow. So please return these volumes after the interment."

Sally nodded while flicking through a few pages. She found them fascinating. They overflowed with love and passion as well as humiliation, fear and pain. Her fingers sensed a strange energy force emitting from the books as if the pages themselves had life. The tingling entered her fingertips, and she felt more alive, as if the sensation had energized her. Sally stuffed the journals into her bag before Lillian could change her mind.

Lillian was still wiping away tears. As Sally lifted her head, she observed a strange expression in Lillian's eyes. With an airy, faraway sound to her voice, Lillian whispered, "Yes, Sally, you do look like her."

"I look like whom, Lillian?"

"You look like Lady Constance, my dear. See the painting over there, the three women sitting around a table?"

With a tear-soaked white handkerchief stuffed in the same hand, she pointed to a picture above the fireplace.

"Do you see the lady wearing the pretty blue chiffon gown on the far right, the one displaying royal demeanour?"

Sally strode toward the painting to get a better look.

"That's Lady Constance. Can you see the resemblance now, dear?" Lillian asked.

"Sorry, Lillian, no, I don't see anything. What am I supposed to see?"

"Oh, child, the resemblance, the resemblance," Lillian said with an irritated tone to her voice. "I'm talking of your resemblance to the Witherspoon women. Tsk, tsk. You young people must learn to use your eyes, not just the eyes in your head but the eyes in your heart."

"What? Don't be ridiculous, Lillian. I'm not a Witherspoon."

"Sally, look at the woman beside Lady Constance in the painting, the one wearing the pink lace gown. That's Beth when she was about your age. The other woman, wearing green, is Duchess Charlotte."

"I don't understand any of this, Lillian. My family name is Witherspane. S-p-a-n-e. Not s-p-o-o-n."

"Sally, I know you were adopted."

"Yes, I was, when I was so young I couldn't even walk. My adoptive mother's name is Mrs. Smith. She never told me who my real mother was. All I know is an elderly gentleman handed me to her and he gave her instructions to baptize me as Sally Wither*spane*. Mother said the old man was nearly a century old."

Lillian nodded in agreement.

Sally continued, albeit in a halting voice. "A fund came with me, enough to put me through university, twice."

"Twice. Why twice, Sally?"

"Well, I failed the first time because I fooled around instead of studying and had to re-sit all the exams. Anyway, Lillian, I succeeded last year, at twenty-eight years of age."

Lillian applauded while smiling, seeming pleased to hear of her success.

"Yes, yes. That old man was Sir Derek Witherspoon. You, Sally, were the last child that he fathered before he died in the latter part of 1971, at almost 96 years of age. The Witherspoon's are renowned for their longevity. I've an idea why he lived such a long time. It was the booze. It must have pickled him."

Both women giggled at the joke.

"Sally, I don't know why the spelling of your name is different. Perhaps your adoptive mother misheard Sir Derek and misspelled it. You are a Witherspoon right enough. Can't you see that, dear?"

Sally screwed her face up as if she tasted a sour lemon and shook her head.

"Where do you think your financial support came from? Your adoptive mother, Mrs. Smith, was not wealthy."

Sally moved toward the painting again. Nothing Lillian had mentioned clicked in her brain. *Why am I in this old house anyway? My adoptive kin were never well to do and no one ever talked about royal ancestors, although I wonder who my real mother was.*

She moved backward away from the work of art and paused to gaze at the painting once more. Lillian seemed to scrutinise her face.

"Can you see it now? Yes, Sally. You can, can't you?"

"I'm not sure," Sally mumbled.

"I know you see it, you darling child. You were the last offspring of Beth's father, Sir Derek. Oh, you're a Witherspoon right enough. One only has to look at you. Look at the two Witherspoon women in the painting again."

Sally studied the painting closer, trying to find a resemblance.

"You see, Sally, Sir Derek Witherspoon was never faithful to Lady Hannah, probably because he married her at seventeen years of age. He wasn't mature enough to enter into marriage and Hannah was even younger than him. Derek sired many children throughout his life and this is why all the kerfuffle began. When you were born in 1971, Lady Sarah's spirit was reborn into you. You were the last child Derek fathered before he died. Sarah's spirit waited for the last Witherspoon birth."

"All what began, Lillian?"

"Sir Derek fathered Beth and you in your last past life. When your soul visited earth in 1899, your life was fleeting. You died at birth in the midst of a raging storm. The convent records stated that three thunderbolts struck the building on the night you were born, or should I say, the last time you were born. You see, Lady Sarah died just as the third lightning bolt struck the convent."

Sally's mind wandered to her fear of thunderstorms. *Maybe it's because lightning killed Sarah and her soul is inside me*. She stopped reflecting as she realised Lillian was still talking about Derek.

"And then Sir Derek fathered you again in this life. Beth's deceased sister, Sarah, was reborn into you. So he fathered you twice."

Sally gasped. "Lillian, those dreams I dream. It must be because I'm Sarah, born again, right?"

Lillian seemed to lose track of the conversation. "Do you have a sweetheart, Sally?"

"Er...no. I've not been back in this area long enough to meet anyone yet, although there is a man who seems to like me. He works at the same newspaper office as me."

"Do you like him, child?"

"Yes, I think so, although I don't really know him too well."

"Then if you and he ever become close with intent to marry, you could both come here to live. This manor is so empty. The old building needs you."

Sally blinked. Why would she live at the manor? She tried to pull the conversation back on track, wondering if Lillian was senile. "Lillian, you didn't answer my question."

"What question, dear?"

"Do I have those strange dreams because I'm Sarah, born again?"

"Nothing in life is set in stone, child. We know the people in the surrounding villages have never liked the inhabitants of this manor. The older families here have said ill luck had descended upon them in the last century, because Derek Witherspoon was an immoral drunk. Plus there's the ..."

"Oh my God, Lillian, what are you saying? Please stop going off topic, you're confusing me." Sally swept a large chunk of her hair out of her eyes, thinking Lillian hadn't answered her question at all.

"Sir Derek was the grandfather and father of Beth, the old woman you met at the past-life meeting."

Sally let out a frustrated sigh. She understood everything Lillian had already said about Sarah and Beth. *Jesus, Mary and bloody Joseph, I don't want her telling me everything all over again. Maybe I should write it down for her. Maybe she's senile. She's rabbiting on a bit too much.*

Sally decided that Lillian must be deaf.

"Do I have to spell everything out to you—again, Sally?"

"Oh good God. No, Lillian. Not again. Please not again."

Nonetheless, Lillian was unremitting with her recollections of the past, although this time she declared, "Sally, there is no maybe. You are the rightful living owner of this manor and grounds."

"What?"

"Yes, Sally. You see, Beth died the night of the past-life meeting." Lillian lapsed into silence, her eyes sad.

Sally shook her head in shock. One minute she learned that Beth was her sister, and in the next, she found that Beth was gone.

"I'm so sorry to hear that, Lillian. Beth came across to me as a nice lady. But I can't just take over her house. Doesn't the law say I can't be the legal owner of everything because I'm an illegitimate adopted child? What about Beth's legitimate children? Shouldn't they be the rightful owners?"

"No. They want neither it, nor the memories it brings them. Besides, they became fearful of the blue—"

"The blue?"

Lillian ignored Sally and continued talking about the living relatives. "So they passed the manor back via their grandparent's genealogy to you. The day you were born the hospital tested your blood. If you're thinking you are not Derek's child, then you can dispel those thoughts. Those genetic tests proved positive."

"But then this means," Sally exhaled long and slow, reflecting on Lillian's words. "This means I'm Beth's half-sister physically, in this life, and—"

"And you were her full sister in your last life, when your spirit was born, albeit fleetingly, as Lady Sarah, Beth's twin. So no one has more right to live here than you, Sally. Besides, the papers were signed by Beth's children to make the transaction completely legal in case your adoption got in the way."

"I'm overwhelmed, Lillian. I can't get my head around this. All I know is I must go home to finish writing my book. My recurrent dreams made me ill. They seemed so real and now I know why. It's because the events were real...for Sarah."

"Please do not leave. Stay. You belong here. You can use Beth's typewriter to write."

"Sorry, but I must finish my story while I'm alone in my apartment. When it's complete, maybe my dreadful dreams will stop and then maybe, just maybe, I can begin to get my head around everything you've said tonight about me being the owner of this lovely old manor."

"This is why the spirit made you come here for the journals, Sally dear. Whether you like it or not, you are part of Beth's family and her children are your kin."

"Yes, yes, yes. I understand, Lillian," Sally said, anxious to get home. Sally was shell-shocked. She was not only the legal owner of the manor, but Beth's family was Sally's blood family as well.

"Lillian. One more thing..."

"What is it, child?"

"I must know how you knew I was coming to see you today."

"I knew because it was written in the letter, Sally."

"Letter? What letter, Lillian?"

"The letter Beth typed two weeks before she attended the past-life meeting. Would you like me to read it to you?"

"Yes, please, Lillian."

Lillian walked toward the bureau and pulled out a folded letter. "'Dear Lillian, Mrs. Harris said I would meet Sally, the reincarnation of my twin sister Sarah, before I die. She will be at a past-life meeting that you will take me to next week. Afterwards, you must insist this girl move into the manor to live. It is where she belongs. My own children do not want it or the memories it brings them. My dear, dear Lillian...a Witherspoon must live here. After my death please search my drawer for another letter. The envelope says "do not open until after my death." Your loving friend, Beth.'"

"Okay. I understand you said I am the owner, but why would she want me to live here when I am only her half sister, in addition to being her full sister reincarnated? I understand her children do not want to live here, but why didn't Beth coax her children to maintain it?"

"Let me read you the second letter. She wrote this letter a long time ago. It will more than clarify things for you." She took a breath. "'My dearest friend Lillian, I know you must feel confused, wondering why I want Sally Witherspane to live here when you think she is not my blood kin. You see, many years ago I overheard a private conversation between my grandmother and Aunt Betsy. I discovered my grandfather, Sir Derek Witherspoon, had fathered a baby in 1971 with a woman called Miss Gertrude Gwen-Don. She was grandfather's last concubine. Blood tests taken at that newborn's birth positively proved the infant was indeed Derek's child, making her my half sister. The female child was given to Mrs. Smith, a childless woman in a nearby village, with instructions to register the baby as Sally Witherspoon. A substantial sum of money went with the baby. A mistake was made with the spelling, hence Sally Wither-s-p-a-n-e. That young woman and my own children are the rightful heirs to the manor and everything our family owns. Please, Lillian, it is of the essence you bring Sally Witherspane to the manor to show her the rest of my mother's diaries and this letter. Thank you. Your dear friend, Beth.'"

Sally glanced at her wristwatch. It was almost time for her bus.

"Sorry, Lillian, I must dash to catch the last bus home in fifteen minutes. I'm tired and don't want to have to make a run for it."

Sally stood up to leave and then turned around. "Oh, whose funeral is tomorrow? It's been more than a week since the past-life meeting when Beth died, so it can't be hers. Did someone else die?"

"No. It is Beth's funeral. We waited until you could visit the manor."

Sally started toward the door again, wondering how they had known she would be coming to the manor that day. She turned back when Lillian spoke.

"Oh, I must tell you this before I forget. Miss Gertrude Gwen-Don was the governess for the children of Derek's close friend, Lord Wilkes. Gertrude was the woman Derek stayed with the longest of all his concubines. Mind you, how Derek got his clutches on Gertie I'll never know. She is a saintly sort of woman and at forty years old, she was much younger than Derek."

"*Is* a saintly sort of woman? Do you mean she is she still alive? How do you know all this?"

"Yes, Sally. Beth and I went on a trip to Kendal a number of years ago. We saw her with our own eyes. She does look saintly, all quaint and proper in her appearance and mannerisms. She was employed as a matron in a girls' school in Kendal."

Sally wondered if her real mother would like to meet her.

Lillian seemed to study her expression and smiled. "I suppose you could write and ask her if she would like to meet you, Sally. She might even have a telephone."

Sally looked at her watch and chewed her lower lip for a moment. "Well, there's another ten minutes before my bus is due. Please give me her postal address before I have to go."

Lillian rummaged through the bureau drawers.

"Yes, here it is, Sally."

Lillian handed her a slip of paper with Gertie's address on it.

"I wonder why Beth waited so long to produce the letter." Sally studied the slip of paper.

"We'll never know the answer to that question. It might have been her private meeting with the psychic that fetched the truth into light."

"I didn't know Beth knew Mrs. Harris. I know her too. It was she who encouraged me to go to the past-life meeting."

"I'm glad she did. The psychic paid Beth a visit some days before that past-life meeting. They were alone most of the time so I don't know everything the psychic said to her. Mrs. Harris left directly after their tête-à-tête, and when I went into the room Beth was sitting at her typewriter, working on the letter I've just shown you. Furthermore, it was Beth who left instructions that when she died, we must not hold her funeral right away. This was to give you a chance to visit the manor first. Perhaps the psychic told her you would come. Beth tried to get in touch with you numerous times when you were studying at Lancaster University."

"She did?"

"Yes, she even sent one letter to the Dean that proved your birthright and asked him to pass it along to you. It was an invitation for you to come here to live when your studies ended."

"I didn't receive a letter, Lillian."

"It must have been lost in the mail. Anyway, Beth cried when you didn't reply. She thought you didn't care."

Sally flopped back into her seat, stunned to realize this was why the old woman had spoken to her at the past-life meeting. Then she felt stupid for remaining in Lancaster after her graduation. She would have found out sooner and could have been living in a mysterious old manor instead of her grotty little apartment. "What a life Beth must have had," she murmured. "Some of it sounds very clandestine."

"It does a bit," Lillian said. "It's understandable this may all be overwhelming for you. Go home and think about our little chinwag today. I heard the weather is about to turn rough again. If you miss your bus, please return and I'll have old John drive you home."

Sally jumped up. *Surely John must be long past driving age by now?* "I must go. I detest bad weather, Lillian."

Lillian rose as well. "It is expected you'd fear it when a storm took your life more than a century ago."

At the door, Sally said, "Oh and Lillian, I will attend Beth's funeral tomorrow. Please call me in the morning and let me know what time the funeral car will arrive. Thank you."

She checked that the journals were still in her bag and waved at Lillian. "Thanks for the journals. I'll return them in a few days." She dashed to the exit and left.

Lillian slumped back onto the couch and sighed heavily, wondering when or if the situation between Sally's father and the past-life meeting would ever end. A flash of insight crossed her mind. *Will Sally come here to live? Someone has to take over running this place. John has almost had it in this life and I'm not staying. So who will look after this beautiful old place when I return to my own little home? Sally must come here to live. She's got to or it will go into disrepair.*

When Lillian ceased her brooding she realised the manor had turned quiet and still so she tottered upstairs to bed. She found a hazy blue glow waiting for her. At first, she paid no attention to it as she prepared for sleep, until the words, "Familiarity breeds contempt," echoed around her room.

"Look here, whichever spirit you are. I'm very tired. Sorry. I must get some sleep tonight."

The glow faded and all became hushed once more.

CHAPTER SEVEN

Sally sprinted toward the bus stop. The last bus would arrive in minutes, and she didn't want to miss it and have to return to let rickety old John drive her home. Confusing and distrustful notions churned through her mind like a butterfly blown out of control by a storm. After the conversation with Lillian, Sally didn't know if she was a Witherspoon or Witherspane, or whether Lillian was sane or for that matter whether the letter was even real.

She saw the bus coming down the hill and forced her legs to speed up. Suddenly, it was as if jet engines propelled her along the winding driveway. The little piebald pony trotted alongside her close to the fence, kicking up its heels as if it was racing her. When Sally closed in on the bus stop, the piebald snorted and whinnied as if to say, "Thanks for the race."

Sally was in luck. The bus driver stopped to drop off two passengers. She climbed aboard, seating herself close to the front. Her chest hurt with running so hard. The windows were murky. She wiped the glass with a paper hankie, revealing a large black rain cloud pushing hard across the pink evening sky. Lillian was right. Another storm was brewing.

Dark, swirling clouds overhead eliminated the pink sky. Leaves whipped from the trees, swirled around as if they were caught in a whirlwind. Just then, the heavens opened and sent a heavy shower.

Sally glanced at the bus driver. His face expressed concern. The bus skidded on a carpet of mushy wet leaves and the driver slowed down. She prayed the storm would not entice any lightning. *Why on God's green Earth have I returned to live in this horrible frigging area?*

To take her mind from the squall, she rummaged in her bag for something to read. All she had were the journals and she didn't want to study them on a bus.

When the double-decker bus turned Hensingham corner, a wind gust hit the side of the bus and the vehicle mounted the sidewalk.

Sally let out a shriek.

The driver got the bus under a control and steered it back to the road, the wheels thumping over the curb. Sally's head thudded against the seat back and her heart hammered hard as if it pursued the very blood it needed to continue beating. The couple on the bus shrieked with laughter, appearing happy with the thrill the journey provided them, like a rollercoaster ride in a theme park.

Although the sky was dark, she could see Dent Hill in the distance. It still looked like the sleeping giant she often saw it to be when she was a child. All of a sudden the road morphed into a shallow river at Scalegill Road End. The driver took a detour up Bigrigg Hill, past Saint John's Church and through Woodend village, on the home run to her neighbourhood on the other side.

Bigrigg Hill was steep and covered with slimy wet leaves from the mighty oaks in Saint John's Church grounds, making the bus driver slow down. Sally turned to glance across the valley on her right, between Saint Bees village and Mirehouse. The water had risen quickly, with flooding on each street as multiple streams of water cascaded downhill. The streets were alive with so much water they looked like the arms of a living river.

She turned her eyes toward the Saint Bees part of the valley. The same thing had happened there, except much worse than Mirehouse. All of a sudden a swift waterfall appeared on the hillside beside the village school, and water gushed toward the streets past the old Priory. Sally despised the predictable monsoon-like Cumbrian climate with a vengeance that belonged to God Himself.

Again she wondered why she had returned to her natal area after graduating from Lancaster University. There are no lakes near Lancaster, so naturally there were no terrible rainstorms like in Cumbria. With her fear of storms, Cumbria was the last place she should have settled in. *It must have been Beth's family beckoning me, using some sort of mind power to bring me here. So the old girl says the manor is my rightful home now, huh. Well, not even a nor'easter could hurt me if I lived in that sturdy old building on the hill.*

The transit pulled into her stop. Sally leapt off the bus before it came to a complete halt. Her feet splattered into the deep puddles. *More bloody soakings,* she thought. *Will my knickers ever get the chance to dry in this godforsaken area? Maybe I should have stayed at the manor after all.*

She cursed as she raced around the corner to her home, unlocked her door and rushed inside, feeling altogether relieved to be indoors again. To take her mind off the deviant weather she drew a bath, played gentle music and began to read one of the diaries as she soaked.

After awhile the water turned cold. She jumped out and dried herself off, put on her nightgown, grabbed a glass of wine and put her feet up to unwind from her puzzling evening, still not grasping the full truth in everything Lillian had said.

When she was ready to go to bed, she noticed her phone blinking. *Oh, I have a message.*

Peter had been worried about her and asked if she would call him, no matter the time. Not wanting to get into anything with Peter so late at night, she ignored his message. For the first time in weeks she slept like a newborn the whole night.

Next morning as she fixed herself a cup of tea, the phone rang. It was Peter.

"Why didn't you call me last night to let me know you'd arrived home all right? The damn storms we're having are the worst I've seen in years. I've been worried about you, Sally."

"Oh, Peter, keep your hair on, lad. Don't worry about me. I'm a big girl and can take care of myself. I am not trying to fob you off with excuses or anything. It was just too late to call you. And to be honest, I need some time alone to think. You see, I might have discovered the story of a lifetime. One of my life's goals is to write a bestseller. I want to do this before I become romantically involved with anyone."

"Really? I had been wondering if you'd like to...but good for you, Sally. What's the topic of your story?"

"Sorry. I'm not ready to have a discussion about it right now. Maybe when I am halfway through the first draft. Remember, this is not for the newspaper. And Peter?"

"Yes, Sally?"

"I do like you, you know. I merely need time to work through a few things first, all right?"

Peter sighed, sounding relieved. "Oh, I see," he said, with a warm, contented tone of voice. "Well, it's really grand to hear you at least like me, Sally. I was beginning to wonder."

"Oh, no, Peter, I do like you. As I said, I just have a few things to straighten out in my life first."

"Well, as long as you know I'm very fond of you. If you need any help, any help at all, then you know my number, all right, love?"

"How kind of you, Peter. Thank you."

She could hear the reluctance to say goodbye in his voice.

Still wearing her nightgown, Sally glided across to her computer and gazed wistfully at the screen. A virgin page was ready, geared to receive reference to a past era, a period of history in which she herself had lived, albeit fleetingly, as Lady Sarah. This time Sally felt that with the diaries and Lillian's help, she had ample insight to put her mental pictures into words.

Like most writers, she wasn't sure how to begin. She flicked open one diary, while slurping her tea, and squinted at the fascinating, although barely readable, brown letters. An idea struck her mind as clear as morning dew on a Lakeland hill. She would type whatever words she could decipher, feeling convinced the rest would surge forth, and so the chronicles of Constance and Beth began once again.

CHAPTER EIGHT

Constance watched her mother drive herself to distraction for weeks with Constance's persistent refusals to marry and give her illegitimate child a name.

"Child, I will not relent until I find a suitor you will accept," her mother said over and over. "I've already said what will happen if you do not comply with my wishes and you're ignoring me. We must force the tittle-tattle to cease. There has been enough scandalous gossip about our family over the years."

Constance's frown declared her indifference. As a fourteen-year-old teenager, she didn't understand what her mother meant. What scandals?

Another power struggle ensued between mother and daughter. Her mother returned to her original threat. If Constance rejected all the available men, then she would admit her into Garlands Asylum. She was convinced that if people thought her daughter had gone insane, the ever-present gossip would stop.

Her second threatened option was to dump her baby into a convent. She believed that if everyone discovered who the baby's father was, the disgrace it would cause the family would be insufferable. She thought her sister, Lady Elisabeth Witherspoon, whom the family called Aunt Betsy, was the only other person who knew the truth about Constance's pregnancy. Constance's father, Derek, would never divulge his incest, for fear of public outrage and imprisonment, so her mother decided the family secret was safe.

Gossip fluttered through the town, like hungry mosquitoes, regarding which man the father might be—at church teas, ladies' sewing meetings, ale houses and especially in the large Glessal's shop.

Her mother harassed Constance time and again, "Constance, marry Sir Mathew Vermont, then everyone will believe he is your child's father and the gossip will stop."

Constance flicked a renegade hair out of her eyes and screamed at her mother. "No. Sir Mathew Vermont is twice my age. I'm just fourteen. He is an old man compared to me."

"Look here, child, Mathew sees you as serene and gentle and the most beautiful young woman he's ever seen. I don't know why he says these things. Thank God he hasn't seen your flashes of temper. Constance, you must listen to me. He has even said he thinks you are more stunning than the *Venus de Milo*. What a lovely compliment."

"The *Venus de Milo*?" Constance said, laughing so hard she had to cuddle her tummy to stop it from hurting.

Her ever-vain mother, with her nose poked in the air, said, "Oh yes, of course you get your good looks from me. Child! Mathew is willing to forget that you're impure. If he is not concerned about your baby born out of wedlock, then you must take him as your husband."

Constance's soul hurt. *Oh, how I hate you, mother. You've always known who my baby's father is. Why, why did you allow papa's animalistic behaviour with me to continue?*

Normally strong willed, she began to weaken and as usual, she ran to her room to vent.

Hannah knew her daughter was as fiery as her hair was scarlet. Although Constance rarely showed her unpleasant side in public, her temper surfaced in her room, where she broke vases and ornaments, chewing over what her incestuous father had subjected her to. She cursed him, wishing a bad accident would befall him while he was away on business.

When Hannah heard more crashing sounds coming from her daughter's room, she thought about her husband. *Derek, you're such a degenerate for what you've done to our family...to our daughter. It's deplorable. Mathew believes Constance is like an angel without wings, with her long limbs and ivory skin, but just listen to the fracas she's making right now. All because of you, Derek!*

Hannah had learned that it was about more than her daughter's extraordinary beauty. Mathew's money-hungry mother, Gretchen, knew about the enormous dowry from Lady Elizabeth, Constance's aunt.

Lady Gretchen Vermont and Lady Hannah Witherspoon met in secret, each with a different motive about the benefits of a union between their two families.

"Gretchen, if your son marries my daughter, then the money she will bring to your family will be a massive addition to your already overflowing bank vaults."

"Yes, Hannah, I understand this. However, we all know your daughter has a fatherless child. There's no doubt people will gossip."

"They will think Mathew is the baby's father and the gossip will stop. Besides, he is much older than my daughter and hasn't been able to find a bride yet, now has he?"

Gretchen twisted her face into a grimace, looking like she was silently loathing Hannah's words.

In a cocky tone Hannah said, "Well, your Mathew is twice my girl's age. What other single females are available for your son to marry—especially a strong young woman like my Constance who would produce grandchildren. There are none. They're all married off or have left to be ladies' maids for royalty."

"You're right, Lady Hannah. My son is over thirty years of age now. I don't know why he didn't marry when he was younger. Yes. I shall wheedle him into marrying your daughter and then no one can spread rumours about either of our offspring."

"Wonderful, Lady Gretchen."

Hannah returned home elated. "Constance, if you do not marry Mathew, then I most certainly will put you into Garlands Asylum. There is no doubt in my mind about that now."

Constance's eyes welled with tears, as if she'd finally realised her mother had really meant every threatening word.

"I had thought this was just one of your idle threats to get your own way. Mother, I'm not crazy. How can you even consider putting me in there when you know who my baby's father is?"

This time around it appeared that Hannah had caught Constance when she felt weary with little defiant stamina left, so she agreed to let Mathew court her.

Both Constance and Hannah knew Gretchen wanted to get her hands on the hefty Witherspoon dowry. That night she said to her son, "Look son, no one knows our family is almost broke. Your brother's wife spends money like it's a guarantee of a place in paradise. Constance's dowry is more than enough to repair our leaking west wing roof. I know you already admire the girl and it will grow into love. Besides, you're not getting any younger. You can't play the bachelor forever"

"Just because I'm over thirty doesn't mean I'm ready to marry, mother. However, to please you I promise to charm the girl into marriage and put an end to your incessant nagging about money."

After many demands from Hannah and frequent sweet talks from Mathew's silver tongue, Constance agreed to tie the knot with him at a private ceremony in Vermont Manor in early autumn, 1899. The marriage was necessary to make people believe Mathew truly was her baby's father. In due course, the gossip ceased, to the relief of both families.

By this time, Beth was an angelic five-month-old infant with chubby limbs and skin as ivory as her mother's. Her hair grew thick and flaxen, the same colour as Mathew's, and her eyes were as blue as a cornflower. The child had no sign of her mother's quick temper.

The newlyweds lived in Vermont Manor, Mathew's ancestral home. It boasted thirty-two bedrooms, a ballroom and a games room, all situated on a hill a few miles north of Whitehaven, on the road leading to Muncaster Castle, near Ravenglass, in Cumberland. Glorious rhododendron trees covered more half the fells to the east, each abundantly adorned with billions of blooms. Every splendid blossom overlooked a breathtaking view of Western Scotland across the Solway Frith, which shared both English and Scottish coastlines.

On the outside, Vermont Manor appeared more like a castle than a mansion, with its lofty turrets and shallow dried-up moat. It was all nestled inside fifty acres of lush, mostly unfarmed arable land, although a small number of cows and sheep were dotted around. Steps from the front promenade, through mowed lawns, led to a clean-cut thyme labyrinth, viewable only from the front windows. An orchard grew at the rear of the property.

Down a narrow winding lane, and running parallel to the manor, were stables that housed a dozen horses. Several were valuable thoroughbreds.

On the surface the family appeared to be the most well to do amongst the entire community of well-heeled, prominent families in Cumberland, yet the Vermont servants were rarely paid.

The most affluent family of them all was the Lathieres. The family's wealthy ancestors had passed down countless properties presented to them by King Henry II. Sir William Lathiere owned Whitehaven Castle, with its countless servants who seemed to leach from the castle's stone work.

The Lathieres changed Whitehaven town from just sixty dwellings into a large, flourishing shipping and coal mining settlement. In 1893, just six years before Beth's birth, Sir William Lathiere replaced many gas lamps with electricity. This made it extra difficult for the thorny Vermonts to contain their jealousy. Especially Lady Gretchen, as their driveway still had oil lighting.

On many occasions, Gretchen Vermont tried to coax Sir William's beautiful younger sister, Lady Margaret, into marrying Leonard, her youngest son, to seize some of the Lathiere riches. Margaret hated the Vermonts. She refused by telling a lie, that she was to become a royal lady's maid to Her Majesty the Queen in her Scottish palace, Holyroodhouse in Edinburgh.

As a result of the Lathieres' prosperity, the ostentatious Gretchen held expensive dinner parties to give the appearance of added wealth and to captivate Sir William's other sisters, Lady Olivia or Lady Anna, into marrying two of her five sons.

Thomas was the oldest and already married with children, then followed Mathew, Leonard, Peter and Christopher. Not one lady of good breeding wanted to marry into Gretchen's family because of her high and mighty attitude.

The Vermonts had to save face the whole time, especially in front of the Lathiere family. More often than not, the Vermont evenings would end with a masquerade ball. Royal guests from Barnard Castle, county Durham, attended only in the summer months as the roads across the Pennine fells were tough to negotiate in winter. Especially Hard Knot Pass. It was the most treacherous switchback road in the county. From its summit, the view all the way to Muncaster Castle was spectacular. The Muncaster family never accepted the Vermonts' invitations. Gretchen hated them for not going to her parties because they were the closest wealthy family for miles.

Now that the Vermonts had Constance's colossal dowry, they rubbed shoulders with the wealthy once more. Gretchen replaced their driveway lights with electricity. Sir Mathew Vermont hired Miss Phyllis Bracken-Thorpe to become a part-time helper to Constance.

After several months it was evident Mathew's teenage wife was growing to love him, although she classed him as a touch unsightly, with numerous scars and a nose not quite in the middle of his face. Nevertheless, Mathew was more considerate than all the Vermonts. He showered his wife and her daughter, Beth, with affection and generosity. Constance enjoyed him lavishing her with jewels, rich silk and fine velvet clothing, and a magnificent white Arabian mare. Constance, the proud teenager, had still not figured out that the money to pay for all her wonderful gifts came from her very own dowry.

Although Mathew's original reason for coupling with Constance was for his mother to get her hands on the dowry money, his feelings toward his young wife grew stronger. They rode together daily, laughing while they raced through fields and woodlands. Later, they took longer gallops over the fells, chasing scores of untamed mountain ponies and sheep.

During one such outing they stopped beside a creak to rest their horses. As they lay on a rug under the shade of an old elm tree, Mathew reminisced. "In the past, my favourite black and white hunting dog, Archer, used to run alongside me. His long legs churned up the grass as he flew out from behind his back paws. When he was young, he could even beat my horse in a short race."

"Oh, what fun!"

"Yes, my love, except now he's old and can't keep up. But he is a clever old canine. He knows every shortcut back to the manor. These days, he waits at the stables and barks excitedly when he spies me approaching. He runs toward me carrying a stick, eager to play catch."

His tale amused Constance. "Yes, I know the dog you mean."

The couple lay in the cool shade together, wrapped in a tight embrace and gazed into each other's eyes. The leaves of the elm tree rustled as if whispering love poems to the gentle breeze. Their marriage seemed made in heaven.

Then Beth reached ten months of age and everything changed.

One afternoon, Constance relaxed with Gretchen while embroidering in the drawing room.

A housemaid entered. "Excuse me for interrupting your afternoon, miladies. Phyllis Bracken-Thorpe wishes to speak with Lady Constance."

"Bid her to enter," Constance replied.

Phyllis had hardly crossed the drawing room threshold with Beth screaming underneath her armpit before she blurted, "Milady, your baby has started to exhibit strange body movements. As you can see, her limbs flail erratically. She clenches her fists and gnashes her teeth and sometimes she screams for hours."

"Yes, I can see, Phyllis. Why does she behave this way? Is she in pain?"

"No, ma'am. I'm sorry to inform you that this is not normal behaviour. I've nursed many a baby. Yours is different and difficult to handle."

Constance didn't get a chance to speak as Gretchen snarled at Phyllis for interrupting her peaceful afternoon.

"Phyllis, she is such an irksome baby. Take the noisy child away! Meanwhile, please keep her as far away from the main east wing as possible. I cannot stand the dreadful sounds the youngster makes. It gives me a headache. I do hope Beth grows out of these noisy tantrums."

"Yes, I'll take her out right away, Lady Gretchen. However, I don't think she'll ever grow out of it. I'm sorry to be the bearer of bad tidings. I fear she needs a physician."

By this time, Phyllis was hugging Beth tightly to her breast. She curtsied and left the room with the child still in a screaming frenzy.

Constance confirmed her silent embarrassment by her flushed

cheeks.

Gretchen said to Constance, "Please do not invite anyone into a room that I am in again without my consent. I must have peace and quiet."

"Yes, Lady Gretchen. I'm sorry but I considered it was all right seeing as Phyllis is my baby's nursemaid and I am your daughter-in-law."

Gretchen scowled and returned to her embroidery without a word in reply.

Constance hated living in Vermont manor, save for it being her husband's home too.

Neither Gretchen nor Mathew seemed to understand why Beth's symptoms had worsened. After a few more months, Mathew began to ride alone more.

Constance noticed his new behaviour, but did not say anything. After awhile, she thought less about Mathew and focused more on becoming acquainted with other ladies living in the outlying areas.

CHAPTER NINE

When Beth reached two years of age, her irregular body movements had turned to intense jerks and she hadn't said a solitary word. A physician wasn't consulted. They didn't want to attract any attention to themselves, especially now Constance was pregnant again. Gretchen grew highly nervous the new baby might have the same problems as Beth. "Constance, what if this child becomes yet another irksome infant like Beth? I cannot suffer another irritable child in this house."

Constance took her words as a warning. Everyone knew what would happen if her baby was born with an affliction in Gretchen's house, although laws against neonaticide were in place. *If my baby was born with an affliction, it would be too horrific to imagine. I just know my baby would not survive in this house.*

Gretchen would instruct someone to steal her baby and do away with it by suffocation or other hideous means. Since Beth's bigger health problems didn't show until she was almost one year old, she had escaped abandonment or death.

That night Constance prayed nothing would be wrong with her new infant.

Constance's Aunt Betsy received news of her niece's latest pregnancy and she arrived at the manor without warning to visit for six months. She hadn't seen her niece for over a year. Betsy bumped into Mathew in the hall. The old woman's face dropped when he said, "You know she is pregnant again then?"

His attitude toward her was cold and coarse.

"If you mean my niece by *she*, then yes, that is why I am here."

A few more words were exchanged. When they finished talking, he stormed away and marched along the hallway like he was going into battle.

Betsy flung the drawing room doors wide open and found Gretchen sitting by the window. "Hello, Lady Gretchen. It's a pleasure to visit your lovely manor."

"Thank you, Lady Elizabeth."

"I'm searching for my niece. Do you know where she is?"

"No, I haven't seen Lady Constance today, but no doubt she will be in the nursery with that boisterous offspring of hers."

Betsy scowled at Gretchen's irritated comment.

"Thank you and pray tell, just where is the nursery?"

"It's on the third floor. I will ring for a maid to guide you. Before you go would you care to join me for tea and muffins?"

Betsy hoped Gretchen didn't engage her in conversation too long.

"Yes, Lady Gretchen, though I cannot stay long to chat. I must pay a visit to my niece soon. There is some important information I must pass on to her. After all, it is she who I have come to visit, is it not?"

"Indeed it is. Do please sit down, Lady Elizabeth. We are both seniors. May I call you Betsy?"

"If you must, Lady Gretchen, and I shall call you by your Christian name too, seeing as we're of similar age and are family now."

Gretchen appeared happy with the knowledge that another senior woman was in the house, especially one riddled with money. She rang a small glass bell on the table to summon a maid to bring them tea and muffins.

Before their refreshment arrived, Gretchen talked of how unruly Beth was and how she constantly screamed. They chatted about the past prior to Constance's marriage to Mathew and about the town gossip that Beth was not Mathew's child. They discussed all manner of other subjects including, of course, money, Gretchen's favourite topic.

When Gretchen mentioned money, Betsy knew it was an attempt to discover how wealthy she was, and concluded that she didn't like her.

However, as soon as Betsy saw Beth, she told her niece she was in agreement with Gretchen. "Beth is either a bad-tempered, unmanageable child or controlled by a demon, or both."

Of course, she made sure that Gretchen did not overhear this statement because she disliked any form of spiritualism, especially devil worshipers.

Betsy advised her niece to put the youngster into an asylum. "It could cure her ills, Connie dear." She paused to gaze into her niece's eyes. "Given time, she might make a full recovery. Meanwhile, you and Mathew can have more children."

"I know about asylums from Penelope, my friend whose father is a doctor." Constance's expression contorted into a display of hurt. "I couldn't stomach the concept of my daughter living in such a place, being beaten and abused the way inmates are according to my friend's father."

"Well, Connie," Betsy continued, "you must do something soon, my girl. Mathew won't take much more. He will leave you. I do not know if his mother knows yet, but when I first arrived here, I bumped into your husband in the entrance hall. He mentioned he's at the end of his tether because of Beth. Haven't you noticed Gretchen's attitude toward your child? The Vermont's are utterly irate because of her."

As Constance began to weep, Betsy's tone of voice softened. "My dear, I've heard about the abnormal fits your child suffers. If you will not commit her to an asylum, then you must at least call a priest. He might tell you the devil is inside her. He could rout it out with an exorcism."

Her niece, still sniffling, looked at her. "Which priest, Auntie?"

"Well now, there's nice old Father McDougal who lives just outside Harass Moor. I heard at a church meeting that he's performed several successful exorcisms in his fifty years as a practicing priest. Write him a letter, dear. Ask him to help you. Tell him you will pay handsomely. If necessary, I will give you the money, although there really should be a great deal of your dowry left for the Vermonts to pay."

Constance stopped crying, her eyes swollen and red. "Auntie, when people are exorcised, do they feel pain?"

The old woman laughed. "No, my dear. It doesn't harm the person. It impairs the evil spirit controlling them. The person writhes around shrieking because the demon inside doesn't want to leave their body."

"Are you sure it doesn't hurt them, Auntie?"

"Yes, child. I'm sure. A priest would never hurt anyone, now would he?"

"Well, I suppose not, Auntie."

"And while you wait for a reply from dear old Father McDougal, you must put Beth in a dark room every day." Betsy's tone turned sharp. "It's what doctors in asylums do. It might make Beth become tired of her persistent screaming and end her bad behaviour. Connie, she may well recover completely. I tell you, child, this is one thing the asylums do, they shock people, and their bodies, back into the real world."

Constance's face flashed with fury. "Auntie Betsy. Have you ever heard of anyone who ever left an asylum feeling well again? I haven't and neither have you!"

Penelope's father was a great deal more knowledgeable than Constance's aunt about asylums. Before Betsy had a chance to reply, Constance jumped up, raced to the door, swung it open with a thud and almost tripped over the hem of her skirt as she left. Her heart was breaking. By the time she reached her boudoir she was screaming hysterically at God. "Why did you allow this dreadful sickness to happen to my baby?"

She picked up a huge porcelain vase with both hands and threw it at the mirror. The loud shatter ricocheted throughout the manor.

Gretchen sent a maid to discover what the commotion was, although Constance knew that Gretchen would have already figured out it was her.

Out of control, Constance ripped expensive tablecloths and threw them into the fire. She hauled her beautiful brocade curtains off their rods and chucked them out the window onto the muddy wet soil below.

Constance screamed at her personal maid. "Get out! Leave us alone." The girl raced away and Constance flung herself on the divan and cried.

After resting for three hours, she calmed down and wrote a letter to Father McDougal, pleading with him to help. The Vermonts' carriage driver delivered the letter right away.

Still plagued with uncertainty but trusting her aunt, Constance went to Betsy's room. "Auntie, I agree to try your suggestion of the darkened room while I wait for my reply from the priest."

"I am so glad, my child. You've made the correct choice. This will certainly help matters until Father McDougal arrives."

"The thing being, Auntie, my Beth is normally only noisy when I'm not with her."

"How strange. Well, do it anyway, dear. It certainly will not hurt and let's face it, you cannot be with the child every minute of the day, now can you?"

The only dark room anything like Betsy's description was the old wine cellar, so Constance allowed her personal maid to carry Beth down there. When the door first opened, a noticeable smell of burned candles and damp wood was distinguishable. Farther down the steps the air smelled ghastly, like old cabbage boiled in sour milk. Water dripped continuously from the ceiling and ran down the walls, leaving deep puddles on the sludgy mud floor. Orange fungus grew on the rotting wooden shelves in the corner. The only luminosity was through the open stout door behind them.

The maid had left first. Then Constance sprinted up the stairs behind her.

Beth was now alone.

Naturally, she cried. Beth felt cold and thought she was there as a punishment, and she didn't know why. Her young mind shrieked, *Mamma, mamma. No leave...it dark...I scared.* Of course, no one heard her screams.

As the door closed, her screams floated on the stale air and the stench carried her thoughts into the damp brickwork. She continued to scream and sob while her mind screamed unspoken words into the blackness, *Mamma, I no like blackness.* Two auditory words escaped from her screaming lips, "No go!" Terrified, she shivered and shook vigorously.

As the last footstep faded, a gently pulsating blue light became visible to her. It warmed her gloom as it shimmered and hummed a tune. Beth ceased her crying, unaware of what the light was or where it came from. She felt warmed by it and from then on, whenever she was scared or alone, the blue light remained by her side.

Since Constance couldn't bear to hear her child's screams, she told Laura, her personal maid, they would not be taking Beth there again. She'd find someone else to do it.

"I'm glad, ma'am," Laura said. "I didn't like taking your bairn down into that 'orrible damp place."

Constance went off to find Gretchen and told her about her plan. "I'd prefer it if Beth was not taken down to that dreadful place again."

To appease Betsy, and in the hope it would work, Gretchen went against Constance's wishes and ordered Ingrid, one of Gretchen's servants, to take Beth to the cellar.

The unhappy trips continued each day for three weeks until white-haired Father McDougal swished in, unannounced, through the terrace door along with young Father Benedict. The older priest wore a long flowing white robe with a purple stole around his neck.

As he sanctimoniously splashed holy water in front of him, he uttered, "*Ego ordo vos decipio genus hominum, recedo ex is creatura of Deus*. Amen."

Father Benedict was a much younger, heavy-set priest with raven hair that shone midnight blue. He walked in behind the older priest. He wore similar white clothing to Father McDougal except his stole was yellow.

"I'd like to see Beth," Father Benedict said.

Ingrid guided them from the front room, along the extensive halls in the south wing and down the steps to the cellar level.

She paused at the cellar door and noticed both priests were shivering.

"It feels cold and desolate compared to the other hallways," Father

Benedict said.

The younger priest's hands shook.

Ingrid pushed the door open and the men walked slowly through the low-hung cellar door and down eight steps. Approaching Beth, they chanted in Latin. "I order you, deceiver of the human race, depart from this blessed child of God. Depart from this infant, whom God hath made a Holy Temple. Leave, you unholy demon, leave in the name of the Father and of the Son and of the Holy Spirit. Leave in the name of Jesus Christ, who reigns forever and ever. Amen."

Ingrid panicked and hyperventilated. She ran from the room when Father Benedict threw sickly sweet scented powder all over Beth. The powder made the child cough and scream. She thrashed her arms and legs. The priests were oblivious that their proceedings terrified the child.

After two hours of continual chanting, Beth stopped screaming and gurgled sweetly. The priest's facial expression changed to that of elation. Ingrid assumed he thought Beth's change in character was due to their exorcism. Both priests smugly smiled at each other. The young priest carried Beth upstairs to her mother and then continued roaming around the manor chanting in Latin while sprinkling holy water everywhere.

When the priests finished, they sauntered back to the room where Constance was sitting by the window embracing her child. Mathew stood beside her.

Father McDougal raised his open hands into the air. "Praise and hallelujah! Our exorcism was successful. The demon is out of your child. She will grow into a normal, healthy young woman. We've blessed your home and need not return. Now you can give a generous donation in thanks to the church." He stuck his open hand toward the couple, ready to take their money.

Constance jumped up and down like an excited child as she glanced toward Mathew, who by this time was already handing thirty British pounds, roughly the amount a schoolteacher earned annually, to the older priest.

"Thank you. God bless you, my children," he said. His long skinny fingers wrapped around the cash and he stuffed it into his vestment pocket. They left as quickly as they first arrived. The door slammed shut behind them with a deafening thud.

The windows rattled in unison as the sound echoed throughout the manor. When the reverberations stopped, the house settled down to the normal creaks and squeaks of an old building once again.

Aunt Betsy looked quite smug and said in a jovial, high-pitched voice, "I told you. I told you the Father would work a miracle for you, didn't I, Connie dear?"

"Yes, you did, Auntie. Thank you so very much." Constance held

Beth tightly. The child's face turned pink and then to red as she struggled to breathe.

Mathew was so overjoyed he hugged Betsy and gave her a kiss her on the cheek. The old woman blushed and let out a girlish giggle as she returned to her room.

Constance turned to Ingrid. "Thank you for watching over Beth."

Ingrid gave her a happy nod and went away to resume her duties.

CHAPTER TEN

Four months later, it was obvious the exorcism had not worked. Apart from a minor spurt of growth or the odd gurgle, Beth's behaviour had not changed.

"Put the child into the cellar again every day." Aunt Betsy instructed. "If you remember, it helped the last time because she stopped her carryings on, if only for a short while. This time continue the treatment for more than four hours over many more months."

Constance didn't know what else to do. Even she was becoming weary of it. However, her stubbornness would never allow her to put the child into an asylum.

Beth's persistent spasms made Mathew believe he was a huge failure, not just as a Christian, but in life. He grew temperamental and visited the Anchor Vaults Inn each day for weeks. He rarely returned before dawn.

In time, Constance birthed twin boys, Karl and Francis, who bore no visible defects. Aunt Betsy lingered until she saw the boys were growing normally. Then one day, she descended the stairs wearing a black feather-trimmed hat and a plush burgundy velvet suit. "Constance, you have two fine, strong sons, my dear. I can return home contented."

"You appear dressed for a journey, Auntie. Are you going somewhere?"

"Yes, Connie. I'm sorry for not telling you sooner, my dear. Thank you for your gracious hospitality but now it is time to return home. I've been here far longer than the six months I'd originally planned. I hope you will bring the boys to visit me from time to time."

"Er...yes, Auntie. I'm so sad to see you leave. Please, can't you stay a little longer?"

Betsy faced the doorman. "My good man, carry my bags outside. I have a carriage waiting." Then she turned to her niece again. "Sorry, Connie, I really should go home." *I can't tell her its best I leave because I want nothing more to do with her noisy disabled child or with her husband, Mathew. For that matter, Mathew has turned to alcohol like my brother Derek.*

"Goodbye, Auntie. We're sorry to see you go and thank you ever so much for helping us. We will miss you." Tears welled in Constance's eyes.

By this time, Betsy had already hobbled down the hall and was standing on the steps ready to climb into her carriage. She turned her head sideways, nodding to her niece. The carriage pulled away with the old woman waving her hankie out of the window.

Constance paused for a few moments on the driveway, knowing it would be lonely without her favourite aunt. She returned indoors to check on Beth and the boys. Nanny Phyllis stood just inside the nursery doorway.

"Milady, if it's all right with you, I would like more assistance with your children now that you have two more. Beth is the hardest of all three."

"Yes, Phyllis, go ahead and find someone suitable. I'm very tired and need to lie down."

"Yes, ma'am. Thank you kindly."

Constance watched Mathew, between drunken hazes, as he noticed his boys were growing normally. Eventually he stopped drinking and displayed a calmer attitude, more like his old self. He did his best to support his wife again and to be a good father to his sons. Every night he read bedtime stories to his boys but continually excluded Beth, toward whom he'd developed a great deal of animosity. It was as if she didn't exist. He wouldn't even allow her to go into the same nursery with her brothers. Mathew completely ignored Beth, even though she must have yearned for a father's love, too. The boys grew quite rapidly and still showed no sign of visible defects.

In the meanwhile, a new neighbour, Mrs. Rosemary Barlow, often visited with her family's nanny and the Barlow girls, three-year-old Phoebe and her older sister, Cynthia. The Barlow's home was a ten-bedroom guesthouse in Gosforth, across the valley. On the highest side of their house was a glorious view of Saint Bees Priory and the Irish Sea beyond.

Since her Aunt Betsy's departure, Constance enjoyed the younger, more vibrant Rosemary's company. Her visits became longer and longer.

It was a blessing when Constance and Mathew moved into the private south wing away from Mathew's mother. Since she hated noisy children running through the halls, she would scream at them to go and play elsewhere.

Constance's son, Karl, was a rough and tumble boy who enjoyed riding his miniature fiery black Falabella horse, a gift from his father. The boy deliberately galloped through the flowerbeds yelling, "Bang-bang. You're dead." Much to the dismay of John, one of the gardeners, who were forever replanting what the animal's hooves had gouged up.

Francis, Karl's gentler brother, played doctors and nurses with Phoebe Barlow in the garden. Mathew and Constance were inspired as to what profession their sons might pursue as adults because of the type of games they played.

For almost five years Mathew appeared to the world to be a doting husband. He supplied everything his wife and children needed until the day his greedy mother told him about Lord Bunting's death.

"The poor man died of an unknown disease. His lucky widow will be quite wealthy now."

Mathew remembered Lady Beatrice Bunting from the time he met her while visiting the Caribbean one year before his marriage to Constance. He knew then Lady Bunting was both sultry and compassionate.

"Mother, Lady Bunting will be so distraught. Perhaps we should visit her."

"Mathew, I do not have time to visit her. Would you go and give her our sympathies? I like to keep the wealthy happy."

"Very well, Mother dear. I will."

"All right. You will represent our family. Take someone along with you. We cannot afford any rumours that might emerge if you're seen visiting her alone."

He went to Bunting mansion the following day and took his manservant with him as a chaperone.

In the weeks to follow, Mathew proceeded to visit the widow by himself in the dark of night so no one would see. Mathew and Beatrice became close friends. He told her scores of touching stories, including the day when his beloved dog Archer died.

"Beatrice, my old dog's heart stopped one day while waiting for me at the stables."

"Oh dear. I'm sorry to hear that, Mathew. You poor man. You seemed so fond of that animal."

He shared the story of Beth, still a crippled child, and how he used to love and admire Constance's youthful fire. "Although now my feelings toward my wife have diminished. I'm bored with her sexual naivety."

Beatrice's eyes glinted when he said the word *sexual*.

Something stirred in Mathew's loins.

Her flushed face displayed her disappointment when he did not continue the topic. Instead, Mathew mentioned his two sons, Karl and Francis. "They're going to a boarding school, so soon there will be little comfort in life for me."

Many nights passed with numerous conversations between the two until they grew cozy in each other's company.

One day Mathew owned up. "I know I shouldn't have married someone as young as Constance."

"Yes. It was a mistake, Mathew. A more mature woman would suit you better, dear heart."

"Well, in reality, mother forced me to marry her."

"Did she really? How shocking. Why?"

Mathew didn't fully answer her question. He was afraid he might alienate her, because his mother was only interested in money, and Beatrice would put a stop to his visits.

He didn't realize nothing could put her off the prospect of having a hulky man in her life.

"Because I was over thirty years of age, Mother decided it was time I married and she chose Lady Constance to be my bride. I hardly had a say in the matter."

Beatrice didn't speak. She seemed to be mulling his words over in her mind.

"At one time I thought my wife was a beautiful, sweet and naive young thing. Forgive me for saying this, madam, but now that infatuation has worn away, a whorehouse seems inviting."

Once again Beatrice's eyes blazed. "Mathew, darling. You need a nice woman who knows how to please a man. Not a whore. You need a decent mature woman with strong sexual desires. I know this because my late husband never needed to call on a whorehouse. He said some of his friends had turned to prostitutes because their wives were not satisfying in bed."

Mathew raised one eyebrow. He moved closer to her, showing his interest.

"Getting cozy, are you?" she said giggling. She rubbed her knee against his in a playful fashion. "Yes, Mathew. I was plenty woman for my husband."

"I bet you were, Beatrice. You're quite voluptuous."

"Oh. Thank you, dear heart. They said he died of the pox..."

Mathew inched away from her, afraid of catching it.

"But I think the doctor's diagnosis was wrong. I'm quite healthy, and if he had died with the pox, then I would be ill as well, right?"

"Well, yes. This is true, Beatrice."

"I do miss him so. A woman like me needs a strong man in her life." She paused in thought. "At least my husband left everything he owned to me. I'm blissfully wealthy."

Mathew glanced around the opulent, scarlet room with its numerous oil paintings and Ming Dynasty vases.

"Dear Beatrice. I'm sorry he died. You must be terribly lonely without him."

"Yes, Mathew. I am lonesome without my husband, although I...I have ways." She touched his knee and her tongue swept provocatively along her upper lip. Her expression was sensual with not even a hint of any dubious scheme.

Slightly blushing, Mathew enjoyed the mystery of her delicate touch. The aroma of her perfume reached far into his mind. He grabbed her hand and looked into her eyes. His eyes yearned for more.

Beatrice kneeled before him and loosened his britches, without a word.

Mathew gasped for air as his mind traveled to a realm where she alone would rule between his bed sheets. He loved the incredible explosions his body felt from her exquisite touch. He was breathless and in ecstasy, savouring her attentions hour after hour.

Beatrice touched and fondled him in ways Constance had never done. She had only been intimate with two men in her life. But Beatrice was a sultry woman with insatiable sexual needs. She played many tricks between the sheets and out of them. Her womanly wiles and manoeuvres more than satisfied Mathew.

Hours later, he slumped back onto the chaise longue beside her bed. When he caught his breath, he said, "What time is it, my beloved? It feels late. I think I should go."

"Mathew, you need not leave every time you visit me. Why don't you come here to live? Bring your children as well. I so love children. Darling, there is more than enough space here for all of you."

A massive smile broke on his face as he thought about the daily sensual pleasures he would enjoy if he lived with her. "Oh, Beatrice, you—"

She interrupted before he completed his sentence. "And I will pay for private tutors for your sons. They needn't go to boarding school either. So you will not miss their presence after all." She smiled. "I hope you'll accept."

Mathew thought her proposal was tremendous. Her offer was too irresistible. *She* was irresistible. He wouldn't turn her down.

"Oh, darling. Thoughts of being here with you every single day...my perfect woman, naked and in bed beside me, and to have my children here as well. Oh Beatrice. It will be heavenly. I'm so excited. I accept!"

As he embraced her, her yielding breasts pressed against his firm, muscular chest.

With a satisfied look upon her face, she gave him what he wanted.

Mathew was in a sexual and emotional buzz, dazed at what had transpired with Beatrice. He returned home to pack his treasured belongings and have his finest horse harnessed. While he packed his clothes, his wife entered the room.

"Mathew, what are you doing?"

"I'm leaving you and I'm taking the boys with me."

Constance fainted hearing his words. The gentleman in Mathew administered her with smelling salts. When she came round she screamed at him.

"No, you will not take my sons away!"

A fracas ensued. She insisted he stay home, if not for the boys, then for her.

"Your girlish charms have no effect on me now. You're pretty but you're so naive in bed. I need a full, hot-blooded woman."

He continued packing.

Constance was breathless from shock and her heart pounded. She picked up a figurine and threw it hard at his face, screaming. "You uncouth bastard!"

Blood gushed from a deep gash in his nose.

Seemingly not satisfied, Constance swiped an onyx ball from the dresser and dropped it on his right foot, bruising two of his toes. She screamed, "You're leaving me for another female?"

"Woman, are you out of your mind?"

When she realised what she had done she cried and beseeched his forgiveness. "Oh my husband, what have I done? I am so sorry. Please, please forgive me."

"You are crazy if you think I will forgive your violent behaviour. Your mother was right. You should be locked up in a sanatorium."

Constance shed sour tears that night.

Mathew hopped out of the room on one leg and headed for Nanny Phyllis to have her tend his injuries. Phyllis grabbed a jar of liniment and smeared it thickly over the gash on the bridge of nose, bandaged his whole foot and handed him a sturdy stick to use as a crutch.

Mathew raced down the hall to grab his boys from the nursery and left to return to the luxurious Bunting mansion.

The housemaid told him that Beatrice was in her bedroom. He left the boys in the maid's care and hobbled upstairs to see his concubine.

When she saw his wounds, she gasped. "Mathew. Oh dear God. What on this green earth has happened to you? Did your horse throw you? Come, dear, lie beside me and tell me what awful thing has happened."

He crossed the room to lie beside her and shook his head, showing his reluctance to talk. Beatrice held him tightly while running her hands up and down his buttocks. Warm happy tears flowed from his eyes as she caressed him. Her affections inspired his body. His manhood erected. For the first time in his life he felt at home with the woman he assumed was born to please only him, both between the sheets and out of them.

CHAPTER ELEVEN

While Nanny Phyllis bathed Beth later that day, she saw another faint blue light. Only this time it was a more intense blue and took the shape of a person. The two other times she'd spotted the figure was when she put the child to bed. At first Phyllis thought the light reflected from the stables. Then she realised there wasn't a shiny surface for anything to reflect off. *Whatever is that light? It's quite extraordinary. I've noticed Beth doesn't scream or make a fuss while it's here either.*

Down the hall, Constance was screaming in her room, still stunned that Mathew had left. She was convinced he would never leave her given his past displays of devotion and generosity toward her. She was still blissfully unaware the purchased gifts were from her dowry.

She decided she didn't want to remain at Vermont Manor without her husband because she detested Gretchen, so Constance left Beth with Nanny Phyllis while she visited her Aunt Betsy.

"Auntie, Mathew has left us and gone to live with that...that Bunting woman. What am I to do? Will you allow us to live here, please? I can't stand that awful Gretchen."

Although Betsy was wealthy, she was growing old and weary. Appearing shocked at her niece's news, she rung for her maid. "Instruct the stablemen to collect Lady Witherspoon's horses from the Vermont stables and bring them here immediately."

The old woman turned to gaze at her niece. "They're fine animals, Connie. I cannot stand the thought of them remaining at Gretchen's. She might sell them because we all know how money hungry she is. Of course I will take you under my roof, you poor dear girl. I know you tried so hard to make your marriage work."

Constance smiled with relief until she heard her aunt's next words.

"Except…oh, Connie, my dear child," Betsy sighed. "I cannot take Beth in. She is much too noisy for me to deal with. So I'm very sorry she will have to live elsewhere. I will certainly give you a yearly allowance to have her housed at another place. Perhaps in a convent. You can visit her as often as you wish."

When Betsy saw Constance's expression, she turned a flushed face away and lowered her head.

Constance's previous gratitude quickly turned to wrath. "You're sorry, Auntie? You say you're sorry? You're giving my horses a home and not us. How can you put two animals before your own flesh and blood? I know you're feeling weary, Auntie, but—" She concluded with an ear-piercing screech.

Following the shrill sound, Betsy exhaled noisily.

Since Betsy rejected Beth, Constance refused her hospitality and the allowance she offered for her daughter. Proud and scared, Constance knew she could never live with her mother again either, after her father's past behaviours. Nor could she lose face by turning to her friends. She marched from her aunt's parlour toward the front door, planning never to return.

The old woman grunted loudly. "Pride cometh before a fall, Connie my girl."

Constance couldn't reply. Offended and frustrated by her aunt's rejection of her firstborn, she ran out of the front entrance and leaped into the carriage without saying another word. She began to wonder how she would manage without any income or a home, because she would never desert her precious child.

Within minutes she realised there wasn't any alternative except to plead for help from Ginns, the gloomy workhouse for paupers.

Constance considered many things on her return trip home. She had developed a huge lump in her throat and so found it difficult to instruct the driver to obtain a fresh horse when they arrived. By the time she reached home she was enraged with Betsy's rejection. Constance raced upstairs to tell Nanny Phyllis to pack a small overnight bag, dress her daughter warmly and put her into the waiting carriage.

"Where are you taking her at this hour milady?"

Constance didn't answer. She collected a few things and returned to the carriage to climb aboard.

"Driver. We must return to Whitehaven before nightfall."

"Right you are. Is everything all right, milady?"

"Everything is fine, driver. Carry on."

He smirked.

They traveled without another word spoken. Beth seemed to search her mother's face for clues as to why they were out so late at night.

As Whitehaven came into view again there was little more than an hour's daylight left.

"Driver. Drop us off one street away from the harbour and leave immediately. Do not look back and do not follow us."

The driver nodded while saying, "You going on a ship, milady?"

"It's none of your business."

He seemed to sense that something was amiss, but he obeyed her instructions and slowly drove away.

Constance walked along the narrow cobbled street away from the carriage toward the grubby-looking workhouse. The crisp sea air smelled of gulls and fish. The sound of waves gently lapping to the shore filled her ears like calming oceanic music.

She didn't feel calm. She questioned if Gretchen had known what her son had done, or if she even cared. *They've obtained what they wanted from me and that was my dowry.*

As she drew close to Ginns, early evening shadows crept across its cold stone walls. Pausing for a few moments and feeling a chill run through her, she pulled her child to her breast. Frightened of Ginns's eerie appearance, Constance wondered if she should march back to the carriage and return to stand her ground with Gretchen so they might continue living in Vermont manor.

Ginns Workhouse was built beside the cliffs near Whitehaven Harbour with an impressive north facing view of the Solway Frith and the Irish Sea. Since its enlargement in 1795, it had grown dark and fearful in appearance, akin to Brahm Stoker's Dracula Castle, without its soaring turrets.

At first the intake overseer refused to accept Beth, stating the rules were that anyone admitted must work for their keep. He spoke with a working-class Whitehaven accent.

"Sorry, ma'am. It be workhouse regulations. Thee can enter, lass. This child cannot. It's obvious this young lass can't pull 'er weight. Rules are rules. And in truth, ma'am, I'm not sure if your unspoiled ivory hands can do menial work either."

Within seconds Constance's inner fire drifted away until only warm embers remained and she collapsed to her knees. As her silk skirt caught the air underneath it resembled an open parachute mushrooming outward around her legs. She clasped her cold and shaking hands together as though in prayer pleading from her soul.

"I beg you, kind sir. Please, please allow us both in. Beth and I cannot live at Vermont Manor anymore because my husband has abandoned us. Oh, sir. I promise under God to work twice as hard as the other mothers. Please, sir. We have nowhere else to go. Please." Tears flooded her face.

The pious, middle class Christian overflowed with pity when he saw her tear-filled eyes.

"Hey, come now lass, dry your tears. You say you lived at Vermont Manor?"

"Yes, sir, I married Sir Mathew Vermont. He left us for a scarlet woman. I simply cannot stay there without him. His mother is dreadfully conceited and she absolutely hates my daughter."

The overseer glanced at Beth and seemed to think about the child's welfare for a moment. "All right, we'll let thee try for six months. In thee go, although a word of warning to thee, milady, do not tell anybody in there thou are both noblewomen. They'll never be off your back about it. Just tell them thee are Connie and Beth, and that thee worked in a fine house and this is the reason thee are well dressed, all right?"

"Oh thank you, kind sir. Yes, I will heed your words. You won't regret this. God bless you!" Constance grabbed his hand and kissed it humbly.

"Aw, come now. Don't be behaving like this. Up thee get and get theeselves through there."

He pointed in the direction of a tall wrought iron gate embellished with scrolls bearing great resemblance to devilish clawed feet. She struggled to pick up Beth, not strong enough to carry her as far as she had already brought her. The overseer grabbed his keys to open the enormous lock. He winked as she walked through, then he clanged the massive gates shut. The loud metallic clatter startled Beth so much she shook violently as if another spasm was about to begin. Constance turned around to look back, unable to keep her eyes off the fiendish-looking scrolls on the gates.

A quiet man wearing a black coat and tall hat approached to guide them down the long outer corridor. At the end, another door unlocked from the other side and opened into a large hall to the women's area. All the while, locks clanged shut behind them. It made Constance think. *Dear Lord, this place is like a prison.*

Three matronly women shuffled toward Constance. They appeared annoyed as they instructed her to strip and bathe.

One said, "Oh, la-de-da. How did you manage to come by such beautiful clothes then, miss? Steal them?"

"No. I worked as a children's governess."

"I know you are lying. You're too well dressed to be a governess. You stole them, didn't you?"

"No, no, they were given to us."

The women laughed and proceeded to scrub Constance's skin so hard her feet bled. When the women finished scrubbing, the star-crossed mother and child were presented with coarse workhouse clothing. Constance's face dropped with shock when she saw how rough and threadbare they were.

The woman smirked. "Hmm. I see a dissatisfied look on your face, missy. Like them or not, these are the only clothes we have. For you. Your clothes will be sold to cover the cost of your food until you learn the ropes and become productive."

"Thank you. I am grateful."

Constance looked at her petrified child, whose eyes were wide and staring. Beth was so scared after her bath that she'd urinated on the tattered cover that one of the women had laid her on. Quick as lightening, Constance flipped the corner of the blanket over to hide the wet patch. She prayed no one had seen, scared they'd be thrown out with no other place left to go but the gutter or a whorehouse. It was then that she remembered the nuns at Saint Bees convent. They took in needy Christian women and children.

It's too late now. We're here.

The woman who had scrubbed Beth, plunged her clenched fist hard into Constance's back. The aggressive action thrust her through another door with such force that she practically fell onto her face, gasping for breath. Her insides felt numb after the blow.

A diminutive, dirty man with food slops all over his clothing met them on the other side of the door. He directed them to the kitchen for a late cheese and bread supper then guided them the rest of the way to a small dingy cell. This was where they would sleep for as long as they called Ginns home.

Now Constance's arms ached with carrying Beth. She felt sore all over after her bath, especially with the fist in her back from the sadistic woman. Nonetheless, she carried her terrified daughter into the cell, laid her on the filthy damp cot inside and cuddled up beside her. Her arms throbbed.

As she pulled Beth to her breast in an attempt to make her feel safe, her thoughts ran amok. *Oh, my dear sweet Beth. Perhaps I should have allowed Mother to put you into a convent after all. At least it would be cleaner there. And anywhere would be better than where we are right now, little one, but we can't go back now, not in these clothes. Gretchen wouldn't let me live it down.*

She hugged her daughter until they both fell asleep.

The next morning their day began with a deafening bell tolling at six in the morning for prayers. As Constance opened her eyes, she spied a cockroach running through a crack in the wall. She snatched a piece of soggy paper from a filthy pile in the corner and stuffed it into the crevice. When she felt satisfied the crack was blocked, she carried Beth into the rowdy food hall for breakfast.

Constance smelled the inmates' repulsive body odour immediately and heard them making unbearable noises while eating, like pigs swilling at a trough. Constance's stomach churned so much she was convinced she would vomit. *What dirty, ill-mannered beasts. The roaches come because these disgusting people spit food onto the floor.*

Each adult stopped work in time for supper and was forced to attend prayers afterward. Children finished work three hours earlier than the adults, in order to have time to learn how to read the bible. Constance wondered if Beth would be included. She wasn't. That night they ate bread and hard cheese for supper again, and Constance contemplated if that would be the only food they would ever receive.

Ginns was the first workhouse in the country that allowed men and women to live under the same roof, although their sleeping wards had bulky doors between them with wardens on either side. After her first few short breaks for lunch, supper and prayers, Constance soon discovered every woman and child ground corn, made sacks and scrubbed filthy lice-ridden bedding and stinking clothes from morning to night without rest. It seemed that they intended the work to be unpleasant, to put off more poor folk from arriving at the workhouse and to remind them of their penniless circumstances.

Constance realised she needn't have worried about Beth wetting herself after her bath because the whole place stank of urine, excrement and sweat. In addition, it didn't take her long to learn that the building housed more than unfortunate paupers and harmless feeble-minded people. There were numerous maniacs and dangerous lunatics residing there, and there she was, eating amongst them. One rough-looking man continually ogled at Constance. Fearing he might approach her, she averted her eyes from his.

Ginns's small, dirty windows made the whole place dark and dismal. It wasn't a nice place for anyone to live, especially children. One or two cried from morning to night. Constance was sure that hearing their cries made seven-year-old Beth wish she could control her arms well enough to cover her ears and drown out the din.

CHAPTER TWELVE

When the other children first laid eyes on Beth, they yelled all sorts of spiteful names at her. "Spastic. Monster. Cripple."

The tears streaming from her daughter's bright, crystal-blue eyes made Constance want to yell, "Please stop! She's human like you. She cannot help her jerks." Especially when she saw Beth was unable to defend herself and could only utter mixed-up words.

"Monster…not…me," Beth said between sobs.

After hearing her broken sentence, the boorish urchins laughed as if she were their personal jester. They laughed even more as tears cascaded down her face.

Constance took her back to their room. "Pay no attention to them, my darling. Everything will be all right. Don't you worry."

Nothing Constance said eased her disabled child's sadness. Beth cried for hours afterward. All Constance could do was snuggle up close and embrace her tightly. Their cell was cool, a welcome feeling that warm summer evening. Each slight breeze that blew through the ample window cracks and the crevices in the walls aided sleep. Yet, although the windows were dirty, at certain times in the day the sun's heat magnified the stink.

When winter arrived, bitter cold winds howled through each gap. Constance complained to the governor. "It is so draughty in our cell, Mr. Titern, sir. We are cold. Would you please have it fixed?"

He laughed mockingly. "There isn't any money in the coffers to pay for every minor repair, and none of the male inmates have stone-worker skills either. Just bung up the holes with damp mud or mushy paper to keep out the draughts."

Constance was shocked that he'd told her to fix it herself and she couldn't find words to reply. Then thoughts came into mind about the rest of the winter.

Titern trundled away without another word.

As Constance returned to work, she found a dirty sack on the floor. She kept it to hang over their cell window in the hopes it would help to keep the cold out.

She came to realize that blankets were in short supply and that any women who had extra night covers were giving sexual favours to the overseers. To retain her self-respect, she knew she must learn to become wily in such a foreboding place as Ginns. At night she stole blankets from the laundry when people weren't looking, and she snuggled close to her daughter to keep her warm and feeling safe.

Woe to any woman, female child, or even a young boy, left alone in the laundry or the sack room. The likelihood was they'd be beaten and abused or even murdered by the dangerous, immoral men residing at Ginns. Some men acted even crazier on the lower workhouse levels. The overseers had no idea why or just didn't care about how insane some of them became down there.

Numerous women banded together to protect their children, and each other, from the criminal inmates. Constance joined forces with them until a mean-natured female discovered she and Beth were of noble birth.

"Well now, 'ows your Ladyship today? Is thee doing all right, milady? Is there anything we can bring thee? Why, where is thee servants, milady?"

With her head bowed low, not wanting to cause trouble, Constance replied softly, "Calamity can knock on anyone's door, even the rich."

Now Beth's face showed great sadness. She seemed to have enormous compassion for her mother since she'd taken so much verbal abuse from the nasty woman.

Many times Constance regretted asking Ginns for help, but she had nowhere else to go now because she'd heard the convent was always full in winter. Neither could she bend to anyone's desire to get rid of Beth just so she could enjoy living in luxury at the manor again. *We have gone through so much sorrow together. I just can't abandon her.*

Constance continued to work quietly, ignoring the women's spiteful jeers. She wanted to say much more to the unsophisticated women, but did not, fearful an overseer would think her a troublemaker and throw her into the coalmines, or worse, onto the merciless streets.

The social, able-minded men of Ginns broke stones on the shores of

Whitehaven to mix with mortar for buildings and road work. In the summer they cultivated the sun-baked fields to feed everyone, including the nuns who taught the children literacy.

Aggressive, temperamental troublemakers, who were unsuitable for farming or working inside Ginns, were forced to work in the coalmines. Sending the rabble-rousers down to the mines was Titern's way of ridding the place of undesirable inmates, as many suffocated with coal gas or the ceiling fell on their weak, underfed bodies. Several corpses disappeared. What happened to them no one knew.

Each time anyone jeered at Constance, she was fearful to say anything as she thought the overseers might blame her for causing trouble.

One day when Constance and Beth were eating lunch to the usual taunts and mocking from fellow inmates, one server, who normally kept to himself, approached Constance. He offered her an extra crust of bread and half an apple. Underfed and disregarding her sophisticated upbringing, she snatched the food from his hand to share with her daughter.

Inmates at the same table shouted, "Hey, Pat, give us more food too."

"Sorry, there's nae more for ye," the server replied in a brawny Scottish accent. "This wee lassie got the last o' it."

Two females with faces swathed in pus-filled acne glared at Constance. She turned her worried eyes away from their repulsive-looking skin.

The Scotsman had a few moments to relax and socialize from time to time because he had a limp. Constance gave him an anxious expression so he would sit beside her, hoping she would feel protected.

"My name is Patrick MacCrinan, miss. I already know yer name because I hear this damn lot ridicule ye every day." His eyes aimed at the jeerers. When he turned to speak to Constance again, a look of apprehension had appeared on her face.

"Aw, don't worry, lassie. They nor me will nae hurt either ye or yer bairn. Why are ye and yer daughter living in this rotten pig hole anyway?"

Constance spotted some inmates across the room glaring at her and she felt reluctant to talk.

"Don't concern thyself aboot that crowd," he said. "They're nothing tae be scared of." He turned around, snarled menacingly at them and they nervously turned their eyes away.

Constance whispered. "They seem frightened of you."

"Aye, they had better be, or their portions will become even littler."

She giggled quietly at his words. "Thank you for the extra food,

Patrick, although I'm not yet sure if I can trust you. We've been ill treated so much here and I don't want to receive any more offensiveness from those boorish people."

"Lassie, it was me who gave ye the extra food, nae them. Sure ye can trust me. It looks like ye could do with a sincere friend and ally."

Beth liberally nodded her head with a big grin spread across her face. "Yes, yes."

Constance peered into his soulful green eyes and saw tenderness there, so she believed him.

"All right, Patrick. Except please don't think I'm being priggish when I say that people here already know we're not from the same background as them, so I will just tell you a little."

He settled comfortably into his high-backed chair to hear her tale.

"We lived in a large old manor with my husband, Sir Mathew Vermont, and his family, a few miles outside of town. After about five years had passed by, he deserted us to live with another woman, Beatrice Bunting, who is nothing more than a common harlot. The worst thing was Mathew took my twin boys with him."

"Oh dear, ye poor wee thing. Why didn't ye stay at the manor then?"

She sighed. "Well, I didn't know it would be this bad here. Besides, my husband's relatives are heartless greedy people, especially his ghastly mean mother, Lady Gretchen. I have my pride. I didn't want her charity, even if she'd offered any, which she didn't. It's because I'm a Witherspoon, Patrick. Her kind does not like my royal lineage. They're covetous of it."

His curious green eyes opened wide. "Anywhere would be better than 'ere, lassie."

"Patrick, if we had continued living at the manor without Mathew, his ghastly natured mother would have sneered at us daily. That would feel much worse than anyone's jeers inside these walls. So we left. I'd already asked my own family to take us in. They said yes to me and didn't want anything to do with Beth, my first child."

Sympathy welled in Patrick's wet eyes as he spoke softly. "Constance, ye are so different frae the other women in here. Will ye let me be thy friend and guardian within these grim walls? Ye and Beth will nae have anything tae fear in here ever again."

"Will the others not persecute you for being friendly toward us, Patrick? I think they would, going by their attitude toward us. They appear to show true hatred."

"Ock nae, lass. They would nae dare say anything tae me, or I'd give them smaller portions o' food. They barely get enough nosh tae eat as it is."

Patrick heard sarcastic moans coming from the far side of their long wooden table. He turned to eye them like a lion about to sink its fangs into its prey. Two people muttered under their breath before looking away red faced. They'd received his message because the food hall emptied quickly to the sound of chairs scraping loudly on the floor.

No one else heard the rest of their conversation.

"Even though you sounded menacing just then, I can see in your eyes you're a kind-hearted man. Surely you can find some work outside these dreadful walls. Why are you here, Patrick?"

He smiled sweetly at her.

"I was hoping tae hear more about ye first, lass. Although if ye want tae know a wee bit about me, then I'll tell ye. See, I first came here when I was fourteen years old." The crow's feet under his eyes began to appear deeper than they should be for his age.

"Then you have been here a number of years, Patrick. It must have been awful to have lived here for that long. I was repulsed the minute I stepped inside this place, although I suppose it is better than having nowhere to live."

"Oh, I agree, Constance. While I'm living inside these walls, I don't have tae worry about keeping a roof over ma head and I don't have tae fret about food either. I work in the kitchen." His belly moved up and down as he laughed.

"I understand. At least we know we have somewhere to live when our cold wet winters arrive. Please, would you care to tell me about your life before you came to Ginns, before you were fourteen?"

"I don't want tae speak aboot life before I was a teenager, although I'll share the rest o' the story I've just been telling ye, if ye like."

Constance nodded and Beth snuggled back comfortably into her chair to listen, seeming engrossed with his tale.

"When I was fourteen years old, I worked as a stable lad for Lord Brinton, the Cumberland public prosecutor o' the time. He lived on the moors just outside Aspatria."

"Oh, no, Patrick. Please start at the beginning. Tell me where were you born and raised, please. And tell me about your Scottish family."

He screwed his face into an unhappy frown, his tone of voice deepened. "Constance lassie. I just told ye I prefer nae to mention any o' that time. Though I will tell ye what happened while I was working for Lord Brinton before I moved into Ginns."

"I'm sorry, was that part of your life painful for you?"

"As I already said to you, I will nae talk about that time in my life. I will tell ye more aboot this story, if ye want tae hear more about it."

"Yes, please tell us."

"One day, when I was behaving foolish like most young headstrong lads do, I drove Brinton's carriage at full gallop doon a winding cobbled lonning that weaved around three ponds. I was young and daft in those days. One o' the coach wheels hit a great big rock and flipped the carriage over on tae its side. I was dragged along by the panicked horses and then I was thrown right over the animals' heads. I landed underneath the horses' pounding hooves and the carriage bounced all over ma legs."

"Oh my God, Patrick! You poor man. That must have been agonizing."

"Well nae at the time, milady. You see, when it struck me in the head, I was snuffed oot like a candle sitting by an open window on a blustery night. A farm hand witnessed the tragedy frae two fields away. He raced over tae find me lying unconscious and bleeding bad. Ma legs were torn tae shreds. He ran for help and ma broken body was taken tae the Brinton's house."

Constance was stunned yet she wanted to hear more. "What happened then, Patrick? Did they take you to the nuns at the old Saint Bees Priory or to the convent at Saint Mary's in Cleator?"

"Nae lassie. I woke up in a lovely soft bed with a bastard of a headache and bandaged frae toe to nose." Patrick ducked his head down fast. "Oops, sorry for ma bad word there."

"I forgive you under the circumstances, Patrick."

"Thank you kindly, milady."

"Oh dear me, please stop calling me that in here."

"I'm sorry. It's just felt good tae talk with a decent woman again. Back tae ma tale now. The whole o' ma body was in agony. And nae lassie. I was nae taken anywhere. I was kept in the Brinton's hoose in a nice room directly beneath the nursery. I could hear the kids playing their music boxes deep in the night. You know, lassie, the Brinton kids often came doonstairs to see me. Their nanny was very kind tae me as well. She gave me morphine for the pain. Aye, Christ was with me that night and thank God for morphine!"

"Good grief, Patrick. I'm amazed. Please, do continue your very interesting story."

"Well, when I got a bit better, I stayed in the servants' quarters to convalesce. I knew it was unusual. Laird Brinton must o' liked me because most toffs don't bother helping the likes o' me. They just send wounded servants tae either o' them two convents ye just mentioned."

"Yes, Patrick. Sadly, it's usually the way of the rich. Most of them cannot be bothered to exchange pleasantries with other people unless they're rich too. Actually, they really don't know how to be compassionate to anyone, especially to working-class people."

"The Brinton's are good folk. Ye are gentry, Constance, and nae a nicer lassie I would wish tae meet in or oot o' here."

Constance knew her face flushed red with embarrassment as she quietly lowered her eyes.

"Patrick, I haven't always been retiring. When I lived among the rich myself, I was as arrogant and pompous as a peacock in a harem of peahens. Living here has humbled me greatly. I'm glad about that, because now I can see people for their characters, not for their money or possessions. Although some of the inhabitants in here are a little bit...er..."

Patrick's mouth opened as if he were about to say something. He didn't make any comment. His grateful smile showed he was thankful she had mellowed.

"You were lucky the Brinton's had a decent nurse living on their property. Did they have young children, Patrick?"

"Aye lass, remember I just told ye? Maybe ye didn't hear what I said because of the commotion the rabble over there made when they came back. After awhile, the wee kids came tae visit me. Two o' them were less than three years old, and my nurse was their nanny. Anyhow, after three months o' rest it was obvious the accident left me unable to work as a stable lad again because o' ma severe limp. They didn't want me serving in their hoose either, even though they mentioned I was highly liked by them."

Constance nodded in agreement.

"Well, lassie, I knew I was nae refined enough tae work indoors in an English Laird's hoose. So they released me frae work with a shilling and a letter of recommendation for employment. I was left with naewhere tae go. So I cut myself a sturdy stick and hobbled miles across country and ended up here and pleaded for help. The workhouse I'd passed in Aspatria didn't have any room. I was lucky tae find this place and even luckier when they took me in. Maybe the Brinton letter helped. I was young, and it was clear I couldn't do hard menial work because of my limp, so I was surprised they give me work tae help oot in the kitchen here. That's a job for a sturdy person and for folks they know are trustworthy. People who would nae steal food tae sell."

"That is an astonishing story, Patrick. I can hardly believe it. Not that I am calling you a liar. The emotion in your eyes tells me your story is true. Please, do carry on."

"Time passed by slowly listening tae the rabble in here until a few weeks ago when I saw ye and your daughter arrive. I wondered who ye were. I knew ye were nae like the riffraff that usually comes here. At first I was nervous tae talk tae ye. By the way, if ye had wondered who fixed the cracks in ye cell yesterday, it was me."

Beth did not twitch nor make a sound during Patrick's whole account. She gazed at him with a distant expression on her face, as if she could see his soul.

Constance's eyes filled with tears. "I don't know what to say right now, Patrick. You've suffered so much in your life, much more than we ever have. Yes, I will be honoured to have you as my friend, and thank you for the work you did in our cell."

Beth nodded in agreement.

They affectionately gazed at one another until Constance said, "Oh my God, Patrick. I must dash off. I'm late for work."

"I'll carry Beth doon the stairs for ye," Patrick said.

Constance trusted his word so she sprinted down the corridor toward the foul-smelling laundry where she would work for the rest of the week. She'd already begun her work as Patrick limped into the laundry carrying her giggling daughter, who seemed to think that a man carrying her was enormous fun.

Patrick hobbled back to the kitchen with a large grin on his face, thrilled he'd found a lady friend such as Constance. When he started work he daydreamed about where he was born in a castle in North Scotland. His family, the MacCrinans, were descendants of Crinan the Thane. A smile emerged on Patrick's face as he remembered the faces of his beloved family members—his father and mother, three sisters and an older brother.

Within moments his happy expression changed to one of horror, as images of violence flooded his mind. He fell to his knees, crawled into the corner and began to weep uncontrollably as he crouched between two sacks full of potatoes.

In his mind's eye, he watched rebels from another clan ransack their castle home. They sexually abused his mother and two older sisters repeatedly, and then stabbed them and burned their bodies, all in front of their bound, screaming father. The rebels forced Patrick's older teenage brother, Bruce, to watch.

When the raiders finished their brutal acts, they pierced Bruce in the gut with a blade long enough to kill an elephant and screwed the razor-sharp dagger around inside his body like they were gutting a fish. He let out screams of agony.

The rebels danced around in merriment looking at the gaping hole where the boy's stomach should have been. The shredded skin of his torso flapped where once strong young flesh was. A large pool of sticky crimson blood spilled out around his feet.

A few minutes later, Patrick witnessed his brother's head drop to his chest as his legs buckled under him. One tall rebel moved closer to Bruce to plunge yet another dagger into his already shredded body. This time Bruce didn't make a sound. Terrified young Patrick knew his brother must be dead.

Four rebels dragged his father into their large courtyard where he was hung, drawn and quartered.

The rest of the marauders hauled Patrick and Bethoc, his twelve-year-old sister, away to the sound of shrieking rebel laughter as his father was torn limb from limb, shrieking and begging them to kill him.

While MacCrinan Castle blazed, black, foul-smelling smoke rose from the once beautiful MacCrinan stronghold home. The wind blew toward Patrick and Bethoc and brought with it the stench of smouldering human carcasses, similar to the aroma of burnt swine.

The rebels kept Bethoc for their sexual pleasure and sold Patrick to a man in a roaming circus. He quickly tired of him and sold him to Gruffydd, a dairy farmer who had originated from Wales and was a cruel taskmaster. Patrick daydreamed about his sister, Bethoc.

Gruffydd caught Patrick and whipped him, accusing him of laziness. The boy ran away that night and travelled south by day and night along the west coast of Scotland. In due course, he crossed the border into Cumberland, England. The boy visited farm after farm and manor after mansion, looking for work and hoping he'd find his sister. Frightened, Patrick, a thin and malnourished child, slept under trees and in haystacks, stealing vegetables and berries from fields and dykes. At last, he reached Aspatria and found employment as a stable boy at Lord Brinton's residence on the moors.

Patrick sighed deeply when his horrifying mental pictures subsided. He wiped tears from his face with his torn sleeve and prayed no one would ever ask about his past again, for the rest of his life. He did not want to remember such pain again.

When he stood up, the kitchen was a mess. As he began to clear it up, Mr. Titern, the governor, entered, looking pleased about something. He didn't speak to Patrick. He didn't need to. Patrick knew money was bound to be on Titern's mind. He grabbed a large, juicy apple from his own personal food store and left without a word to Patrick who felt relieved that Titern didn't notice the mess.

CHAPTER THIRTEEN

Constance toiled long and hard each day doing laundry or scrubbing floors. On hard-hit days she reflected on Mathew, because she hadn't heard a solitary word from her so-called Christian husband, who had helped her as an unmarried mother back in 1899.

Some inmates were loaned to farmers as cheap labour. And in 1910 they sent Constance to the Pack-Horse farm a mile away, to be a personal maid for a gentleman farmer's wife. Constance received no payment, just better food and the ability to return to the workhouse each evening. Otherwise she would never have left her child in Ginns. She hated leaving each day, although by this time Beth was in the kind care of Patrick, their trusted friend.

The farmer paid Ginns a handsome price for a whole month for Constance because she was beautiful and ladylike. His wife, Becky, had a good heart, but she was frumpy and a bit rough round the edges. He seemed to hope that some of Constance's genteel politeness would rub off on his spouse.

Working on the farm every day was a blessing for Constance, like a holiday sent from God. She not only breathed fresh, clean air, she ate decent wholesome meals as well. Every day she sneaked apples or a cake into her apron pocket to take back to Ginns for her daughter and Patrick.

The farmer's wife enjoyed many meaningful conversations with Constance. Constance showed Becky how to dress in a cultured fashion and how to fix her hair into a chic bun. Her husband seemed pleased.

After a few weeks had passed, Becky said to Constance, "My husband is to leave for London on business soon. He doesn't want me to remain here by myself. We would like to offer you a permanent full-time position as my companion. Would you like that?"

Constance's face lit up like a haloed moon on a wintry night. In a split second she knew the farm was a much better place for Beth and herself to live. She was about to accept when Becky continued, "Although I'm sorry, your daughter would take up too much of your time, so she cannot live with us."

Constance remembered her aunt saying the same thing. "Ma'am, if I cannot bring my daughter, then I'm afraid I must turn down your kind offer. I'm sorry."

When Constance returned to Ginns that night, the workhouse governor was outraged because he already knew she had turned down a job offer.

"Constance, why didn't you accept the situation? Your daughter would be well taken care of by me and the rest of the workhouse staff."

Her mouth fell open in disbelief. She turned her head away from him in disgust. Mr. Titern certainly would not look after her daughter properly. He was just interested in the money he'd get from the farmer. In addition, as long as she worked hard, then Titern could not throw her and her daughter out.

The following few days were warm and muggy. She continued going to the farm for another month, then another and another. Before long, summer was almost at an end.

One evening when Constance prepared to return to Ginns, Becky said, "My dear lady, did you know Florence Nightingale died on the thirteenth of August?"

The information struck Constance's soul like an ice-cold bullet and she was unable to reply. She had always admired Florence Nightingale, ever since she'd met her in Hampshire at a party held in her honour.

This was the onset of a life-changing condition for Constance. She returned to Ginns with a slow gait that night, feeling sad and depressed. Constance grew skittish and withdrawn, and she felt suicidal, but for her daughter's sake she knew life must go on. Each evening when she finished work at the farm, she always said to Becky, "Thank you, ma'am." With a quick curtsey she walked back to Ginns more than a mile away along a dark cobbled lonning.

Roughly one week after the devastating news about Florence Nightingale, Constance took much longer to walk back to the workhouse. Her mind bogged down with each heavy step as if her shoes were filled with lead.

It was pitch black when she finally passed by Patrick, who was sitting directly outside her chamber guarding Beth. When Constance passed him, she said, "Patrick, I'm so sorry to return this late. I thank you from my heart for watching over my little one. You are such a dear, dear friend. Heaven will repay you."

He smiled as he strolled along the halls to his own cell for some much-needed rest.

Constance felt worn out but had the strength to give her daughter her usual goodnight hug before snuggling beside her to sleep. As she slipped off to sleep, Constance heard strange unearthly noises echo along the corridors. She was so tired she ignored it.

Very soon, autumn showed its chilly pink nose. Beth always had a great deal of thinking time while her mother worked on the farm. Although she was pleased her mother was escaping the depressing workhouse daily, Beth blamed herself for their predicament in the first place. She was convinced if she had been born normal like her half-brothers, Karl and Francis, then Mathew would not have deserted them nor treated them so abysmally.

Each time her mind raced, she was thankful that the blue phantom she had first seen in the manor's cellar appeared to comfort her. Her familiar spectre consoled her many times as she waited for her mother to return each night. While she passed the time, the continuous singing of workhouse songs drove Beth to distraction. She moaned under her breath about the caterwauling, especially when they sang,

By day I must dwell where there's many a wheel,
And female employed to sit down and reel,
A post with two ringles is fixed in the wall,
Where orphans, when lasted, loud for mercy do call,
Deprived of fresh air, I must there commence spinner,
If I fail of my task I lose a hot dinner.
Perhaps at the whipping post then shall I be flogged,
And lest I escape my leg must be clogged.
While tyrants oppress I must still be their slave,
And cruelly used, tho' well I behave,
Midst swearing and brawling my days I must spend,
In sorrow and anguish my days I must end.

After several years of tough, repetitive work, Constance suffered a complete debilitating breakdown. Her Aunt Betsy was informed. Unbeknownst to the rest of her family, and especially Constance, Betsy regularly sent money to Ginns Workhouse for their keep. Betsy insisted that Constance be moved to Saint Luke hospital. Even with servants to take care of Beth, Betsy considered the child would be too much to handle and was still secretly convinced Beth was possessed by demons. So Betsy paid Mr. Titern, Ginns governor, a handsome fee to look after her instead.

Betsy was unaware Constance had a close friend in Patrick and that he would never allow Beth to be hurt. He had been busy in the kitchen the day Constance was taken to hospital and Patrick didn't know she'd gone until Titern told him to move into his own cell once again. Patrick assumed his new friend was now in good health and had moved to the farm with Beth. He wished them luck in his mind. However, contrary to the governor and Betsy's financial agreement, Beth was left alone and defenceless inside the bleak workhouse walls for hours at a time, forlorn.

Not one of the overseers appeared to give a damn whether she lived or died. The other children's mothers couldn't care less about her either.

Mr. Titern pocketed the money from Betsy without ensuring an overseer looked after the child. Yes, they paid her the occasional visit, mostly to feed her and to check she was still alive, then locked her inside her cell to prevent anyone from hurting her.

Fortunately, two mornings after Patrick last saw Constance, when he returned to his own cell after cooking breakfast, he heard Beth yelling at the top of her voice.

"Help come."

Patrick raced as fast as his gammy leg could take him along the hallway and was unable to open her locked door. He went to speak to the overseer in charge that day.

"Git that lassie's flipping door open right now or I'll kick it and ye in!"

The overseer's face turned pasty with fright. He knew Patrick had a temper as fiery as his flame-coloured hair, so he gave him the key. Patrick returned as fast as his lame leg allowed, to open the door.

Beth smiled gratefully. "Miss you. Mam gone."

Patrick grew incensed but held his anger in because he didn't want to frighten her any more than she seemed to be already. No one had taken care of her lavatory needs so she was soaked from the waist down. The whole room reeked of bodily waste. Her blankets had fallen onto the dirty floor. Beth's bright-blue eyes reached out to him in desperation.

"Pat cold me."

"Not to worry lass. I'll return with some clean dry clothes and washcloths soon."

He locked the door and headed for the laundry. The administrator in charge wasn't going to let him take any bedding. Patrick walked up to him, pushed his face against the man's and demanded, "Give me some dry bedding and female clothes, ye Sassenach pig, or I'll knife ye. I mean it. You'll find yeself with nae guts the next time ye need them. So ye'd best give me them. Now!"

Without another question, the overseer unlocked a cupboard door and handed Patrick clean female clothing, three clean woollen blankets, two linen sheets and a pillow with a cover. Patrick snatched them from his hands, then visited the main storeroom to drag out a dry mattress. One male inmate who passed him in the hallway wondered what Patrick was doing. Patrick snarled. "Help me carry this stuff or ye will find yeself dead when ye wake up."

"There's no need to get angry with me. I've done no harm to you. What is going on in this place today?"

"Nae ye mind what's gone on. I've nae time tae explain except tell ye that it's about wee Beth. Just help me now!"

"Yes. I will help."

He brought Patrick a laundry cart and attempted to calm him down with quiet conversation as they moved the cart down the corridor together. At first, Patrick ignored the man's chitchat. Farther along the way Patrick spoke with a frustrated tone of voice to his helper. "Them Sassenach bastards left wee Beth on her own o' the time these past couple o' days. I thought Beth had gone tae the farm with her mother, but I found oot Constance is in hospital. The overseers were tae take care o' Beth and they didn't. The poor wee lassie is shit and piss up to high heaven. So she is."

The inmate had a milder temper than most men in Ginns and shook his head with disbelief.

"That's terrible, Patrick. Didn't you know Constance was in Saint Luke Hospital? If you need any help again, just let me know."

"No, I did nae know. I thought all sorts. Besides, that Titern and his crew were paid tae look after her."

Patrick thanked the inmate for his help and the man left. By this time the noise had attracted a nun who'd arrived to see what the commotion was about.

"Begging your pardon for the noise, Sister. I'm upset they Sassenachs left wee Beth on her own ever since her mother was taken to hospital. Titern was paid by her great aunt tae take care of her and he hasn't."

"She's been on her own? What do you mean, Patrick? We nuns haven't been here for two weeks because his Eminence the Cardinal had visited our diocese."

"Ye should have shown him this unholy place, Sister. We might be treated kinder if he witnessed all this for himself."

"His Eminence didn't have time to visit the workhouse, Patrick, although we told him about some of the goings-on here. He said he will come the next time he is in this area."

"Let's hope he does. If only for wee Beth's sake."

"Aren't Titern's wardens taking good care of her? Didn't Mr. Titern keep his word?"

"Nae, Sister. They have nae washed nor changed her. They've done nothing except feed her. It looks like it's been going on since they took her mother in to hospital a couple o' days ago. Awe, you should see her, Sister. The wee lassie is in a bad way. She cannot look after herself. It's a crying shame. So it is. She has food slops o' over her clothes and her cell stinks o' rotten food and shite. Sorry for ma use o' words there, Sister, but I speak God's honest truth tae ye."

A horrified expression came onto the nun's face. She lifted the hem of her habit and briskly marched to Beth's cell to witness it for herself. When she opened the door, she broke her vows and swore with such anger the devil would have been pleased she'd fallen from grace and would have offered her a chair at his side.

Patrick laughed hearing the nun use bad language. She turned her red face away, clearly ashamed that she'd cursed, and she blessed herself.

"Patrick, do what you think is best for this unfortunate child. I will go and see Governor Titern immediately. This kind of thing must never happen. No human being ought to experience such treatment. And to think, Titern will have been paid a handsome price to look after the child by her wealthy great aunt."

"Right ye are, Sister. It's all right. I will look after her maself. Thank you kindly. Bless ye, Sister, bless ye," he said while bowing his head a few times as he continued to drag the squeaky laundry cart into the cell.

The nun marched to the governor's office as if she had a legion of nuns beside her. Patrick heard Beth giggling. She seemed to think it funny the nun had used profanity.

Patrick attended to Beth's toilet needs first, then took the wet bedding away and replaced it with the best he found, as he reflected about Beth. *Awe Christ, I don't want anything bad tae happen tae this wee lassie. When I first came here, I was able tae fend for maself a wee bit but she can nae.*

He placed Beth in a chair and covered her with a clean warm blanket while he swilled the floor in an attempt to get rid of the stink.

"How would yer mother feel aboot our friendship if I don't take care o' her wee lassie until she returns? Nae, Beth, ye are safe now. I'm so sorry ye got in this state. I've been so busy in the kitchen and was certain yer mother and ye had moved tae the farm. I didn't know she was taken bad and took tae hospital."

When he finished cleaning, he picked up Beth and placed her into her now clean, dry bed. "I'll nae let anything bad happen to ye again, wee-yen. From now on ye will be in the kitchen with me. Into bed you go, lass. Ye will have a sound sleep tonight and every night frae now on."

He thought it had been awhile since she'd felt so cozy. When she looked at him with big blue smiling eyes, he could see she knew he meant his words. She drifted into a warm, sweet sleep while Patrick sat in a big old chair in the corner, watching over her during the night, with only one heavy blanket draped around him.

Directly after breakfast the next morning, Patrick marched right up to governor Titern, grabbed him by the throat. "I know ye have been getting money tae keep the wee lassie and ye pocketed it all. Ye greedy Sassenach pig!"

Titern's skin colour took on the appearance of white emulsion. The other inmates fell into shrieks of laughter and were unable to swallow their food for laughing. Patrick grabbed Titern's shirt firmly by the front and continued to yell in his hulky Scottish accent while shaking him like a rabid dog killing a rat.

"Listen, Titern. I'm looking after the wee mite frae now on. Ye best get somebody to help me in the kitchen. I will have Beth in there with me frae noo on, so I'll need mare scullery help. And if ye throw me oot o' here because o' what I just said, then I will take wee Beth with me. If she isn't living in here, then you get nae mare money frae her wealthy family."

The Scotsman released his grip on the governor's throat and Titern fell to the floor in a daze. Patrick appeared full of himself and had finally found the courage to stand up to Titern. Patrick cocked his head upward as proud as the king of the jungle and put his massive clenched fist toward Titern's face. "Ye got any problems with anything I just said to you, Titern?"

The governor's face ran red, but he didn't say a word. He rose to his feet, shook his head like a beaten dog with its tail between its legs and ploughed out of the room, banging doors along the way. He snarled and hollered at anyone he passed in the hallways.

In subsequent days, Patrick added wheels to an old chair, which made it easier for him to move Beth around. The nuns applauded Patrick for his resourceful ingenuity. Then something unheard of happened. Patrick received authorization from Mother Superior to move his cot into Beth's cell instead of sleeping in a chair beside her cot to guard her each night.

Apparently, the workhouse governor didn't want to allow it because

Patrick and Beth were not relatives. But the nun had told Patrick that she had insisted and had pointed out to the governor that she had seen other children pinch Beth until she bled. She told him the child needed protection and that she couldn't run away from this sort of mistreatment.

Moreover, the smart nuns knew that Beth would be in peril from immoral males now her body was blossoming into young womanhood. Many people knew certain inmates wanted Beth dead. They called her the Devil's Spawn because of her spasms.

Neither Patrick nor the nuns could believe the terrible things the Ginns's inhabitants said about Beth. Patrick felt glad she was with him in the kitchen or safe in her cell at nightfall.

He sometimes witnessed a blue glow appearing inside their cell during the night. He didn't tell anyone about the apparition. He thought they'd deem him insane. Each time the blue glow appeared, it had the shape of a female.

Sometimes the entity showed itself in the kitchen and it watched Patrick like it was sussing him out. Beth seemed to know he could see it too and wanted to talk about it. But each time she tried she almost went over the edge because she couldn't talk coherently.

"Blue Pat woman."

"Sorry, lassie. I'm not sure what ye mean."

He hadn't yet learned how to fully understand her so early in their friendship. Beth's mind was as sharp as a razor's edge, yet she was unable to speak a complete, coherent sentence. He couldn't understand it.

Beth was now twelve years old and she could speak few words, which always came out back to front. She sounded like a toddler learning to talk or like someone a doctor might label as soft in the head. Her inability to speak steadily drove her to distraction. No matter how hard she tried, her mouth just wouldn't produce the words she wanted to express.

One day Patrick threatened the inmates. "Ye best leave the wee lassie a-lain. If ye don't leave her in peace then I'll give ye o' smaller helpings. And ye parents will get nae fruit frae me for ye kids either. To make it clearer for ye all, I'd slit yer throats when nae body is watching if ye hurt Beth again. So I will."

They stopped taunting and the hall fell silent, except for Beth's giggles. She knew she'd found a true friend in Patrick. Her laughter annoyed the inmates even more.

Time sped by for Patrick and Beth while Constance was in hospital until after Easter in 1912, when Titern made a public announcement.

"It is with great sorrow that I must inform everyone of some dreadful news. The great unsinkable ship, the HMS Titanic, has sunk and more than fifteen hundred lives have been lost."

The whole place buzzed with sighs of disbelief. Beth's mother was still in hospital, so there was no way she could know if any of her relatives were lost in the catastrophe. None of the other Ginns residents had relatives aboard the grave vessel, although some had dreamed of sailing to far off lands on such a ship.

Conversations whirled round the workhouse for weeks on the mystery of the unsinkable titan ship, now sleeping on the floor of the Atlantic.

By this time séances were popular in the northern counties of England. Two new arrivals to Ginns, Mary Crab and her cousin Linda Hobbs, held a séance in their cell just about every night. They knew dabbling in the paranormal was against Ginns rules, and if the nuns ever caught them, they'd chuck them out by their ears onto the street.

Although intrigued by the mystery of séances, Patrick would have no part of it, mostly because he didn't want to leave Beth alone even in a locked cell. He also knew the nuns would be angry with him if he joined in what the church in those days deemed as unholy acts punishable by eviction.

Patrick didn't mention anything about the séances to Beth, as he thought she'd be frightened. He really hadn't the slightest idea she'd already experienced the supernatural herself as a baby in the Vermonts' cellar as well as inside Ginns. He'd failed to remember that Beth wasn't alarmed when the blue figure appeared in the kitchen. But by the warm look in her eyes back then, he felt she could see it too, so he believed the blue spectre to be angelic in nature.

Soon after the séances began strange events occurred in the workhouse laundry room and dimly lit areas, especially on the lowest level at night. Inmates shouted and shrieked that there was a demon in their cells. Two laundry women said they watched boorish men floating two feet above the laundry room floor, wearing full Viking warrior attire, complete with iron axes. Equipment was said to have mysteriously moved by itself. The laundry was a scary place to be, especially after eight o'clock at night. Even the maniacs were petrified to go near the lower levels.

The night screams grew louder and louder as the days passed by. The nuns had neither heard nor seen anything, as they returned to their convent an hour after dinner each evening.

One night Patrick heard ear-popping screams and limped into the hallway yelling, "What is going on oot there? It's late. We're trying to kip in here."

A woman sounded terrified as she shrieked, "Help me, Patrick. Something invisible and clammy just touched my leg. It felt horrible.

Damn that Mary Black and her brainless séances. I think she's opened the way into Hades itself!"

Patrick shouted back to the frightened woman, "Maybe Mary has opened the gates of hell. I know there's a strange looking door on the lowest level. Anyway, it's entirely yer own fault for dabbling in the ungodly along with Mary and her sidekick."

"My God, Pat, what door? I've worked everywhere in the damn laundry and I've seen no door."

"Shut up about it, woman. Ye can nae see it. The damn thing's been bricked over. I first heard the tale frae an old geezer in here. He said his father told him of it years ago."

The woman fell silent. Patrick glanced into the cell at Beth who appeared uneasy. Her face contorted as she said, "Patrick here stay me."

Even as he watched over her, life in the workhouse was becoming a frightening place for her yet again.

Patrick yelled to the now-silent woman up the corridor, "I'm going back to my cell now, so I hope ye lot shut up. I'm knackered with all yer carryings-on."

He turned to enter the cell. From the corner of his eye, he glimpsed something moving toward him in the corridor. Patrick paused for a moment to get a better view. When it drew closer, he saw a dark shape inside a cloud of black smoke. It had the form of a large man with an even denser black smoke-like substance hovering along the ground behind it.

"What in the hell is *that*?" Patrick muttered.

When it drew nearer some of the dark, hazy matter grew clearer. He saw a creature with cloven hooves and tentacle-like horns that moved snakelike on either side of its head. It made indescribable noises like a tortured hellhound would if its fangs were ripped from its jaw. All of a sudden, the beast pierced Patrick's soul with flame-red eyes, so sharp he thought they'd penetrate his flesh. Alarmed, he swiftly re-entered his cell, closing the door hard behind him, only to find Beth with a beaming smile.

"What did ye just see that made you smile, lass?" Patrick soon realised why she smiled. In the corner of his eye he saw a familiar bright blue entity at the far corner of their cell. *Can wee Beth see it too? Without any doubt, that blue spectre is from the light. I wonder if it materialized to protect us from the sinister being in the lobby.* The blue being wasn't from the same place as the ugly creature he'd just seen in the hallway.

The sinister entity in the corridor stopped for a moment outside their door and sniffed, as if searching for food...or a victim. The blue entity flew toward their door and grew colossal in size and immeasurably bright. Their whole cell lit up as if a thousand candles burned all at once. "Do not fear, Patrick," the entity said. "I was sent by Briathos, the angel who thwarts demons."

Patrick could not believe either his ears or his eyes.

Within moments the evil creature outside moved away from their door, whimpering like a wounded dog. It travelled along the hallway, snarling and munching as if it was tearing at flesh. Patrick heard a few more male and female screams—and then silence.

"Scared me. Pat, you?" mumbled Beth.

"Nae, not noo lassie. Whatever the thing oot there was, it's gone noo. Don't bother yer wee self either, Beth. Ye go back tae sleep, me la'arl wee love. Hopefully, the rest of the night will go by quietly. By the way, lass, did you see that big, bright blue light in here a few minutes ago?"

Eager to mention the blue spectre to someone, she nodded her head. Patrick felt relieved to know she was aware of it too—proof he wasn't going crazy, especially after it spoke to him.

"Are you scared of that being inside the blue glow, Beth?"

She shook her head while smiling and uttered a shaky, "Pat, no before seen manor lots."

He climbed into his bed to return to sleep, alternating between watching the door and staring at the crucifix hanging on the wall opposite. The workhouse was completely silent. When his tired eyes began to close, he noticed that the blue glow had moved from the door to the other side of the room, between the door and Beth's cot.

Patrick had never been concerned about the goings-on in the place before. Until that particular night nothing bad had ever happened to him or Beth, except for dirty looks and comments from inmates. Now something much worse had occurred—the appearance of the unholy dark creature. He grew nervous for their welfare and felt relieved he had not attended the spirit meetings himself.

At dawn Patrick heard frantic screams. He placed Beth in her chair, locked the cell and headed toward the voices.

"What in the hell's been happening in here lately?" he said to a passerby in the hall.

"Awe, it's just terrible, Pat. Somebody found a female with her throat ripped out in the laundry this morning. They couldn't tell who it was because her facial skin was torn off and one of her legs was missing."

Beth screeched with fright.

The passerby continued tearfully, "One woman said her roommate wasn't in their cell this morning. Then she wept buckets realizing whose body was discovered, or rather, the pieces of a body. The floor down there is drenched in blood and is strewn with half-eaten flesh. Blood's everywhere, Patrick. Everywhere!"

"Dear God, this place is turning horrific!" Patrick turned to look at Beth in an attempt to conceal his own fear of the dark forces lurking in the shadows inside Ginns. "Don't you bother about this wee one. I won't let anything bad happen to you."

Beth gazed at him in silence. Her ashen face confirmed her feelings of trepidation.

Sister Francesca summoned Father McDougal. When he arrived, he blessed the woman's remains and instructed staff to take her to the morgue. Then he made the two new women, Mary and Linda, clean up the blood splatters on the floors, walls and ceiling before anyone could begin work.

The Father announced at lunchtime, "I will be questioning everyone to discover if anything ungodly has been practised here. The carnage last night didn't just start last night. Something or somebody brought that malevolence in here and I intend to find out who it was."

A young novice sister said, "I'm sure it must be a rabid dog that sneaked in or a wild animal that escaped from a zoo. I mean, what else could be responsible for that much carnage, Father?"

"You'd be surprised, young Sister," said Father McDougal, with one raised eyebrow and a nod.

After the floor was scrubbed, Sister Francesca and the novice visited the laundry. They overheard two women whispering about the creepy events during the night and the terrifying dark creatures that had floated around the workhouse for weeks. The novice shivered in dread.

Sister Francesca asked if anyone knew who had participated in anything ungodly, like the Ouija board or any form of black magic.

A woman pointed to Mary and Linda. "They've been holding séances every night since they arrived here a few weeks ago."

Enraged, Sister Francesca approached the two women. "I insist you stop your black gatherings immediately, or you'll leave Ginns. Matter of fact, I should throw the both of you out right now."

Mary and Linda bowed their heads as though in shame and followed her orders. There was nowhere else for them to live except a whorehouse or the street with the guttersnipes.

Sister Francesca added, "Everyone who participated in these women's witchery must take part in prayer meetings instead. This will begin immediately."

Prayers did not prevent further unspeakable events occurring. The nuns pleaded with Father McDougal to perform an exorcism on the building and on several angry inmates in an attempt to cleanse the place of evil. The nuns were lucky they didn't have to contact the Pope and have to wait for a reply. After Father McDougal's previous success with exorcisms, the Pope had granted him prudence to use his own judgement to execute them.

The priest ordered nonstop prayer meetings day and night for a whole month. Work came to a virtual standstill because the majority of their time was used up in prayer.

Three days passed by after the first exorcism. Then Father McDougal informed Patrick and Beth inside their cell, "You can safely return to your duties now. Everything in the kitchen is back in operation."

To Sister Francesca, Father McDougal added, "The people who are still disturbed during the night must be suffering from nightmares because there is no sign of any physical malevolence. What's more, I checked the carved archway on the lower level and all the outer walls three times since our last cleansing ritual. An uneducated person would never understand what those carvings down there mean, but to be safe, I've drenched the whole room with holy oils every day. We've cleansed the whole place with prayers and exorcisms. Nothing, not even Asmodeus the Archdemon, whose name is carved down there, will ever pass through that devilish arch again. It's cemented shut."

"Thank you, Father. I hope this is the end to all the unpleasantness here," Sister Francesca said with a relaxed expression on her face. She paused then asked Father McDougal, "Father, I wonder if Mary and Linda recognized those carvings, because they performed their rituals directly on top of them."

"I shouldn't think so, Sister. I dare say it was sheer luck or ill-luck. Mary does have a nursing degree, so she will have some intellect, but I doubt she is fully versed in the black arts. She wouldn't recognise the demon name, Amadeus, written in Latin. Frankly, those two women seem like novices to me. Besides, as long as Mary and Linda do not begin their wickedness again, we must be good Christians and allow them both to stay here."

"Yes, of course, Father. If we do not show kindness to them, what chance would they have outside these walls?"

People suffered nightmares after the exorcisms, so screams continued throughout the night. None of the washerwomen would enter the laundry later than suppertime for weeks. Many inmates retained ill feelings toward Mary Black and Linda Hobbs. Unable to withstand everyone's hostility, they both left Ginns workhouse for pastures new in southern England.

After awhile, the remaining inmates' nightmares ceased with no additional reports of any negativity or poltergeist activity, and the rest of the year passed uneventfully, especially for Patrick and Beth. They kept to themselves after the evil creature had appeared wreaking havoc. The only extraordinary event was that a blue radiance lit their room every night thereafter. No one other than Beth and Patrick ever saw it, and they slept sounder than everyone else. Neither of them enlightened anyone in Ginns about their protective blue guardian angel.

In 1913, while Constance was still convalescing in Saint Luke's hospital, Christmas Eve morning broke. At breakfast Sister Francesca ordered, "The chapel floors must be scrubbed and the pulpit polished until it glistens for Midnight Mass tonight. Do I have any volunteers?"

Everybody gawked at their emptied plates, not wanting to lend a hand. Patrick offered, because he had plenty of time on his hands with having extra help in the scullery.

In preparation for the special day, the nuns scurried around like renegade spinning tops, searching for decorations. Sister Monica handed Patrick a box of sparkly ornaments.

"When you've finished your cooking and cleaning, I'd like you to hang a few holly decorations in the dining area, with Beth. Please add a few of these bright trinkets to the chapel as well."

Beth watched Patrick climb ladders to suspend the colourful fringes. With her eyes fixed on Patrick's derrière, she began to giggle uncontrollably. She'd found something comical about the shape of his rear end, although she couldn't tell him why it was so humorous. And he didn't have any idea why she was giggling. Beth was almost fourteen now and more aware of the differences between men and women. Her bubbly, contagious laughter set off Patrick chuckling as well.

With laughter in his voice, he said, "Be a good lassie. I'll fall if ye don't stop trying tae make me laugh."

She bubbled up a chuckle. "Sorry me Pat."

Of course, Patrick still didn't know what she was laughing at.

He almost choked with laughter. "It's o' right lass. I love tae hear ye laugh." He continued fixing the decorations.

The place looked like a home with all the tinsel and baubles. The Scotsman had been artful and it looked pretty.

"Purple. Nice."

"Aye, lassie, it is. Did ye know purple represents the Good and High Spirit? This is why churches use it. They say the colour protects people from negativity, giving everyone a wee lift. We should hang purple all the time to keep our spirits up."

"Me tired."

"I know, lass. I'm tired tae. We'll be sleeping afore ye know it. I just need tae put these boxes away first." Patrick gazed at her long and hard, inhaled a deep breath and sighed. "Ye are so pretty, Beth, and yer eyes are as bright as a summer sky. I wish ye could talk better than ye do, lass. So the doctors did nae find oot why ye can't talk, huh? Because I know ye are intelligent."

"Pat. It all right, me."

"Aye, lass, ye seem happy enough even though yer mother is still in hospital. She'll be well cared for in yonder and there's nowt as sure as that. And ye have me taking care of ye in here. Let's get back to oor cell. We have a busy day on the morrow—it's Christmas!"

Beth gave him a slight *Mona Lisa* type of smile and without warning her eyes turned sad. When Patrick saw her face, he knew her heart weighed heavy. Perhaps she remembered Christmases past at the manor, with gifts, singing and banquets.

He silently stroked her cheek, then put the boxes away and wheeled her to their room to rest. As they passed by each door, they heard singing from the cells, most likely because there was no work in the morning. Workhouse inmates had few days off. Christmas was one of them.

Hours later, at midnight, thunderous bells woke them. It was their sign to attend Midnight Mass. The weather outside was cold and ugly, and a storm was brewing.

One overseer, wrapped in a double sheepskin, pummelled on everyone's door. "C'mon, you lazy lot, out your beds. Those who don't go to Mass tonight will receive the usual porridge in the morning, not the special breakfast we have planned. You'd best wrap up. It's snowing."

Many inmates wanted to remain in their beds because it was so cold, but they didn't because they'd miss the special Christmas breakfast. Good food wasn't provided too often in Ginns.

Beth squealed with excitement. "Chris-mast Pat. Chris-mast merry."

Patrick wrapped his young friend in another blanket. "Aye, me wee lass, it is and a merry one to ye. Now close yer eyes and open yer mouth. I have something for ye."

The previous day he'd found a small piece of chocolate on the floor in Titern's private food cupboard. He placed it inside her lips as her Christmas gift. His gift from her was a wide grin as she sucked on the sweetness. When it melted on her tongue, some chocolaty goo escaped out of the corner of her lips and skated down toward her chin. Patrick wiped it off with his sleeve then hopped around on his good leg like a court jester to make her laugh. She hooted and chuckled, which pleased Patrick even more.

He lifted Beth from her bed and tucked her blanket around her for the cold journey along the draughty hallways to the chapel. His lame leg hurt much more in damp, cold weather and he limped all the way.

In spite of his pain he cheerily said, "At least they'll nae be singing them miserable workhouse songs tonight, Beth lass. Nae, tonight we will hear joyful hymns! 'Joy Tae the World' is ma particular favourite. But you're ma main joy in this foul pigging place."

With sparkling eyes, Beth bounced a gleaming smile at him and tried to hum his favourite hymn. An advancing seizure made her stop because she had produced too much saliva and almost choked on it. She murmured, "Daft Pat me."

"It's all right. Ye tried. Come on, lassie. Let's get ourselves in to the front pews. That new nun, Sister Benedict, has a wonderful voice and I want to make sure we both get to hear her sing."

He tucked Beth's blankets snugly round her shoulders as they entered the chapel. It was bitterly cold, but they both enjoyed the hymns.

When the ceremony ended, everyone returned to their cells to slumber for a few hours under extra blankets that Patrick had swiped from the laundry earlier that same day.

The following morning at seven, an hour later than usual, the bell rang for Christmas Day prayers.

In the morning Patrick discovered that their windowpane was adorned with frosty winter beauty, partnered with lengthy icicles hanging from the sills. Condensation had run down the inside of the windows and before it reached the bottom, it had frozen, filling tiny cracks in the glass. No icy blasts would pass through their window until winter was over.

A cheer rose when the workers saw the special breakfast. It was eggs, not gruel. Patrick gave his eggs to Beth, since they constipated him, so he preferred to go hungry until lunchtime.

After breakfast, he and Beth returned to their cell as the inmates began to sing.

It is Christmas Day in the workhouse,
And the cold, bare walls are bright
With garlands of green and holly,
And the place is a pleasant sight:
For with clean-washed hands and faces,
In a long and hungry line
The paupers sit at the tables,
For this is the hour they dine.

"There they go again singing them depressing songs. I knew peace would nae reign in here for very long."

Beth nodded her head in the direction of the corridor, pointing the way with her eyes and muttered, "Back go Pat, no worry now."

Patrick placed her in her heavily blanketed bed to snooze before returning to the kitchen to prepare lunch.

Feeling snug, she rolled over to stare at the cross on the wall and then wondered what sort of Christmas her mother was having in hospital. *Dear God, it's been so long since I've seen Mama. I want her back. Please make her well and let her return. Amen.*

CHAPTER FOURTEEN

Unknown to Beth, her mother's life was growing more abysmal. For almost three years Constance fixed her eyes on the plain tiled grey walls, rocked herself back and forth, and droned like a bee in a one-note continuous hum without uttering a single coherent word. The nurses force-fed her from the very first week.

One morning one of the doctors spoke to the nursing Sister while he observed Constance.

"Does this woman ever attend to her own personal care, Sister?"

"No, Doctor. Lady Constance has been disinclined to do anything for herself since she arrived. Mother Superior assumed that in due course she would speak to me, because I am friendly. Sadly, she hasn't spoken a solitary word to anyone since she arrived here, approximately three years ago."

"I see, Sister."

He turned toward his colleague, who by this time was shaking his head. "Then consequently we have no alternative other than deem her unfit of mind. She originally came from the workhouse, so we will admit her into the communal wards of Garlands Asylum."

The Sister gasped loudly. It was obvious they hadn't read Constance's medical history, so she retorted, "Doctors, her aunt pays for her to stay here."

"Oh, I see. Well, that doesn't matter now. We need the room for someone with a chance of recovery. Three years have passed by and I do not think this woman will ever improve."

Money was on their minds more than their patient's health or the need to free up a bed. She'd seen it happen there many times before. Money ruled them.

The years in the workhouse had taken a heavy toll on Constance's body and mind. Outwardly she didn't appear to care but she understood the doctors' conversation and knew the asylum would be bleaker than Ginns. So consequently, a few days later, she woke up in Garlands Asylum in a ward colder than the workhouse.

Two nurses dragged her by the scruff of the neck, from her bed to the therapy rooms, to receive what the doctors called "freezing water therapy." The doctors said the cold baths were shock therapy, designed to jolt a patient back into the real world. At least they wrapped her in a thick blanket after each ice bath or she'd have caught pneumonia.

During and after therapy, Constance was the quietest patient in the entire asylum. Other patients screamed and wailed relentlessly. One patient, who the nurses called the 'Window Woman,' would stand banging her head against the wooden window frame, until it bled. Constance watched with a blank expression as three nurses subdued the woman with a straight jacket and then dragged her into a padded cell to medicate and quiet her.

Another female patient sat in an old scruffy chair all day, quietly rocking herself back and forth. Suddenly, for no apparent reason, she jumped up, raced to the middle of the room and emptied her bowels on the floor. No matter how often they scrubbed the floor the room smelled like a cesspit.

Then there was the 'Fly Woman,' who liked to catch flies buzzing past. If she found a spider's web, she ate that creature as well as its home. Then she'd smack her lips as if she'd eaten a juicy steak. Her breath stank.

Those were terrible times for Constance. She was fully aware, she just didn't want to speak. Weeks of cold baths passed by before she eventually spoke to nurse Penelope Smith, her old friend and the daughter of the doctor Constance had mentioned to her aunt before she and Beth deserted the manor forever.

One day, Constance grew alarmed when she overheard two physicians talking about operating on her. Although she hadn't spoken a word, she realised it was crucial her aunt was informed quickly or she would be minus a few organs, or worse—she'd be dead. At long last, she spoke a complete albeit stuttering sentence. "Penelope, m-may I...c-can I have permission t-to write a letter to my Aunt Betsy p-please?"

"Oh, Constance my dear. It's really wonderful to hear you talking again. Yes, wait a minute. I will fetch you some paper."

Moments later, Penelope returned with a short wax pencil and two loose sheets of paper. "Here you are, dear. It is against the rules to give a patient a pen because the doctors say they might use it as a weapon."

"Th-thank you, Penelope."

"I'll return in ten minutes and if you like, I'll deliver your note to your aunt personally."

Constance nodded while scribbling a few lines and promptly passed her note to Penelope.

"Oh, you're finished already?" Penelope seized the paper and eagerly ran outside. She clambered into the motor car that her father had given her on last birthday and delivered the vital communiqué within the hour.

Betsy was pleased to see Penelope and welcomed her like a distinguished guest.

"I have a letter for you from your niece, milady."

Penelope passed the missive to Betsy, who sat in an old velvet wing chair and read it out loud. "'Dear Aunt Betsy, the doctors in Garlands are going to operate on my brain tomorrow. I implore you, please help me. Your loving niece, Connie.'"

Old Betsy slipped backward, sinking deeply into her chair, shocked with the note's contents.

"You look pale, Lady Witherspoon. Shall I fetch you a glass of water from the table over there, or perhaps some smelling salts?"

"Yes, thank you, dear. Water...please. You really are a true friend to my niece."

When Penelope returned with the water, Betsy said, "Thank heavens you work in that dismal Garlands or I might never have gotten to learn of Constance's plight."

"I am indeed her friend, Lady Witherspoon. I knew you would be concerned for her welfare, especially since the doctors are about to operate. I'm repulsed at some types of therapy they use on their patients. You see, after the procedure, many of them have the intellect of a cabbage and a few have died. As a normal rule, they just perform this type of operation on state patients, except they plan to do this with Constance because she was brought to Garlands from the workhouse, so they think she is a pauper."

"I see. And what kind of operation were they about to perform on my niece? Constance didn't write the name."

"Well, Lady Witherspoon, Dr. Henry Cotton is the nation's notable mental health surgeon. He discovered that bloodletting is not as efficient as removing certain glands or other bodily parts to fix mental illness. The asylum doctors plan to do a gland-removing procedure to fix Constance's silent gloom. The only reason for their decision is that she doesn't speak to anyone, although she did speak to me today. It's no wonder she doesn't speak. The poor lady is dreadfully unhappy and adding to everything else, her nasty room is damp and without a fire."

Lady Witherspoon's face changed to mauve with anger.

"You're right, Penelope. I'm exceedingly alarmed hearing your report. I will not have my niece treated in such a fashion, nor will I allow her to suffer any barbaric medical procedures. And she must have a fire in her room. Ye gads, this time of year the temperature drops heavily during the night. Please return to that damned asylum before it's too late and inform those despicable doctors that I'll visit my niece on the morrow."

Betsy reached across the table beside her to get a sheet of paper from the drawer and began to write. Moments later, she handed the letter to Penelope.

"Here, my dear, please take this letter to the asylum. It states the surgeons must not touch my niece with a knife or any other inhumane implement. If they do, my generous yearly endowment to them will cease. Please make sure they read it right away."

Penelope's face beamed in elation. As she was leaving, Lady Witherspoon called out, "Don't forget to tell those damn doctors that I am visiting my niece tomorrow."

"With pleasure, milady!" Penelope returned to the asylum to deliver her important message with a wide grin firmly planted on her face and a giggle inside. *The doctors will not like the contents of this correspondence. The chance of the asylum losing money is enough of a threat.*

Many wealthy benefactors would also stop their donations if Lady Witherspoon asked them to because they held her Ladyship in such high regard.

Penelope handed the note to a doctor and watched as he threw the note onto the fire. She knew they would never have the nerve to touch Constance now.

The following afternoon Lady Elizabeth's car squealed to a halt at the front entrance of the asylum, and she entered the building as if she rode in on a whirlwind. The expressions on the doctors' faces displayed their disapproving annoyance. It was best to say nothing, because Lady Witherspoon's eyes bulged as she glared at them, showing she was angrier than they were.

An orderly escorted her to where Constance rested. Betsy found the room cosier than Penelope had described, with a soft bed, several covers and a comfortable chair beside a roaring fire.

Due to Constance's debilitated condition, the only words she could muster when she saw her aunt were, "Thank you, Auntie."

The elderly woman sat by the fire warming her hands, silently deliberating for an hour. Without a word she suddenly stood up, hugged her niece and left the room to bellow acidic words at the doctors in their office.

"Look here. My niece must be kept in a warm room at all times, do you hear? She must not be returned to the wintry cell you heartless scoundrels normally lock her in."

The doctors assumed that Constance had somehow informed her aunt about her previous living conditions and so kept her in the better room from then on. They continued to plunge her into iced water daily and treated her as if she were completely insane. Penelope knew the truth, that Constance was weary from undergoing too many traumas over the years.

A few months before Betsy's visit to the asylum, she had met Sir James Forsythe Jr. at a séance and the two had forged a close friendship. Betsy believed in omens and deemed James as special because a dream he once had saved his life. He had dreamt his close childhood friend, Adam, was on the brink of death and an angel had told him to rush to his friend's bedside. He'd already purchased a ticket for the RMS Titanic's maiden voyage and had the dream the night before the ship put to sea. James was disappointed he'd miss the first sailing, but his friend's welfare was more important to him. When he had arrived at Adam's home, he'd found his friend merely bedridden with a simple cold and not dying at all.

Five days later James had heard the RMS Titanic had sunk with thousands of people drowned. At the time, James said to Betsy, "My dream story was plastered over the tabloids, including the church rags. I felt a little embarrassed by it. Although I'm thankful I paid attention to that prophetic dream and avoided the terrible catastrophe and possibly my own demise."

Betsy said, "We had an elderly cousin that we lost to the Titanic."

He didn't say a word and just embraced her.

His loving reaction made her realize that James was a kind-hearted man and made her feel confident she could confide in him about her niece. "Constance has had a terrible life James. She doesn't belong in Garland's asylum. You live closer than I do. It's obvious you're a good-hearted young gentleman. Would you visit my niece on my behalf to keep and eye on her wellbeing?"

One of James's eyebrows rose upward, showing his intrigue. "Certainly shall, my dear."

Thus after more than three years of distress and suffering, Constance received the answer to her silent prayers through his regular visits. She began to talk more each passing day as she and James became friends.

In time Constance told James details about how her husband, Sir Mathew, had deserted her to live with Beatrice Bunting and had taken her sons with him.

James's facial expression grew somewhat vacant with the shock of learning a woman would take another's children. "Constance, I heard about Beatrice's droves of male visitors from my friends. They said she is a widow and a harlot. You're so beautiful. Why on earth would he leave you for such a wayward woman as Beatrice?"

"Beth, my first child, was young and hard to handle," Constance said. She flushed red with embarrassment because he had used the word *harlot.*

James noted her embarrassment by her plum-coloured face. He put his arms around her shoulders. "And to take your sons with him into...into such a whorehouse. Well, it was a deplorable thing for a gentleman to do. Ye gads. He is no gentleman. He's a cad."

After a while, James helped Constance to procure a divorce from Mathew on the grounds of abandonment, and in time, James grew devoted to her. He realised she didn't belong in Garlands and that she was not insane at all. She was just a desperate mother struggling to keep her daughter alive and safe.

When James thought he'd heard enough of both sides of the story, he was sympathetic toward Betsy's side. *So this is why the old lady didn't want to have Beth living in her home. The child was young and it would have been far too much for her at that time in her life.*

James didn't understand that there was much more to the story than anyone had previously shared with him.

When the scandal of Constance's divorce died down, young James proposed to her. "My dear, would you do me the honour of marrying me? I require a soft-hearted, determined wife, one endowed with a true and noble countenance such as yourself. And you already know how to entertain my wealthy friends. I promise I'd never disappear from your life."

"Yes, my love, I accept. You would never behave the same way as Mathew Vermont."

They decided to wed the following month.

Constance insisted their marriage service should be held in Saint Nicholas Church, on Lathiere Street in Whitehaven, and not at the more ancient Saint James Church. Her reason was that Saint Nicholas was where George Washington's grandmother, Mildred Warner Gale, had been laid to rest in 1701. Constance had always admired George Washington's deep understanding of humanity and his love of God. His mother had insisted her black slave girl, Jane, must be buried inside Saint Nicholas's cemetery.

"That would have been quite the surprise for the community in those days, Constance," James said. "I loathe prejudice against the coloureds. So, darling, I don't care which church we marry in as long as we do marry."

In addition to selecting the church, Constance insisted that Patrick must be present during and after the ceremony. He had been a faithful friend and he would be there to take care of her daughter. James had just heard short stories about Beth—mostly that she was quiet and used a wheelchair. He didn't meet her in person until the day of the wedding. He likely assumed her excessive twitching was just nerves because of the wedding. No one had divulged the truth about her medical condition to him.

On the wedding day the nuns instructed that Mr. Titern had to have transport ready, promptly at noon, to carry Patrick and Beth to Saint Nicholas for the service.

For the ceremony Beth wore a russet-coloured dress and coat with a matching short-brimmed hat and gloves that Glessal's store had delivered to Ginns.

Patrick looked like a dashing prince wearing the grey suit Mr. Titern had loaned him. He didn't loan it to be kind. Sister Benedict had ordered him to do it.

After the wedding the two chattering nuns rushed around collecting Beth's few belongings. She was ready to leave the poorhouse forever. They behaved like excited children at a birthday party.

"Sister, she must take the statue Patrick carved for her."

"Indeed, Sister Benedict, and the little Bible I gave her, she must take that too."

"Yes, yes. But don't let her take that awful grubby blanket she has grown attached to, Sister, it's so grimy. If she needs one, James will provide her with another."

Later on inside the chapel, the nuns held a private service to thank God that Lady Constance had met James. Now her future would be brighter than her recent past.

CHAPTER FIFTEEN

It was a clear fine day as James, Constance and Beth moved into Forsythe Manor, the vast white mansion that James's grandfather had bequeathed his mother. The old manor was situated on the hill that overlooked the workhouse and the Irish Sea. The newlyweds took Patrick with them to be their chief stableman, since he had been a devoted friend. He would be in charge of inexperienced stable hands and garage employees, and still be their close friend and confidante.

As they approached the manor, it glittered like a magical fairyland castle in the sunshine, even though it was more than two centuries old. It glistened and sparkled in the light, as if thousands of diamonds were trapped inside each stone.

Moving into the manor dramatically changed their lives. Beth would bear the name Lady Elisa Vermont-Forsythe, because her mother was descended from royalty. She possessed her own large, airy room. When she first saw the décor, she figured she'd died and gone to heaven. Flames licked up the chimney of a roaring fire in the corner. Two silver candlesticks stood proudly at either end of the carved mantel, throwing light onto the mirror on the wall above the tall fireplace.

A large, golden fur rug graced the front of the hearth. Deep pink cotton velvet curtains hung at the grandiose windows, with a pink rose pattern painted on the walls, three matching Persian rugs scattered on the floors. Beth's eyes popped wide open when she spied the huge bone china vases brimming with blooms on every surface, including the window ledges. The flower colours complemented the deep pink velvet chairs and couches. Opposite the largest window stood a massive, heavily carved four-poster bed, adorned with silken sheets and plush feather-filled pillowcases.

As the sun's warm fingers poured light across her bed through squeaky clean windows, the room grew bright and warm. The sun's gift appeared to turn her ivory-coloured sheets into gold. For a long time, Beth had longed to lie in a proper bed again, with pillows. Now she had this beautiful room all to herself.

Next to the bed stood Ruth, a pretty redhead, who was her personal maid and temporary nurse. Contrary to numerous tales about the temperaments of red-haired people, Ruth was a serene and patient woman, one who took time to understand Beth's needs.

In the weeks to follow James hired Miss Rachel Penny-Feather as a full-time governess for Beth. Rachel was the spoiled daughter of a once affluent banker who had unfortunately lost his wealth. The girl hated doing any kind of work, except now with her father's calamitous circumstances, there was no way she could support herself. No one knew where Rachel's father had gone after she took the position at Forsythe Manor, not even her.

The manor servants enjoyed gossip and Constance often eavesdropped on them, considering it a great way to discover who was who, and who did what. The first chitchat she overheard was between two maids outside in the hall.

"Francis—'ere. Did you 'ear what 'appened when Lady Constance's first husband, Sir Mathew, went to live with that Bunting slag?"

"Nay, Alice lass, what went on?" Francis said with a girlish giggle. Her co-worker always told great tales.

"Well, Francis, Mathew slapped that Bunting temptress two kiddies right away. Bang-bang. One right after the other. He couldn't look after the first two lads he had wiv our lovely Lady Constance here. Bunting. Oh aye she's a right slag that one. No man can go near her wiv out 'er getting into his bleeding britches. Well, she fell right in it when Mathew 'ammers 'er not one kid, but two. I'm surprised she never had kids before Mathew banged her up, the stupid slut." Alice concluded her tale with shrieks of laughter that echoed as far as the scullery.

Constance struggled to hold back her chuckles and was forced put her hand over her mouth to prevent detection.

One kitchen maid heard the hilarity and ran upstairs to listen in on the conversation. Constance ducked behind a pillar just in time so she wasn't caught snooping.

"You're too funny, Alice lass. So wit did they call them kids?"

"Elisabeth and Victoria."

"Did them wee mites 'ave any defects, Alice?"

"No, Francis. And because of missus fancy hot-pants Bunting's wealth, they was ordered to the royal household to further their education."

"I heard the royal household didn't miss any wee detail in Elisabeth and Victoria's education. That 'ome will have been the complete opposite of where our la'arl Beth lived for most of her life, God love 'er."

"Aye. It will 'ave been," Frances said. "Many of us were sickened each time anybody spoke of how badly Beth was treated by that ghastly two-timing Mathew. A right bastard he is. Them two wee ladies should never have 'ad to live in Ginns. Never."

Constance giggled softly and thought, *How curious. I wonder what other things I'll learn from these talkative servants.*

Life was splendid for Constance again. Later that same year she bore yet another set of twins, James Jr. and Martha.

James Sr. ordered that a section of the garden, with a swing and round-about, be fenced off as a play area for the children. As soon as his spoiled son reached three years of age, James presented him with a piebald pony. Selfish James Jr. ignored it, not even giving the animal a name. He attempted to steal his sister Martha's King Charles dog. She adored her puppy, which she had named Miss Pooches. This was the day when his sister finally stood her ground and fought back. She pulled her brother's hair, not allowing him to take her dog away. He ran away crying. He'd met his match that day.

In time, Constance noticed her children's behaviour toward each other and it infuriated her.

The year the twins turned four years of age, the family took a Christmas cruise of the Mediterranean on the steamship Tegucigalpa for six weeks. Two weeks before their departure, the accompanying household staff was presented with white clothing. The majority of Beth's clothes were pastel pink, to complement the stillness of her ivory complexion. Constance favoured blue or russet red and large white sunhats complete with a veil, to keep the insects away from her face.

The first leg of their cruise was visiting Spain and then onto Greece, followed by Italy. Their travel plans went without a hitch.

They hopped happily ashore in Italy and checked into their hotel.

Beth loved the warm temperature. Patrick disliked the hot nights, as he found it difficult to sleep and the heat made him cough and wheeze. To relax before bed, he would stand close to an open window, enjoying the heavy scent of honeysuckle flowers wafting by on a warm breeze.

On their first morning Beth inspected the many brightly coloured butterflies flittering effortlessly around the patio overhead. At times it looked as if they were inside a coloured snow dome. After breakfast they travelled inland to take in the surroundings and discover Italian wildlife. Everyone was happy, particularly when they saw the Hoopoe, a long-beaked parrot-style bird with an orange and black crest on its head, and bold striped wings. Beth chuckled, watching the bird's antics as it pecked at grass roots and bobbed up and down hunting for insects.

Patrick did most of the work, instead of Rachel. He liked pushing Beth's wheelchair along the hotel's private sea walkway after dinner. He enjoyed hearing the sound of waves crashing onto the rocks below and hearing Beth giggle when significant amounts of sea mist sprinkled on her face. "Wash me, get Pat ha."

He placed his hand on Beth's shoulder, pleased she was happy. She gazed upward with a cheeky glint in her eyes. "Shut now up," protesting against the seagulls' piercing squawks.

Her mother enjoyed relaxed chats with other guests or lounging in the hotel reception area, because the pale colour of the walls against the dark emerald green carpeting cooled her. When James arrived they both admired the view from the lobby across the gardens. This was when they met a young English family from Cornwall, Mr. Edward Bartholomew and his wife, Margaret. Edward was a successful businessman who dealt in fabrics, particularly fine silks from the Far East.

"Our children are in the hotel crèche today," Edward informed James.

"Our twins are there today as well," James said. "Would you and your wife care to stroll the gardens with my wife and me?"

A few days later, Edward presented Constance with a bolt of his finest royal-blue silk.

"My goodness. It is a spectacular shade of blue, Edward. This fabric feels divine, but I'm sorry, I cannot accept it." Constance stroked the fabric.

James interjected. "It will be all right to accept Edward's gift, my dear, now we're all acquainted and becoming friends. I must admit, it is such a remarkable shade."

"Yes," Margaret said. "Purplish blue is the colour of Spirit you know, so you must accept."

"Thank you, Edward. See how the fabric glistens in the light, James. It will make a spectacular gown."

"I'm so glad you like it, Constance," Edward said. "It was originally made for an Indian princess. Sadly, she died from a broken heart. Legend has it that she was in love with a man way beneath her station. Her father didn't want him near her, so had him executed—or so the tale says.

People declare when it is a full moon the ill fated lovers walk the palace terrace together hand in hand. Her father never witnessed this himself."

"Really, Edward, what a sad but tender story," James said. "We shall not wait until we return home. I will instruct the hotel dressmaker to turn it into a special gown for my wife to wear at Christmas."

In no time the four grew extremely close as if they'd known each other all their lives. James invited the Bartholomews to Forsythe Manor for a long visit in the spring the following year. They accepted.

Beth sat in her invalid chair beside the hotel pool.

"Why is she here?" Margaret asked Constance. "Is she a servant's daughter? Or has the girl been in an accident?"

"Beth is my daughter from a previous marriage."

"I've never heard of someone from high society keeping a crippled child. I'd assumed all babies born to rich families with an affliction were cared for in convents or the like."

"Beth's disability didn't appear until she was older, Margaret. By then it was too late for doctors to help her and I'd grown to love her. I couldn't bear to let her go."

"You were very brave to keep her. What would you have done with her if you had been underprivileged?"

Constance changed the topic, not wanting to remember the workhouse or that part of her life.

After four delightfully warm weeks, the Forsythe's said goodbye to their new friends, the Bartholomews. James and Constance left the hotel to continue the rest of their holiday on the Orient Express.

The train seemed to invigorate Beth as it chugged along, rattling on the track's joints. *Chu chu chug ka, chu chu chug ka.* She enjoyed the high speed they travelled, laughing each time the shrill whistle resonated through the Bulgarian mountains and valleys. It tickled as it buzzed inside her ears.

She enjoyed the spicy, aromatic meals. "Different home food."

After each banquet-type meal, Patrick pushed Beth up and down the train aisle for his exercise. Numerous passengers glared at her as she twitched and writhed in spasm. Once they were informed she was Lady Elisa Vermont-Forsythe, they stopped ogling whenever she convulsed and smiled at her instead.

Beth overheard two passengers talking together. What they said made her feel uncomfortable.

"The poor thing, Cynthia. She is not just a lowly passenger, you know. She has a title, so she must be terribly wealthy."

"She's slender and looks like she is a horse rider. Perhaps she's been hurt in a riding accident."

Beth frowned. *What's the difference if I have money or not? I am who I am, regardless if I have any money or none.*

She voiced in broken English, "Me all time always me. A thing no."

They didn't grasp what she said, or even notice Patrick's glaring eyes declaring his distaste for their attitude toward her. He removed Beth and returned her to the family's compartment with a growling tone to his muttered whispers. "What rich bastards they are. They don't know my bonnie wee lassie at all."

After that day Patrick walked the train aisles without Beth for his exercise to free her from further embarrassment or pain.

Each time he left their compartment she smiled at him and said, "It okay, Pat." She was content with not going with him.

CHAPTER SIXTEEN

When their holiday ended, the Forsythe's returned to the manor.

Each time Rachel was near, Beth cried out, "No me hurt no."

Constance was oblivious to her daughter's half-spoken plight, unaware of Rachel's spitefulness toward Beth when she was alone with her. Rachel complained bitterly saying she wanted an extra twenty shilling per annum because Beth was much harder to look after now that she was growing older.

All Constance could hear was complaint after protest from Rachel. Constance blushed with shame when she heard about her daughter's hysterical screaming so agreed to Rachel's demand for a higher salary.

Weeks passed by yet Constance still had no idea Rachel was mistreating her daughter. It seemed that although Patrick could understand Beth, Constance could not.

Even the other house staff knew about Rachel's wickedness, along with Patrick. They were too nervous to stop her after Rachel's threats that she would have them discharged if they said anything to their employers.

"You should take your daughter to see a physician," Ruth suggested. "After all, milady, doctors have made great advancements in recent years."

After deliberating, Constance considered it a great idea and took her the following week. And so for the first time in her life, tests began on Beth, who was now a young teenager.

The doctors probed and prodded, testing for this and that, while hours ticked by. At last one of them spoke. "Well, milady, we do not know what ails your daughter."

Another doctor noticed Constance's dejected expression. "It might have happened while you were pregnant, milady. We are sorry. We'll not risk guessing what her spasmodic disorder is."

When the doctors finished speaking, Constance's stomach churned. It was all her fault that Beth was the way she was. *Did it happen the day I fell down the stairs? I dare not say anything to these doctors about it as mother would nag me for causing another scandal.*

"Doctors, might it be because Beth's biological father was a drunk and his seed was bad?"

"It's quite possible, milady. However, there is nothing more that can be done for your daughter. Take her home and care for her."

Beth was so agitated that she couldn't utter a single syllable. She wanted to scream aloud and say, *Doctors, I'm not deaf, you know. I can hear you. Tell me too. After all, this is about me. And, Mother, what do you mean saying my real father was a drunk? Mathew Vermont is my father, isn't he, Mother?*

She had not known any other father except Mathew, and now James. She felt so frustrated that it made her go into spasms. She wished she could say something, anything. But again, her spasms prevented any words from escaping her mouth.

On the journey home, Beth mumbled repeatedly, "Mother, Mathew dad me yes?"

Constance didn't answer because she was unable to cope with Beth's garbled words. She didn't turn her head to even acknowledge she'd heard her. When they returned home, she left Beth with Rachel, who was standing just inside the front door.

Beth squirmed, screaming, "No hurt."

"See what I mean, milady?" Rachel said.

Resentful and with deaf ears, Constance grabbed her long dark skirt, pulled it up to her knees and raced upstairs to her room.

Patrick was standing outside beneath the open window to Constance's room when he heard her scream. This was followed by Constance's loud pleas. "What will happen to my daughter if anything grave should happen to me? God, why are you doing this to me? What have I done?"

He realised she'd forgotten the vow he had made at the workhouse, to always take care of Beth no matter what transpired in life.

Two hours later, Constance left the manor with puffy red eyes.

"I'm off to visit Aunt Betsy," she grunted to Patrick as she passed him.

Wary of Rachel's threats, Patrick knew he couldn't help Constance by himself. Maybe he could get the other staff on his side. *I don' think I can do it alone. I'll ask them at supper tonight.*

When Rachel realised Constance was well out of the way, she threw Beth onto her bed, irritated with her screaming. "In you go and there's no supper for you, to teach you a lesson not to scream like you do."

Beth snarled at Rachel. She thrashed her legs, trying to kick her.

Rachel laughed and ran downstairs into the scullery to eat her own supper. The house staff didn't speak to her as they scarfed down their food. Their narrow squinted eyes and their dour faces showed growing dislike for Rachel. But she ignored them all and finished her meal in peace.

CHAPTER SEVENTEEN

The following morning Beth awoke to a hungry, rumbling tummy, having had nothing to eat since teatime the day before. She heard two housemaids gossiping outside her bedroom door. As she listened, their topic forced Beth to forget her hunger pangs for a short while.

"Fanny," the older maid said, "did you know Beth's actual father was her grandfather, Derek Witherspoon? I know because I used to work for her grandmother, Lady Hannah. One night a few months afore we knew Constance was pregnant, we heard him come home from the tavern, drunk. He forcibly took his own daughter and the lass just fourteen year old at the time. Men!"

"Oh, that's terrible, Miriam. And Beth is such a pretty wee thing too."

Beth reflected. *Thing? I'm not a thing. I'm a person, like you.* She didn't make a sound, for fear she'd miss the rest of their conversation.

Miriam continued talking. "Well, it was Susan, the dressmaker, who first heard the commotion. She just called me to go and listen. Susan said that young Lady Constance must've asked for it because if she was a good girl then it would never have happened. Though with all the commotion it sounded like Lady Constance put up a good fight. After a minute or two we heard a loud thud and then everything went deathly quiet. The next thing we heard, a few months later, was Lady Constance was having a bastard baby and Sir Mathew Vermont had offered to marry her. His reason was kept hush-hush, but we knew he had been paid money to wed her by Lady Elisabeth Witherspoon. What a carry on. We was entertained for months by it all."

"What in heaven's name do you mean by saying, if she was a good girl it would never have happened? Miriam, that horrible man had no right to violate any girl, least of all his own daughter. Tsk, tsk."

"All right, ol' lass, keep your hair on! I'm just telling you what folks said, is all. People have always blamed the girl."

Fanny roared. "Well, I don't like the way some men express themselves. They get away with it too. Some people say that any assault is always the girl's fault and that she asked for it. What is the world coming to? I know Lady Constance well and she has always been God-fearing. There's no way she asked for any of it. Never in a million years. Not then. Not ever."

She paused, taking a deep breath to compose herself. "Sorry I lost it there, Miriam lass. It was nice that Mathew came to her rescue though, wasn't it? So there's at least one kind gentleman in this town. I don't like his snotty ol' mother though."

"Aye, Fanny, but Sir Mathew did not remain nice. He changed. And hey, I heard old Hannah blamed Constance for the assault by saying she dressed provocatively. I remember it well. We were having sweltering weather that summer. If she didn't open at least one button on her bodice, she would've felt like she was choking. Men always say it's the girl's fault, no matter which way girls dress or behave. It's such a shame."

"Here. Did you know when Constance was five months pregnant with la'arl Beth that damn Hannah pushed her down the stairs to make her lose the baby? The poor girl was ill for weeks. When that didn't work, ol' Hannah forced Constance to give birth secretly in France because she refused to marry just any man to give her bairn a name. And that lying ol' git told everyone her daughter had gone to visit relatives."

"Miriam, are you telling tall stories again?"

"Nay, Fanny lass. I know I sometimes lay it on thick, but what I'm telling you today is the whole truth. Lady Hannah knew what had gone on right enough. She knew who Beth's father was and she was glad when Constance lost the wee mite's twin sister, Sarah. Oh hell. We'd best shut up, Fanny. I can hear Beth waking up and she might hear us. I don't know how much she understands what's going on around her. She seems to say no and yes at the right time though. Have you noticed? Anyway, I don't want to upset the poor wee mite. She's been through enough."

Beth was stunned at their conversation. *They're wrong! It's just idle gossip. It didn't happen.*

Regardless what she thought about their words, she was unable to stop crying and wanted her mother to come home to tell her the truth.

Fanny heard Beth crying and realised she must have heard them nattering. She rushed into her room to console her.

"Gossip, wee one, is just...well, gossip. So don't you worry about what you heard us say, all right?"

She stared right through Fanny with dagger-like eyes, unable to shun her feelings of resentment at hearing their untrue words. She couldn't understand why they said such things. *And now she says none of it is true?*

Beth chose not to believe them. *Although if what they said was true, then this might be the reason grandfather appears objectionably cold when he looks at me.*

Shivers raced up her spine with visions of the two of them together. *Mother...and him...touching her intimately. Now I'm glad Rachel doesn't allow grandfather to be alone with me when he comes to visit. She might be mean to me, but she doesn't like him, especially when he's drunk. So if what they said about him and mother is true, then Rachel keeps me safe.*

One beautiful sunny day in June, Rachel felt trapped with being in the house all the time. Beth's personal care was her only duty, so she could leave the house whenever she wanted for a break from her manor duties.

Rachel said to Helen, a housemaid, "Get Beth ready. We're going for a drive in the new horseless carriage. Mr. Forsythe hasn't driven it himself yet, so I will."

Helen pulled a face and let out a shriek that could raise the dead, as if to suggest that Rachel should dress Beth herself.

Beth giggled, seeming not to caring who dressed her. She shouted, "Hurrah horse no ha yes."

The maid dressed Beth in a white camisole blouse and a pink skirt. Despite the fact she was living in luxury, she had never been inside a new-fangled horseless carriage before. She'd seen them pass alongside the grounds but had no idea her stepfather owned one.

"You must come too. I don't want to go alone," Rachel said to Helen, who jumped at the offer, apparently pleased to get time off from her household chores.

"Yes, Rachel. I'll come but you wouldn't have been alone because Beth would be with you. And I hope I don't get into trouble for leaving my chores."

Rachel gave Helen a cold look as her eyes turned into slits. *Beth can't talk, so I feel alone. Is this maid stupid? To hell with her chores*

When they set off, Beth grumbled, seemingly disturbed by the noise from the engine.

Rachel stopped the automobile outside a quaint café on the far side of Whitehaven Castle Park. She instructed Helen to put Beth into the invalid chair and then push her to a table inside. The maid gave Rachel another dirty look. Beth saw it and grinned.

While the three women ate strawberry jam and scones, a few people ogled at them from across the tearoom. They probably weren't used to seeing an invalid eating in a public café. Jam dripped onto the white serviette tucked inside Beth's collar and was about to fall down onto her clothes. The people across the room mumbled as if the sight revolted them. Rachel did nothing about it.

Helen leaned across the table and wiped the jam away with her own napkin. "There you are, Beth. The jam is off now."

The maid turned to Rachel. "This is your job, you know. You should not have left Beth looking like that. It looked awful. What would her Ladyship say if she found out?"

"And are you going to tell her? You should be doing your chores instead of being here. She'll fire you if she finds out."

Helen's face ran red with silent indignation.

"Hmm, I thought you'd have nothing to say. Just keep your mouth shut, Helen. As long as Lady Constance is happy, then my prosperity will continue. So I don't give two hoots what anyone in here thinks."

A well-attired young man, wearing a navy suit and a pale-grey shirt, smiled and approached their table. He introduced himself as Terrence Hatter. "Please, may I join you ladies?"

Rachel's eyes flashed with desire when she noticed his expensive clothing. "Yes, please do. How long have you been in town, Mr. Hatter?"

"My company in Carlyle is flourishing," Terrence said, "so I intend to open another branch in Whitehaven. I'm searching for an agreeable companion to show me around, since I've never been here before."

Rachel jumped into the breach. "I will help you, sir. My name is Rachel...Rachel Penny-Feather."

"Excellent, Miss Penny-Feather," Terrence said as he rubbed his palms together. "Please call me Terrence." He glanced across at Beth and the maid.

Before he could ask anything, Rachel said, "I nurse this woman. The maid is here to do the menial work."

"Oh, I see. I did wonder what your relationships were for a moment. I will meet you at this café tomorrow, at precisely one o'clock. Is that time agreeable to you, Rachel?"

"Yes, Terrence."

Helen gave Beth a probing wink combined with a grin, like she knew that greed was on Rachel's mind.

After that day, Rachel spent all her time with Terrence Hatter. Just the cook, Helen and two scullery maids were left to watch Beth, and none of them had nursing training. Helen grew particularly disgruntled with Rachel for not undertaking her own duties every day.

On one such day Helen said, "Look, Rachel. I'm pleased you have a young man in your life but I 'ave my housework to do. I don't 'ave time to sit with Beth. She is your responsibility. I can only keep her company for short periods and she is growing decidedly bored. If her Ladyship learns of your behaviour then she'll be furious wiv you."

Rachel shrugged her shoulders and sauntered away. Helen couldn't believe how impolite Rachel was for leaving, especially without a word in her own defence.

When a month had passed by Helen couldn't stand Rachel's behaviour any longer. She sent a message to Betsy, to enlighten Constance what was going on behind her back. Constance returned posthaste to discharge Rachel as governess.

"Oh ta Mother ta," Beth said, happily thanking her mother for sacking Rachel.

"She has gone at long last!" cried Helen.

Cheers filtered upstairs from the scullery staff, pleased that Constance had fired Rachel.

Afterwards Constance found Beth's personal maid, Ruth. "I enjoy your company myself, but would you step up to look after my daughter until I can find a replacement?"

"Yes, milady. I'd be delighted. I hope you'll be patient wiv me until I learn how your daughter prefers things done."

"Of course I will. The most important thing is you are kind-hearted and she already likes you."

Ruth had always known that Beth grew desperate to exchange words other than just in broken English. As the days passed by Ruth received a flash of inspiration and asked Lady Constance's permission to buy a typewriter. "I'm sure it will help your daughter."

"How so, Ruth?"

"Beth can control some of her head movements, milady."

"Yes, and she moves her head in the same direction as her eyes, Ruth. What do you think it means? Do you think her health is getting better?"

"I'm not a doctor so I cannot tell you, milady, but I do know a stick could be placed in your daughter's mouth as a pointer to type wiv."

"It sounds like a good plan, Ruth. Very well. Purchase the contraption and charge it to Mr. Forsythe's account. I'll give you a note to produce to Glessal's shop stating the purchase as valid."

The following day Ruth and Beth went to Glessal's to select her machine, and the store delivered it the same evening before dinner. Beth was so excited about the machine she was unable to take her eyes from the letters on the keyboard. Ruth proceeded to teach her the alphabet and Beth made wonderful progress. Ruth felt confident that Beth would be quick to learn the words she wanted to say.

In just a few days she learned to type one short, correctly written sentence. "I love you, Mother."

After Ruth read it herself, she ran across the hallway to show it to Constance, and tears welled in Constance's eyes. She sprinted to her daughter's room and flung the door open. Feeling great joy, she kissed her daughter tenderly on the brow. "I knew it! I knew you were clever, my angel. I must take this to show Aunt Betsy."

Beth giggled and squirmed with elation, looking happier than she'd been in years.

Constance set off the same day to Betsy's house to prove her daughter had a much higher intellect than was previously assumed by everyone, including some doctors. The news astonished Betsy. Her face glowed with gladness, then suddenly her expression changed to one of sad embarrassment and tears tracked down her cheeks.

"Oh, Auntie, whatever is the matter? Please, sit down." Constance sat beside her.

"I'm feeling bad because I remember the times I've wanted you to get rid of Beth."

"Auntie, it's all in the past now. Please don't fret."

Betsy reached over to clasp Constance's hand. "I'm so thankful to hear you've forgiven me."

The two relatives enjoyed a weeklong visit reminiscing before Constance returned home and watched Beth typing hour after hour, all with hardly a twitch. Constance's eyes sparkled in awe. How quickly her daughter learned mystified her. She held Beth in her arms. "I'm getting to know you at last, my daughter, after so many years of silence."

Beth hummed a chortle with a joyful grin plastered across her face. "Me you miss," she said, clearly thankful Constance had sought her company.

Beth typed an inspirational quote by Elbert Hubbard for her mother. *"A little more persistence, a little more effort and what seemed a hopeless failure may turn to glorious success."*

Constance was determined to spend more time with her daughter in the future.

After dinner the same day, Constance's attentiveness wandered back to her aunt. On her last visit she'd realised the old woman was growing frailer as the progression of her winter years ploughed on, so she decided to return for another visit.

"I'm sorry, Beth darling. I can't get Aunt Betsy out of my mind. She seemed so frail the last time I saw her. I hope you will not be offended if I dash off to see her again?"

"Me too come?"

"Oh, I'm sorry, dear. I'm obliged to say no because you need to practise your typing. Besides, the sound of your typewriter might disturb Auntie's rest."

"No machine take," Beth said, in a futile attempt to keep her mother by her side.

"No, dear. After you've suffered so many unvoiced years, you need to continue communicating with everyone. You know as well as I how important conversation is—especially for you."

Beth sighed. "Yes."

Constance wanted to take Ruth with her, except who could take care of Beth in her absence?

CHAPTER EIGHTEEN

James did not take adequate time to study candidates for locating an alternative nurse for Beth. Without checking her nursing credentials or references, he hired Mary Crab.

Everything happened so fast, Beth knew her mother hadn't noticed Mary's appearance. She looked like a storybook witch with a slightly hooked nose and olive complexion.

Doesn't Mother use her eyes? Mary will not fit into mother's elegant way of living. Why did she hire a nurse who seems to have emerged from a cocoon like a disfigured moth in a nurse's uniform? Surely Mother can see the crooked wart on Mary's chin. It resembles a miniature pulverized turnip and smells mouldy.

Without any more ado, Mary Crab moved into Rachel's old room and Constance returned with Ruth to Aunt Betsy, who was pleased to learn of the speedy replacement to take care of Beth.

Mary unpacked her things, then trundled into Beth's room and spoke to her in a sharp, condescending tone of voice. "Hello, Lady Elisa. I've seen you before. You don't remember me, do you?"

Beth shook her head, although she knew Mary's face, but couldn't remember where she'd seen her before. Right from the start Beth did not like Mary.

"Can't you remember seeing me at the workhouse?" Mary cackled mockingly then changed the subject.

Beth hated Mary's tone of voice and a gloomy feeling passed through her. She didn't know why she felt that way and was unable to remember it was Mary who performed the séances at Ginns and conjured the beast that caused such mayhem.

"I hope you're in good form today, girl. Oye, can I call you Beth like everybody else?"

Beth turned her head to gaze at the flowers in the garden without answering her. She missed having her mother around and wondered why she couldn't go too. *Aunt Betsy would never have known I was there except for my typewriter clacking away and I could have even left it at home.*

Beth heard strange noises coming from Mary's room each night. The sounds troubled her. Mary completed her duties correctly, except Beth had weird feelings of impending doom from the moment she first clapped eyes on her.

After a week or two, Constance sent a message to Patrick stating her aunt was in better health than previously assumed and she would return home by the end of the month. Patrick was about to tell Beth when Mary snatched the note from his hand and issued him with a threat.

"Stay the hell away from this house. If you don't, you'll find yourself with no job and back in the workhouse." She glared at him as if daggers flashed from her eyes. "Do not tempt me, Patrick, because I'll personally see to it."

Ever since he left Ginns, Patrick never got over his luck of moving into a posh house again. The risk of homelessness was too great for him to bear. So for the time being, Patrick thought he'd keep his mouth shut. He stayed close to the stables, keeping his mind firmly on his work to blot out his fears.

It didn't take long for Mary to glean the sin Sir Derek committed with his daughter years earlier, and that Beth was the result. Mary grinned hearing the news and wrung her palms together as she cooked up a malicious scheme.

Unknown to the rest of the staff, Mary sent a note inviting Derek to visit the house while James was away on a business trip. He wouldn't return for two months.

This was a convenient time for malevolent Mary, who practiced black magic in her room each night, communicating with the dark forces. The Archdemon Asmodeus promised her riches if she brought forth Pharzuph, the demon of lust, to enter into Derek Witherspoon's body. Mary couldn't resist the promise of wealth.

That evening Derek left the Anchor Vaults in Whitehaven at around ten and headed toward the manor. When Pharzuph materialized in front of him and entered Derek's drunken body, he gave little resistance. By the time the demon reached the manor using Derek's body, he reeked of sweat mingled with stomach-churning stale whiskey. The pong permeated every part of him.

As the drunken demon staggered toward Beth, she gasped. His shirt was swathed in brown drool stains. She shuddered with trepidation.

"Hello, lovely little girl," Pharzuph said with a hissing tone of voice.

Beth knew about her grandfather's drunken activities, but she didn't know he was possessed by a demon. Her inner spirit alerted her to something—something that made her feel so uneasy that she wet herself in dread. *How could this vile drunken man be my father as well as my grandfather?*

Cold-hearted Mary enjoyed watching Pharzuph touch Beth in private places, places she didn't want touched—at least not by him.

Mary knew the demon would never chase her for sex, because she could defend herself with witchcraft. Her pact with Asmodeus had sealed the deal.

"Pharzuph, you are here because Asmodeus wanted you here. He will rip you apart if you touch me."

Asmodeus was an Archdemon and much stronger than Pharzuph was, so Pharzuph left Mary alone. But there was no reason for him to leave Beth alone.

He moved toward the crippled girl and then it began again.

Patrick didn't hear a thing as he snoozed at the back of the stables. Neither did the other house staff.

Beth trembled violently and cried out, "Pat Beth hurt come."

Amused, cold-hearted Mary picked Beth up and tossed her onto the bed like a sack of potatoes.

"Patrick doesn't like you anymore," Mary snarled.

The teenager's legs flailed as she attempted to kick Mary. But the nurse was nippy and steered well clear of Beth's thrashing legs.

"Mary bad you," Beth stuttered, sobbing with anger and pain.

Mary cackled. She left the room, leaving Beth alone with no nightwear and her breasts still uncovered. She didn't even give the frightened young woman a blanket to shield her from the night chills.

Thankfully the night turned warm, but Beth still shivered with fright. *Why doesn't Patrick love me anymore? What did I do?*

All of a sudden the blue entity appeared, its bright glow shining throughout the room. It hovered by the window for a moment and then drew closer to Beth, softly humming a gentle tune that seemed to say, "Visible or not, I am always with you, my twinsie."

Beth didn't understand. If the spectre had come to help her, why had it not prevented her grandfather from hurting her?

The blue entity said in reply, "Patrick does love you. Ignore that evil woman's lying words."

Beth despised both her grandfather and Mary, and considered many notions. *Why is my life like this? Am I paying a penance from a past life? Is it because I was as evil in a past incarnation as Mary is?*

Beth awoke the next morning alone, undressed, cold and traumatized. The blue spirit appeared at her side immediately.

"Why me no you help?" Beth asked.

A melodious voice filled the room. "Oh, I am helping you, twinsie. I am. Can't you feel the warmth of my love as it rushes toward you? I'm here to watch over you."

Beth felt calmer, though she didn't reply.

"I will weave a magic charm around you," the spirit said, "to help you forget all the trauma from your grandfather."

Exhausted, Beth quickly fell asleep once more.

When she awoke again much later, she was cold. *Why am I not dressed?*

All she could remember about the previous night was that she didn't like Mary.

A small bird singing outdoors grabbed her attention until Mary sauntered into the room. With a sarcastic mocking pitch to her voice, she said, "And what can I disturb you with today, Beth? Why, child, you're not even dressed yet." She giggled like the crazy, insect-eating patient that Beth's mother had told her about at the asylum.

What is Mary blabbering about? And why did she leave me practically naked all night?

"Oh, I do love nursing you, Beth. You can't tell people how I take my hatred out on you without your typewriter. By the way, you look like a waif. Did you know your blouse is torn?"

Beth remained silent.

"Oh yes," Mary said with a scowl. "And after your grandfather has been to the Anchor Vaults pub tomorrow, he is coming with his friend for sex with you. Isn't that nice? What a lucky girl you are. You'd best make yourself look pretty. He pays me well for it." Mary gave a wild screech of laughter and skipped back to her own room.

Beth quivered like a willow in the wind, with thoughts of her grandfather returning for sex later. She couldn't remember anything about him visiting her in the first place. *What is that horrible Mary talking about now? I've never had sex with Grandfather. Besides, what is sex? And who is Grandfather's friend that Mary mentioned? I don't understand why she says such nasty things to me.*

After a few moments Beth yelled at Mary. "Pee me." At the same time she wished Mary could hear her thoughts. *Please, please. Don't leave me to sit here soaking wet again. I'm cold. I need to get dressed.*

Mary ignored her appeal, but could be heard still throwing up.

Once again Beth's mind screamed for her mother to return.

Later on, when the drunken nurse awoke, she entered Beth's room with a lit cigarette and burned the teenager's arm with it five times.

Beth screamed. The pain set off more spasms.

Mary laughed wildly. She told the other house staff that Beth's burns were a new rash she had developed.

Beth seethed inside. *Mary, when you burn me I don't even try to control my spasms. I let them happen and pray that my feet will strike your face hard. People will catch you one day and I'll be free of you. I hate you, Mary Crab. I wish my thoughts could kill you!*

Beth typed countless letters while Mary slept, hoping one would break free from her room with a housemaid. But later, Mary grabbed the notes and destroyed them all—except one. Gloria, one of the manors many chambermaids, shoved it into her apron pocket.

Later on, she rushed to see Constance when she finished her work. "Milady, I observed Beth's pitiable expression while cleaning the fireplace. So when Mary wasn't looking, I stuffed this half-burned note into my pocket. I do not know what it says."

She passed the note to Constance, who turned pale and keeled over when she read the contents.

"Why in Hades would anyone behave in such a despicable way? And why didn't the rest of the staff know about this, Gloria?"

"Sorry, ma'am. I don't know what the letter said. There's only Ruth can read and she's here with you. I just noticed your daughter's heartrending expression as she was half dressed and shivering, ma'am."

"What? She was half dressed?" Constance gritted her teeth. Her heart burned with rage. "I thank you for being so observant, Gloria. It's not your fault you can't read."

Beth's note went on to say, "Mother, Mary has been in your room stealing our family heirlooms and has sold them to buy booze. She hid her pilfering with black magic. I know because I've heard chanting coming from inside her room. She also said grandfather is returning with a friend. Whoever that is."

"And why didn't the other cleaning staff know about this?" Constance demanded of Gloria. "And who is this friend of my father's?"

"I don't know who the friend is. None of us knew what Mary was doing, milady. She never let us near Beth except to clean her room and she was always there watching. Except for today when she was lying on the floor intoxicated."

"Intoxicated!" The sharpness of Constance's voice could have cut a hole through a stone wall.

She returned home and barged into Beth's room to find Mary standing at the foot of Beth's bed. Mary's chin dropped. "H-hello, milady."

Constance screamed at her. "Why has my father been here?"

"He came to visit your daughter, milady. To...keep her company while you were away."

Constance's mind raced with memories of when she was a teenager and her father kept her company. With that memory she needed neither explanation nor reason.

"You are fired, Mary. I curse both you and my father. I pray neither of you has any peace for the rest of your lives for what you've done. You're an evil fiend!"

Beth's face lit up like a beacon in the night. One of her messages had got through. Her suffering at Mary's hands was over. *Oh God. Thank you, mother.*

But Beth had no idea what her mother meant when she said her grandfather was evil and cursed him as well.

The blue entity on the balcony glowed more than at other times and smiled because it knew the magic enchantment had worked. Beth had forgotten the horrors of her possessed grandfather molesting her.

At that moment Patrick limped through the door crying. Beth threw her arms out excitedly to greet him. "Pat! Miss me you."

He hobbled across the room with a pained expression on his face and hugged her. "I'm so sorry, wee lassie. I was frightened I might make things worse for ye. See, Mary used wicked threats tae force everyone tae stay away, that she would hurt ye and she'd have us all fired as well. I had tae stay away after that warning. I did nae want her tae hurt ye."

The other house servants, alerted by all the commotion, stood at the doorway nodding and mumbling in unison.

Open mouthed and bewildered, Mary wore an expression of wonder at how Constance had found out. She panicked and lifted her skirt to make a run for it. Patrick stood in front of the doorway snarling to block her exit, but she ran into the next room, likely to try to rescue some items she'd stolen

She was too late. Before Constance had returned to the manor she'd sent a letter to Constable Bob Greer to report the thefts. She had just mentioned the pilfering and nothing about her father's visits.

Everyone at the house knew Derek was Beth's grandfather. Constance thought if any gossip leaked to the public it would damage the

Witherspoon family's status forever. Constance made an announcement to her staff.

"I will give each of you five pounds to hold your tongue about anything you've ever seen or heard while I've been away. If anything leaks out of these walls that my father has been here, then you will all be fired. You may only talk about Mary stealing. Have I made myself clear?"

"Yes, milady," was their unanimous reply.

When Constable Bob Greer arrived, he pushed his way through a flock of house staff that was guarding the door to prevent Mary's escape. The constable was a devout Christian and had already learned about Mary's character from his friend, a Ginns overseer who'd told him she practiced witchcraft. Bob said nothing to Constance's family about the tales he'd heard concerning Derek and Mary. He thought the family had been hurt enough.

Mary screamed uncontrollably when she caught sight of the chains the constable carried. He put her in irons and dragged her away struggling.

"Get off me! Let me go! Somebody help!"

"Be quiet, woman. No one here will help you, you vagabond."

Bob hurled Mary into a windowless cell at the police station to await her judgment in court. The cell decor was grim, with dark walls, a thin mattress on a metal bed frame, one blanket, no pillow, a rusty toilet bucket in the corner and no other comforts.

The judge was a close friend of Constable Bob. He reminded the judge about the Witherspoon scandal years earlier, so the judge guessed what Derek would have been up to with his granddaughter even though Beth didn't write much about what happened. Bob told the judge Mary had allowed the old man to visit Beth and asked if he would give Mary the longest penalty allowed, no matter what.

Constable Jeffrey Martin was a co-worker of Bob and behaved vindictively toward all criminals, no matter what crime they'd committed. He acted like it was his Christian duty to rid the world of wickedness. When Jeffrey was on duty, he would not give Mary water. If he was in a good mood, he fed her once a day. Most of the time he made her go hungry.

"Please, Constable," she begged. "I'm famished. So thirsty. Give me a drink, sir."

"You deserve nothing, Mary."

She tossed and turned each night for weeks, terrified of the phantoms that tortured her in nightmares. In time, the same black visions appeared in her waking hours. Monstrous creatures with blood-red eyes appeared in her cell like the one in Ginns workhouse when Beth and Patrick lived there.

Claw marks appeared on Mary's cell walls right in front of her eyes. It sounded like knives scraping against metal. Her tormented soul screamed for someone to help. No one arrived. Constance's curse had firmly attached itself to at least one of its targets, although no one had any idea just what had attached itself to Mary.

By the day of the court case Mary was a skinny, nervous wreck with bulging eyes. The police dragged her, covered in scratches, into the courthouse while she screamed. "There are monsters among us. Can't you see them? Get 'em off me! Get 'em off!"

The citizens in the gallery laughed mockingly and stamped their feet loudly on the floor.

"You'll be taken to Garlands Asylum if you're not careful, Mary Crab, and you would not get out of there in a hurry." Constable Jeffrey laughed at her attempts to lift her bodice and show him her skin.

"Look, look. I have scratches all over my body from the demon's claws."

The constable averted his eyes. He clearly didn't want to look at the body of a half-naked madwoman who hadn't washed in weeks.

By this time Judge Black was present. A Ginns overseer was brought in as a character witness for Mary. He told the courts what she had done to the people at the workhouse.

Judge Black said it was nothing to do with the case and told the jury to disregard it.

Mary screamed like a ghoul, tearing at her chains, making her wrists bleed. The judge would not tolerate her behaviour in his court. He instructed the constable to remove her until she calmed down.

While she was out, the jurors were unanimous. Guilty!

When Mary calmed down, she was returned to the courtroom. The judge declared her guilty of thieving and practicing black witchcraft. He gave her five years in Blackmore jail, inside Garlands Asylum grounds for the criminally insane. Blackmore was a horrifying place fit only for murderers and rapists.

The judge placed an addendum order. "Mary Crab, when you have served your time, I'll make sure you will never have a nursing position in Cumberland County again. That's if you live long enough. The Blackmore inmates could make short work of you. You might be dead in less than a week because you have such a spiteful big mouth."

Everyone in the courtroom laughed and cheered. Mary panicked and fell to her knees sobbing as the tight chains around her bleeding wrists clanked and rattled.

Constance and Beth were present for the verdict. Constance watched her daughter and noticed a confused yet happy smile on Beth's face when the judge mentioned what the wild Blackmore prisoners might do to Mary.

Following the court case, Constance grew troubled as she mulled over what might have happened to her daughter. She fretted so much she stopped eating and grew seriously ill, with no strength to stand up.

James didn't seem to understand. "Constance, why do you allow everything to get under your skin, especially now when it is all over?"

All she said was, "Father hateful." She had never told James what her father had done to her when she was a teenager and she wasn't about to tell him.

He had employed the best physicians to tend to her and hired two quality lady's maids to be her companions round the clock.

A few weeks into their work, one lady's maid informed James that his wife had sat up unaided. His face beamed with jubilation.

"This is wonderful news!" he said. He didn't have much time left to stay around the manor because he'd planned another business trip. His job was important to his sanity. He decided he could leave now that his wife was getting better and he knew she was in safe hands.

Before the court case, Constance had given Mary's position to Ruth, knowing her daughter needed a gentle and loving companion more than anything. Most important of all, Ruth knew how to look after Beth the same way Constance would.

The new position meant that Ruth had more money in her pocket and an easier job—no scrubbing floors or other house cleaning. As the weeks passed by Ruth and Beth enjoyed their times together and the teenager recovered from her ordeal with Mary.

Although old and weak, Aunt Betsy visited her niece as often as she could, which seemed to please Constance. As she grew stronger, she confided in her aunt, telling her that Mary had confessed to inviting Derek to visit her daughter.

Betsy's mind rolled back a few years and she came to her own opinions as to what could have happened. She had often thought about Derek and Constance. Now she wondered if the same thing that happened to Constance could happen to Beth.

No one knew that Derek had been possessed by a demon all those years ago and that Betsy had banned him from ever setting foot in her home again. The old woman pondered on whether she should disclose her reason to Constance and decided it best left unsaid and in the past.

One day, when Constance's condition showed much improvement, she and her aunt embraced lovingly.

Betsy confessed, "My dear, when you asked me if I'd take you and Beth into my home all those years ago, I was afraid of people's reactions. I followed what some people in church recommended. Connie, my dear, it was members of the congregation who suggested the exorcism for Beth. Some of them said I mustn't go near your child for fear the demon inside her would release her and leap into me. I felt frightened by it. I'm so sorry."

"Auntie, my daughter was never possessed. She is physically ailing. That is all."

"Yes, I know, child. Your life just went drastically wrong and especially for Beth. Now I know her sickness is neither contagious nor dangerous to anyone. In those days I was terribly fearful. When I learned she could use a typewriter...well dear, it pained me so much as I came to realize I'd damaged both of your lives. Things came to pass so fast, Connie. When you were admitted into the asylum, I couldn't...I just couldn't..." Her eyes welled up and the lump in her throat threatened to choke her.

Constance interrupted by reaching for her aunt's hand and saying in a soft voice, "Let's forget the past, Auntie, and move on to a brighter future."

The two relatives agreed and talked for hours over sherry. Suddenly an idea came to Betsy's mind, a plan to build a hospice to help others like Beth.

The following day Betsy enlisted the support of Mr. Thomas Fortigue, a banker and a close sympathetic friend. Thomas set to work sending letter after letter to every wealthy family in the country with news of Beth's ability to communicate with a typewriter. Thomas pleaded that they contribute to the fund.

When the news broke of the pending hospice, it gave hope to other parents with disabled children like Beth. After many months the account grew to a considerable sum. Yet it was still not enough.

Someone at the house had shrewdly informed the Holyroodhouse Palace staff about their plans. One morning an elegant-looking carriage pulled up outside. Everyone was surprised to see Duchess Charlotte alight from it. Her visit caused quite a stir in the household. When Her Grace entered, everyone bowed and curtsied as they guided her entourage into the blue morning room. Two muscle-bound guards carried a heavy, bulging carpetbag.

Duchess Charlotte ordered, "Put the bag down and someone have Beth brought before me immediately."

She watched them place the bag on the floor. "No, no. Put it onto the table instead and then wait for me outside. My ladies-in-waiting will remain here."

The Duchess looked around to see everyone gobsmacked with shock. "Well, don't just gawp. Hasn't someone gone to fetch the girl yet?"

James snapped to attention and called for Ruth, who brought Beth downstairs along with her typewriter, which a housemaid carried. Beth bowed with one of her unsteady head jerks and proceeded to type a note. When she finished Ruth passed the letter to Duchess Charlotte.

"Good day, Your Grace. I am Lady Elisa but I prefer being called Beth. Thank you for visiting us today. Please forgive my inability to curtsy. I hope you will take refreshment with us."

A lengthy silence ensued. The duchess appeared grief stricken as a lone tear escaped her eye. No one dared invade her private pain, even though it was displayed so openly.

After some minutes her Grace spoke with a sad sigh. "My baby died at birth. They said it was an unknown breathing difficulty."

She paused for a moment to wipe away another tear with a white silk handkerchief. "When he was born one of his legs was twisted. The nurse whisked him away from my arms. They...they told me he had died. I sensed he was murdered. I couldn't do anything about it, but you..." The duchess exhaled noisily, her tears almost choking the breath from her. "Oh you, my dear lady..." As she gazed at Constance with wistful eyes, she blurted out, "You were so brave. I was very young and cowardly."

Her Grace wiped away many more tears, as did Constance. To avoid embarrassment for the duchess and for his wife, James told his staff to leave the room, save for Ruth.

Duchess Charlotte paused, heaving a sigh and then instructed the carpetbag be moved over to where James and Constance sat at the opposite end of the table. The two ladies-in-waiting left the room and returned with the two muscle-bound guards.

"Move the bag over there." Duchess Charlotte pointed to James and Constance. "Now you may go." When the door closed behind them, Her Grace continued, "Please open the bag, Clarissa dear."

The maid unbuckled the straps and flipped the bag open. Everyone, including the ladies-in-waiting, struggled for breath at what was inside—more money and jewels than any of them had ever seen, including Mr. Fortigue, the banker. His legs turned to rubber and he keeled over when he saw the jewels sparkling like prisms beneath the chandeliers.

Once again Her Grace praised Lady Constance. "My dear, I've heard numerous stories about your past. I cannot even begin to understand the painful experiences you have endured to keep you and your daughter alive all these years. It's quite beyond me. Your resilience while living in the workhouse was quite admirable."

Constance couldn't speak and wondered how she knew.

"I'm overjoyed you did not give your child up. Look what Beth can do. Because of this, I pledge to make a generous contribution every year to your cause. The contents of this bag will get you started."

Half choked, Constance made a long, drawn out curtsy.

"Your Grace, thank you for your outstanding generosity." Constance's knuckles turned white as she gripped the back of a chair to stop herself from falling over. She was surprised to see so many gems and so much gold in one place.

"Would you partake in some tea and muffins with us, Your Grace?"

The Duchess shook her head silently and left, leaving everyone flabbergasted with the bounty she'd left on the table.

Minutes later she returned still looking tearful and joined them in refreshments after all.

Beth's face beamed a dazzling crystal-white smile, never once dreaming she would be in the presence of such an important person as Her Grace.

Thomas Fortigue found buyers for the exquisite jewels. They fought over them because they were once owned by Duchess Charlotte. Thomas found a suitable building in the countryside with wonderful views of the Cumbrian fells. Then work began to turn it into the Beth-Charlotte Refuge, a place where eighty disabled children would live and learn in safety.

The hospice was a great success. Youngsters became skilled at music and other creative pursuits as well as the normal school curriculum.

One child, a boy with no arms, excelled beyond anyone's wildest dreams—he learned to play the violin using only his feet. That boy was Beth's favourite student, because his music sounded heavenly, like dragonflies dancing on water droplets left by a rainstorm.

Duchess Charlotte visited the hospice bi-monthly for a whole year to check on the children's progress. On each visit she insisted they play for her. Their melodies sent her floating into minutes of thoughtful meditation.

One sunny day weeks later as Ruth strolled with Beth in the park, they met Jonathan Brown, a kind-hearted clothing merchant. After that, Ruth and Jonathan were in each other's company every day. She frequently spoke about him to Beth when they were alone together.

Beth often replied, "Me like."

"Oh, me too, milady," Ruth whispered, giggling like a teenage girl with her hand over her mouth.

Three months later Jonathan asked Ruth to marry him. This was no surprise for observant Beth, who noticed things other people did not. She knew she would miss Ruth terribly after she got married, even though Beth wanted the best for her special friend and nurse.

CHAPTER NINETEEN

Lady Constance asked Ruth to be present to choose another new nurse for Beth. Many women applied. A nanny agency near Ambleside, almost thirty miles away, sent Miss Jennifer Thompson. It would be a long return journey if she did not receive the position.

Beth eyed Jennifer up and down, scrutinizing her every move, listening to her every breath, knowing what to look for with having previous knowledge of ill-tempered nurses in the past.

Jennifer's eyes sparkled like bright emeralds. Her glossy red hair was combed into a bun and shone like it had been burnished with gold. A simple white blouse and a full grey skirt covered her strong, formidable body.

Beth particularly liked Jennifer's warm smile. *Surely a woman who looks like she could be an angel couldn't possibly be ill tempered or cruel.*

Beth typed a note. "I want to try Jennifer out."

The choice was made. They gave the new nurse a room on the far side of the house. Ruth would be rooming next door to Beth's quarters until after her marriage to Jonathan.

Ruth taught Jennifer how to understand Beth's needs with her few words and facial expressions, especially if she didn't have her typewriter beside her. Jennifer was quick to learn.

One afternoon as Ruth, Jennifer and Beth walked through the dancing shadows in the garden, Beth saw Patrick on his knees tending flowers beside a willow tree. She was in a playful mood and uttered no sound, hoping for a comical reaction from Jennifer.

As the three women watched the sun set beneath the willow trees, the heavy scent of evening blossoms floated in the air. When Jennifer reached to smell a rose she screamed and ran back toward Ruth and Beth.

Beth laughed at Jennifer's skittish reaction.

Ruth asked, "Have you pricked yourself, Jennifer?"

"No, Ruth. There's someone lurking about in the bushes over there," Jennifer said, pointing in the direction of Patrick.

"Sorry if I startled ye young ladies," Patrick said, limping toward the women. "Just tending the roses. The wee one here loves them, ye know." He nodded his head toward Beth, with a smile. "Please don't tell Mr. Forsythe. He asked me tae clean the stables today and he might fire me for nae doing it. Then what would I do? I have no place tae go except back tae the workhouse."

"It all right," Beth said. "Not away send. Workhouse no."

"Patrick, you made us jump, that's all," Jennifer added.

"You scream scared Jen. Me laugh."

Jennifer playfully stuck her tongue out at Beth then turned to Patrick. "Don't be nervous. I know Mr. Forsythe would never discharge you for doing such a charming thing as tending the roses for Miss Beth."

Patrick smiled as he ambled through the bushes back to the stables, looking somewhat relieved.

A housemaid called out, "Beth, please return to the house immediately. Your Aunt Betsy is here for Ruth and Jonathan's wedding."

Regardless of her health, the old dear had decided she didn't want to miss the ceremony after all. Beth had long since forgiven her for forcing them into the workhouse and gave her great aunt a huge, giggling smile.

When Ruth and Jonathan's big day arrived, the street was festooned with pink and white ribbons, and flowers for their wedding. A white horse and buggy adorned with pink rosebud garlands stood outside the front door—their wedding gift from Mr. Forsythe and Lady Constance. When the happy bride hit the road for her journey to church, the horse pranced as if it knew the valuable prize it pulled.

When the service ended, the bride and groom exited the chapel as Mr. and Mrs. Jonathan Brown. Their spiffy entourage glided along the aisle behind them as if floating on air. Sunshine pouring through the huge stained-glass windows cast rainbows all around. The coloured lights dazzled the eyes of the priest as he stood by the doorway.

Beth winked at him as Patrick pushed her decorated wheelchair covered with blooms past the man. The priest stood open mouthed, looking dumbfounded.

Her face glowed. *I would love to marry, but that's not meant to be...not for such as me.*

She turned to Patrick. "Ruth beautiful. Service nice Pat."

"Aye. 'Twas a lovely service, lass. Really lovely."

Everyone headed for the manor to attend a party that Mr. Forsythe was throwing for the newlyweds. All Ruth's friends were present—housemaids, chambermaids, butlers, gardeners and even stable hands.

In the most unusual role reversal, the gentry served the servants. No one had seen anything like it before.

"Fun," Beth said while laughing with no sign of a spasm.

Jennifer pushed her to the red velvet chaise longue in the corner, beside the window, so she could see outside and also view the wedding party.

Father McDougal entered the room and the music stopped abruptly. He bid them to continue. As he caught sight of Beth he briskly strode toward her.

Beth's mind ran amok. *Sometimes that priest puts the fear of God in me. I hope he isn't coming over here.*

By the time her last thought was completed, Father McDougal stood directly in front of her with his hands clasped together, smiling at her. There was nothing for her to do but smile back.

"My dear lady. I'm saddened at the atrocities you've suffered throughout your life. I know many people, including myself, believed demons had possessed you. When you were in the chapel today, you winked at me and I saw a strange light shining on your face. Many colours glimmered above your head and then I felt a great weight fall off my shoulders. I don't know what it was other than the light seemed to open my eyes. I could see your innocence. I don't know what your sickness is, my child. It is obvious to me now there has never been a demon inside you. I feel so proud to know you."

Beth blushed at his words.

The Father continued. "I do not mean to embarrass you, my child, but I must speak of this. Many years ago when I first heard you were living in the workhouse, I studied Mark 2:5, which says, 'When Jesus saw their faith he said unto a man sick with the palsy, Son, thy sins be forgiven thee.' Beth, my child, if the Lord says you are sinless then who am I to state differently? I hope you can forgive me." He dropped to his knees and cried.

Beth's eyes watered and a few perspiration droplets rolled down her brow. "Up no. Father."

By his bemused expression, Beth guessed the priest did not understand what she meant, so she used her typewriter. "Thank you, Father. Please get up. My soul is at peace and I hope yours finds the same peace."

While Father McDougal read it, he sighed long and heavy, then arose and sat beside her. He gazed into her eyes. A lone salty tear ran down his cheek and settled on his lips. He licked the tear away.

For a brief moment a hazy blue image hovered in front of Beth's face. She wondered if the priest saw it too.

He sat with her for over an hour until Jennifer escorted Beth to her room.

Through the bedroom window, Beth watched the newlyweds leave. She felt enormous sadness, mixed with feelings of great joy and happiness. *Ruth will never look after me again. And now I have Jennifer to take care of me...completely alone and unaccompanied. Will Jennifer turn evil like the others did when we are alone? I wish my blue entity would return.*

Jennifer placed a gentle hand on her shoulder. "Come, my dear. Let's get you to bed. It's been a long, exciting day for us all. You must rest now. Tomorrow we will go to the rose garden. The one Patrick planted for you. Would you like that? I heard he also planted lilies in honour of the newlyweds."

Beth sighed heavily and nodded without a word. Jennifer laid her on silken sheets and for the first time she was tucked in by Jennifer alone, without her beloved Ruth there. Beth grew nervous and a spasm ensued. But then it faded and Beth drifted off to sleep.

Halfway through the night Beth had nightmares about her grandfather and the demon in the workhouse. She woke up screaming.

Jennifer rushed in and held Beth close. "Everything is all right. I left your door ajar in case you needed reassurance. Beth, I know I'm new in your life. You will become accustomed to me. I'll never allow anything to hurt you."

Beth returned to sleep thinking. *This one appears like she cares. Time will tell.*

A brilliant blue radiance glowed by her bedside until she slumbered, then it nestled beside the window until dawn.

The following day Beth awoke before the birds. Jennifer entered her room, yawning. She hummed as she appeared to float across to the window.

"What song is, Jen?" Beth asked.

"Why, it's called 'I Sing a Song of the Saints of God.' Would you like me to sing it for you?"

Beth bobbed her head.

Unbeknownst to Jennifer, the blue entity materialized behind her while she sang.

I sing a song of the saints of God

Patient and brave and true
Who toiled and fought and lived and died
For the Lord they loved and knew
One was a doctor and one was a queen
And one was a shepherdess on the green
They were all of them saints of God—and I mean
With God's Grace to be one too.

Jennifer's eyes glowed with sparkling hues of green and cobalt blue. It made Beth feel warm and snug inside. Beth wanted to applaud, although she couldn't. Her arms flailed around as she screeched with glee. "Good, Jen. Song nice."

"Thank you, milady. I'm glad you enjoyed it. Is it all right if I call you Beth? I'd like to...if we're to become friends."

Beth's head nodded rapidly while she searched the room, looking for her blue night-time spirit visitor. *Perhaps the spirit knows something about Jennifer that isn't yet apparent to me. It usually shows up when I need comfort or solace.*

"Did you see that strange pulsating blue light last night, Beth?"

Unsure if she could trust Jennifer, Beth resolved to not tell her about the blue apparition. "Know not, Jen."

"Strange. I saw the same blue glow at Ruth and Jonathan's wedding. Did you?"

Beth directed her gaze toward the birds without answering.

"Shall we eat breakfast in the grounds today, Beth?"

"Yes yes, Jen," Beth said, glad she had let the spiritual topic drop.

After dressing Beth, Jennifer was strong enough to take Beth and her wheelchair down the twelve winding steps with no assistance from anyone.

Although it was a warm sunny morning, a gentle breeze blew. They took shade beneath the willow tree, one of Beth's special places where she felt at peace. She watched the sunlight filter through its arrow-shaped leaves and wished she could flee from her world of muddled words.

"It will be autumn soon, Beth. Do we spend autumn and winter indoors?"

"Cruise Orient Jen. Train. Express. Fun great."

"My goodness, Beth. Are you telling me we will be going on a train ride this winter?"

"Know not. Busy wedding all. Ask."

"Yes. I'd prefer you weren't stuck indoors for months on end. You need air and sunlight. Without it you could become off-colour."

Jennifer covered Beth with a blanket and hurried indoors to see if breakfast was ready and to ask Lady Constance if she had any plans for the winter months.

While Jennifer was gone, Beth watched two dragonflies flitting around chasing mosquitoes. *Those nasty bloodsucking bugs never bother me.* Her notion was that the mosquitoes thought they'd be infected by her sickness, so they didn't go near her.

A few minutes later Jennifer returned with a pot of Earl Grey tea on a small tray. A maid followed behind with eggs, toast and marmalade.

"Beth. I have some thrilling news," Jennifer said. "I've just spoken with your mother. We are going to Europe in September—Paris to be exact, then on to Italy to spend the rest of the winter there. Isn't that exciting?"

Beth couldn't care less about the holiday. She glared hungrily at the tray of food, needing the hole in her tummy filled.

Jennifer turned into an inexhaustible chatterbox, chitchatting about this and that the whole time she fed Beth, which drove Beth to distraction. As soon as Beth had had her fill, Jennifer drifted into siesta. Pleased, Beth thought, *Peace, perfect peace.*

Jennifer awoke an hour later and Beth said, "Snore you."

"Oops...sorry, milady. Hope I didn't disturb you too much."

Beth shook her head. "No all right." She chuckled when she saw a bug land on Jennifer's shoulder and bite her.

"Ouch! You beastly creature," Jennifer cried. "Go away!"

Her reaction sent Beth into a fit of uncontrolled laughter.

"That wasn't funny, Beth. It hurt."

A long silence ensued.

The morning turned cool, so they returned indoors to eat lunch. Jennifer put medication on her mosquito bite. Afterwards they nattered about the clothing they'd take to Paris.

Later the same day they travelled to town to buy hair decorations for their trip. They patronized the newly modernised T. Glessal's store instead of the dreary old-fashioned Lamb & Burkett shop.

When they finished, they strolled around town to window shop and stopped at a tea house. A young man winked at Jennifer.

Beth frowned. *Here we go again. Jennifer will meet this man every day and then she will leave me on my own, just like Rachel Penny-Feather did.*

She didn't yet know that Jennifer was nothing like Rachel at all.

"My name is Edwin," the young man said to Jennifer. "Will you allow me to take you to a tea house on another day?"

"Sorry, Edwin. Although I thank you for your interest, I view my job quite seriously and never have any time to spare to develop relationships of my own outside of work."

Edwin left the café. As the two women headed home, he walked on the opposite side of the street and he dashingly tipped his cap as they passed by.

Once again Beth felt distrust. *Will Jennifer desert me every day like Rachel did? Why does she want to work with me when she could have any nursing position or even marriage?*

She watched Jennifer's every move through the following weeks, hoping to uncover clues to her true intent.

CHAPTER TWENTY

September arrived quickly. Graceful autumn leaves fell to the ground, embroidering the earth with hues of red and gold.

After breakfast Jennifer wheeled Beth to her closet. "It's time to pack, Miss Beth. Our holiday begins tomorrow. Have you decided what clothes you will take?"

As Jennifer pulled out one outfit after another, Beth moved her head to indicate a yes or no. It wasn't long before their trunks overflowed and Jennifer had to sit on the lids before they'd close. Their day dragged, until it was time to catch a good night's sleep.

When morning broke the following day, Lady Constance made everyone eat a hearty breakfast of bacon and eggs. Then she flipped open their trunks to make sure they had everything they needed for their trip, especially Beth's typewriter.

James was so excited he couldn't eat. He stood at the door smiling like an excited school boy just presented with a new catapult. When Constance deemed everything was in order, they loaded their vehicle and set off on their European adventure.

They arrived at the harbour without any hitches and boarded a large brilliant-white ship. When they reached their deck level and quarters, Beth and Jennifer couldn't rest for the excitement of sailing across the channel. They sat by their portal to watch the waves gently rippling below, and at night they silently gazed at the stars above. Beth thought it was very romantic. She wished she could have a man to share her starry vision with but thought it would never happen to her. No man would want a crippled wife.

Their maritime journey passed smoothly and on a beautiful, sunny morning they exited the ship's ramp to climb aboard their Paris-bound train. To Jennifer's surprise, Edwin, the man they had previously met in the café, exited the ship. He had been aboard the steamer on a lower-class level.

What is Jennifer up to? Beth wondered. *Has she secretly brought this man to date whilst we are abroad?*

Beth needn't have worried. Jennifer ignored him and walked by as if she didn't see him. She was in awe and wondering what sort of holiday it would turn out to be.

The train ride was bumpy with a smidgen of a chill in the air. Beth hated it. Upon reaching their hotel, wearied from their trip, they slept late the following day and remained at the hotel to relax from their journey.

When daylight broke on the second day, Jennifer was already awake and looking at a cloudless blue sky through the window opposite their beds. She turned with a smile when she heard Beth stir.

"Good morning, Miss Beth. Are you ready to get dressed?"

Beth wriggled like a garter snake and returned to sleep. Jennifer remained by the window, watching couples on the hotel grounds as they admired the autumn flowers.

Thirty minutes later she heard Beth waking up again.

"Is there anything I can get you, Beth dear?"

"No," Beth said with a raspy croak to her voice.

Jennifer rushed to her side. "It sounds like you're not having a good start to your day. Your breathing seems shallow."

"Jen no twitch. No breath. Tired me."

Jennifer tucked her in and went down the hall to Lady Constance's room to give her the bad news. "Having no spasms is fantastic. On the other hand, milady, Beth's breathlessness could be the onset of something grisly."

"Please fetch the hotel doctor."

The doctor admitted Beth into hospital immediately. After a thorough examination the doctor's diagnosis was pneumonia. He instructed that Beth must be away from drafts and she must have a massage three times a day to prevent bedsores. Her window was always left slightly ajar to circulate air. Each day the hospital staff fussed around her. She was barely conscious most of the time. Medication prevented her from feeling anything. When they rolled Beth over to massage both sides of her body, she lay peacefully and didn't stir.

Constance was never far away from her daughter's bedside and neither was Jennifer. Constance knew she had chosen the right nurse this time because Jennifer catered to Beth's every need.

Approximately two weeks passed by before Beth felt like her old self again and wanted to return to the hotel to enjoy more of their holiday. Late one afternoon the reluctant doctor released her into Jennifer's care and insisted that if there was any change in her condition, he must be informed immediately.

When the two women left the hospital a man dressed as a nurse followed them to their hotel entrance.

"How odd, Beth," Jennifer exhaled noisily. "Did you notice if that man over there has followed us? His uniform is the same as the hospital nurses."

Beth shrugged her shoulders in reply, feeling hungry and wanting to eat. "Jen food eat dinner miss. Hospital starve me."

In the dining room, Jennifer ate like a bird and Beth ate enough to sustain a giant. When she had finally eaten her fill, they headed to their suite. As Jennifer pressed the elevator button, she glanced across the hotel foyer. The man who'd followed them was heading their way. He ignored Jennifer and looked directly at Beth. "I waited here until you had eaten dinner," he said with a strong French accent. "You remember we met in ze hospital, mademoiselle Beth? I was one of your masseurs. I would like to lend you a hand while you visit France."

Beth smiled.

Jennifer said, "How do you propose to help us? We have everything we need right here at the hotel."

"I am a highly skilled masseur and also a qualified nurse."

"What's your name, sir?" Jennifer demanded. "Please show me your credentials."

When the man displayed his documents, his eyes were transfixed on Beth. "My name is Jacques Madeleine, mademoiselle. I felt an instant bond between us ze minute I set eyes upon you in ze hospital."

Beth turned away, embarrassed. She couldn't remember him.

Jennifer read his documents. "He's telling the truth." She turned to Jacques. "I'm sorry. I didn't recognise you. Well, don't just stand there, my good man. Help me get Beth into the elevator."

The lift was slow to move. As it lingered for a moment, Jacques gazed at Beth the whole time. She felt uncomfortable with his gaze and looked away.

When they arrived at their level, Jennifer laid Beth on her bed to relax. Jacques wanted to do it except Jennifer wouldn't allow it. When she informed the family of Beth's return, Constance and James walked down the hall to see Beth. When they reached her suite door, they changed their minds and didn't enter to allow Beth time to rest.

Jacques sat in a chair opposite Beth's bed and couldn't take his eyes off her. Noticeably uncomfortable, she wriggled around red faced. After awhile she screamed at Jacques, "You stare no."

He chortled apologetically. "I not stare at you in ze unkind manner. I am gazing into your soul, my lady."

This surprised Beth. She turned her head and closed her eyes, pretending to sleep and wondering why he was paying her so much attention.

Jacques remained in the chair for the rest of the evening and left only minutes before the stroke of midnight.

He returned to the hotel the following day. "It is ze lovely warm morning. Shall we all go for ze walk to ze Place de l'Étoile? I know Beth loves ze stars."

"Yes," Jennifer agreed. "It will be all right to take her out on such a warm day as this."

Even though it was warm, there was a breeze. They wrapped Beth in a blanket and strolled along the avenue. Jacques spoke of his attraction to Beth, who was mildly interested in what he had to say.

Suddenly the sky turned cloudy, and a heavy downpour followed. They took refuge under the Arc de Triomphe, where Beth's mind wandered. *What a romantic place to be stuck with a man who finds me appealing. But I am handicapped. Why would he be interested in someone like me?*

In a matter of minutes the temperature dropped sharply. Jacques covered Beth's shoulders with his jacket. It wasn't enough. She began to shiver.

"We should make a run for it and return to the hotel," Jennifer said. "It would be better than staying outdoors in this weather."

By the time they returned, they were saturated. Beth sneezed and shook vigorously. Jennifer gave Beth a hot drink and Jacques called the doctor.

"It's my fault Beth has relapsed," he said to Jennifer.

"No, it's not," she replied.

"No," Beth said, shivering.

Jacques shook his head sadly. "But the excursion was my idea."

When the doctor arrived, he was furious they'd taken Beth outdoors. "You are both ze health workers. You should know better. Especially you, Jacques. I know you are ze qualified nurse at ze hospital."

Beth noticed that Jennifer and Jacques didn't dare say a word in their defence, likely because of the doctor's bulging eyes and the veins protruding from his neck.

"Take this woman to ze hotel steam room immediately. Make sure she has ze hour-long hot bath. Then put her into bed with plenty of covers and a hot drink."

The doctor left, mumbling profanities in French. Jennifer didn't understand what he said. Jacques did and his face flushed scarlet.

After Beth's visit to the hotel spa, Jennifer dried and dressed her. Although Beth was ill and feeling dreadful, she grinned from ear to ear as Jacques carried her to bed. She enjoyed his attentions, and for her, time stood still. She felt as though she were in a vacuum, except she could breathe and felt surrounded by love. He held her hand until she dropped off to sleep.

Jacques visited her every day and they talked for hours until she fully recovered. The strange thing Beth couldn't understand was how he knew what was on her mind as if he were telepathic.

"Mademoiselle Beth, I know you from somewhere. Perhaps from many centuries ago."

Beth grinned. His words intrigued her. She'd had a lot of time to meditate all her life and had often pondered on past lives and soul mates. Beth puzzled about such things especially since she'd repeatedly seen the unworldly blue glow and its opposite, the demon of Ginns. So she knew there was more to life than just an earthly plane of existence.

From the first day Jacques and Beth were alone together, she felt she was a complete woman. A romantic episode had begun—one she had never known before and had never expected would happen.

Jennifer's soul smiled as each new life experience for Beth unfolded. For Jennifer, it was easy to see that Beth experienced wonderful feelings of affection and belonging. Her face shimmered with love for Jacques. Neither he nor Beth could know whether it would become a lifelong bond of devotion.

Days, then weeks, passed by as the two became inseparable. They visited the opera and ancient monuments, and Jennifer was their chaperone. Jacques was tireless with loving gestures toward Beth. He'd pick a daisy or another flower to tickle her nose, which threw her into fits of laughter.

Jennifer felt left out and unneeded, like piggy in the middle. She grew despondent and questioned whether Jacque's feelings were real or just male hormones.

By this time the only work Jennifer did with Beth was her personal care, because her Ladyship would not allow Jacques to bathe her daughter, even though he was a nurse.

Jennifer decided to find friends of her own to help master her feelings of dejection. She couldn't join James and Lady Constance, as they had their own agenda. So she asked Patrick if he would join her at a nearby café. He didn't get to see much of Beth either but seemed pleased she looked happy.

He accepted Jennifer's invitation. "Aye, lassie. That sounds like fun. Beth seems happy enough, so it's time ye had some fun."

"Let's meet for coffee at ten tomorrow morning, Patrick. Beth will be out with Jacques by then."

Right from the first day, Jennifer realised the trips with Patrick were not a good idea because his accent was so thick. For entertainment, she chose to stay in the hotel foyer by herself to watch the other guests' antics.

One afternoon, just after dinner, two female hotel staff approached her in the foyer.

"We are wondering why you are always sitting alone, mademoiselle," the blonde one asked in a strong French accent.

"I am a nurse for an English lady on holiday here and my attentions are not needed much these days. My patient has someone new in her life and spends all her time with him."

"Ah...a wee romance perhaps," the brunette one replied with a British accent that made Jennifer feel right at home.

"Seems like it. I'm left by myself in one of the dreamiest cities in Europe. I don't know anyone except the people I travelled with and they have their own schedules."

"This is too bad," the blonde said. "Why don't you join us at ze hotel bar tonight, chérie? A great singer will be there. You will have fun."

Her companion nodded. "My dear lady, it's not good to be alone. It's almost Christmas."

"Yes, I know."

Jennifer had nothing to lose, and since she was already staying at the hotel, she smiled and said, "I can meet you at seven o'clock in the hotel's theatrical bar."

"Wonderful," said the blonde.

Just as they left, the brunette woman turned round. "By the way, Jennifer, I am Gretchen and this is Marietta. She is from Paris and I am from south London."

"How did you know my name?"

Gretchen chuckled. "Oh, from the hotel register. See you tonight at seven. Bye."

The two left the hotel, boarded a red cab at the entrance and sped away.

Jennifer returned to her room to bathe in a lavender flower bath. Afterward, she put on her best dress. She dried and prettied up her hair with trinkets and stepped into her shiny black shoes. By this time it was almost seven o'clock.

With growing excitement she skipped downstairs to meet her newfound friends.

The bar was dark. She didn't want to go inside past the entrance because she couldn't see Marietta or Gretchen anywhere. Musicians began to play a waltz, and a man put his hand on her shoulder and whispered, "Would you like to dance?"

Jennifer quivered with nervous excitement as the unknown man touched her with his strong hand. Her eyes adjusted to the dim lighting. He was exceptionally handsome and tall. So she danced with him before she even knew his name.

As they danced he said, "My name is Giorgio. I am with one of the acts booked to play here later this evening."

"I'm a nurse."

"Shall we sit down and talk?"

Jennifer nodded. He placed his palm in the middle of her back and guided her to a small corner table with a candle at its centre.

She scanned the room looking for Marietta or Gretchen and perceived neither one.

"What would you like to drink, miss?" He hadn't asked for her name yet.

"Just a coffee please, Giorgio. Thank you."

He went to the bar and returned to place a coffee on the table in front of her with a smile. They twittered the evening away while discussing the cultural differences between France and England.

"You have a great command of English, Giorgio."

"Yes. I was born in England. My parents moved to France when I was a child, so I had to come too. At first I didn't like it here, but now I have become so used to it I couldn't imagine living anywhere else."

She looked at him with an unbelieving expression on her face.

"I'm sorry. Here I am talking with you and I do not even know your name."

"It's Jennifer."

"Paris is so romantic. Would you agree, Jennifer?"

It was almost nine o'clock and she felt taken aback that he was showing her so much interest so quickly. Romance fled from her mind in a trice as she focused on Beth and Jacques, wondering if they'd returned yet. Jennifer realised he had asked a question she hadn't heard. "I'm sorry, could you repeat your question?"

"This country, Jennifer. Don't you think it is romantic here? The nights are long and cool, always with heady scents of flowers wafting by. Love and music float in the air here. Jennifer, are you listening?"

"Oh, sorry, Giorgio. I was thinking of my charge. I've never really thought about Paris. I guess it is quite romantic here. You know, we are travelling elsewhere when our holiday in France ends after Christmas. We're going to Italy. I hear it is also a romantic country. Have you been there?"

"Ah, yes. Italy is hotter." He reached across the table and stroked the back of her hand.

She pulled it away nervously. "You mean the...er...climate is hotter?"

"Yes, yes, dear lady. The temperature and the music in Italia is bellissimo."

"It will be my first visit. I hope it's not much hotter there than it is here—tonight is practically unbearable."

Giorgio gazed into her eyes and changed the subject.

"You need a good man. No, you need a great man, Jennifer. One who will be attentive toward you...a man like me."

The dimly lit room hid the blush of her hot cheeks. He was flirting with her and she liked it.

His hand stroked the inside of her wrist. "Do you have such a man in your life, ma belle dame?"

"What did you just say Giorgio? What does belle dame—"

"I said you are a beautiful lady," he interrupted. "'Ma belle dame means my beautiful lady. And you, Jennifer, are stunning with your red hair."

Jennifer giggled like a schoolgirl, thinking she had never been beautiful. She deemed herself as a bit of a plain Jane and so decided he might be a player of hearts.

"Thank you for the compliment, Giorgio. I'm afraid I have to leave now. It is late and I must return to my suite. My patient will be waiting for me. Thank you for the evening."

"Will I see you again, belle dame?"

"We'll see. Perhaps tomorrow. Now I really must leave."

Giorgio gripped her hand tightly while it rested on the table. He raised his other hand to stroke her hair. Then slowly moved it downward to her face and gently caressed his fingertip across her eyebrow oh so slowly.

His action triggered a bomb inside her and she quivered with pleasure. It was the first time she had felt the sensation. It unnerved her. She wrenched her hand from his and strode from the bar to the elevator to the rhythm of her racing heart.

Giorgio chased after her. As she was about to step inside the open elevator, he seized her firmly but gently around her waist. "Do not leave, Jennifer. Please return to the table and spend more time with me. The night, it is young."

Jennifer's heart practically stopped. "Giorgio, please unhand me. I have told you the reason why I must leave. Now if you will excuse me, I have my work to attend to."

He didn't let go.

Annoyed, she raised her tone of voice. "Sir! Take your hands off me, or I will be forced to call for assistance."

He released his grip and stood silently with his head bowed in what seemed like a stance of shame. Jennifer felt bad about his hurt feelings because she never took delight in hurting people, whether she knew them or not. Many notions crossed her mind. *Does this man really like me? Should I stay a little longer or should I leave? Beth must have returned by now.*

Her most important thought won.

"I must leave, Giorgio. My patient. Perhaps we might meet tomorrow."

Giorgio looked at her with tear-filled eyes. "I'm sorry, Jennifer. I didn't mean to appear obstinate. I am so lonely. I have no friends here."

Jennifer wanted to hug him. Her women's intuition told her not to and she entered the elevator.

"Perhaps tomorrow, Giorgio. Goodnight."

He smirked. Then he spun round on his heels and walked away.

Beth hadn't returned yet and Jennifer felt wound tighter than a pair of twisted knickers. *I could have stayed with Giorgio a little longer.*

She prepared for their usual night-time routine at ten o'clock, just as the door opened and in wheeled Beth with Jacques. They were laughing.

Jennifer lost control. "Where the hell have you two been? I've been worried sick about you."

"Shout no. Fun had."

"I'm sorry, Beth. I didn't mean to bark. I've been so worried. Anything could have happened. Why didn't you return sooner?"

"Not fun know."

"Jennifer," Jacques called out in a soothing voice, "there is no need to be annoyed at ze lady Beth. It's not her fault we are late. I was ze one pushing her. We were having fun and we lost track of time. That is all. No harm is done."

Beth nodded her head feverishly in agreement. Jennifer glared at Jacques as she spoke to Beth.

"C'mon. Let's get you into bed, Beth, before your mother discovers how late you have returned. You know fine well how she feels about things like this."

Jacques reached out to kiss Beth's hand to say goodbye. As his lips touched the back of her hand, her eyes grew large.

"I'll return at nine o'clock tomorrow morning, my love. Please be ready."

"Hmm," Beth mumbled with a hesitant but happy smile. She had probably been expecting Jennifer would say something that she didn't want to hear and must have been relieved when she heard nothing except silence.

Despite the fact Jennifer wanted to tell Jacques to stay the hell away, she didn't want to get into anything so late at night. So she allowed him to leave and then locked the door. She washed and began to dress Beth without speaking.

"Nice Jacques, Jen," Beth said.

Jennifer finished dressing Beth in silence and put her to bed. Then she headed to her adjoining room and turned out the light.

Beth quietly reminisced about her day with Jacques. *Our picnic in the park was divine. Jacques has such strong arms. I feel so safe with him and his body...hmmm, his delicious body. It felt so warm next to mine while we were lying on that blanket so closely entwined. It was fantastic! When we talked 'til dusk it was like I had known him forever. I think I love him. But why is he so taken with me? I'm a cripple. I wonder...perhaps we were lovers in a past life. Nonetheless, I did have fun today. We kissed so much I cannot remember the performance of the show we saw together.*

Still feeling his body close to hers, she wriggled her hips and giggled. Beth's memories of her day made her chuckle loudly.

Jennifer barged through the door. "Beth! Stop making so much noise. I can't sleep."

"Me sowey."

"What's wrong, Beth?"

"No Jen hurt."

"Aw, do you mean you're sorry for hurting me, Beth?"

"Yes."

"You didn't hurt me, dear. I'm just tired, being up so late and worried about what your parents will say tomorrow. You know what your mother can be like. Please get some sleep. We'll talk about it in the morning, all right?"

Jennifer kissed her brow. Beth nodded and heaved a happy sigh as she snuggled deep inside her bedcovers. Within minutes she was blissfully dead to the world.

Jacques arrived bang on, at nine o'clock the following morning. Beth was keen to go out with him on such a clear, blue-skied day. Jennifer hadn't had time to speak with her about the previous evening.

It was the week before Christmas and the two lovers wanted to shop for gifts.

As they left the room, they bumped into James, her stepfather, in the corridor. He presented Beth with a note to make credit purchases anywhere.

"Beth, with this note you can buy anything your little heart desires—within reason of course." He winked.

She presented her generous stepfather with a huge smile.

James turned to speak to Jacques.

"Just make sure you sign the credit notes each time she buys something. All right, Jacques? I will not pay for anything that has not been signed for."

"Yes. I will make sure of this. You will not be billed for any of ze items milady does not buy."

The lovers left the building and moseyed along a narrow road behind the hotel. Something in a window on the opposite side of the street shone brightly as the sun's rays hit it. Its glare was blinding. They crossed the road to investigate and found it was a sparkling crystal tiara with a flower and leaf pattern. Beth loved it.

"Do you wish to buy this, my love?"

"Mother for yes," Beth nodded eagerly.

"Ah. You wish to buy this for your mother."

Jacques produced the note to the shop assistant.

Beth bought a gold tiepin shaped like a sled for her stepfather and a pair of cufflinks that Jacques liked from the same store. She didn't tell him why she bought them.

"You have already purchased Mr. Forsythe ze gift, dear one. Why you need these too?"

"Me like two. Paper blue."

He thought she wanted to give James two gifts.

"You want this one wrapped in ze blue paper as well, my lady?"

"Jacques yes."

He chuckled. "You're crazy for ze colour, aren't you, my love?"

"Blue love me."

The store owner apologized because he had no blue paper left. Jacques signed the purchase notes and placed the items into the shopping basket hanging on the arm of Beth's wheelchair.

A little farther along the cobbled road they found another quaint store. They could hardly get through the door because the shop was packed full of items. Beth spied a snow globe containing two reindeer scratching the ground beneath a tree. Her mind wandered back to Jennifer. *She will love it. Jen adores animals.*

Jennifer was pleased Beth gave the impression of blissful happiness with Jacques as she grew through her first romantic period of her life. But she was unsure what would happen when they left for Italy. She hoped neither would break the other's heart.

CHAPTER TWENTY-ONE

When Christmas Eve morning arrived, Beth was up with the larks. Jennifer popped her head inside the door.

"Have all your gifts been wrapped, dear?"

"Jen no," Beth replied, giggling.

Jennifer was glad Beth laughed more since she'd met Jacques

"All right. Show me which gifts still need to be wrapped and we'll do it together."

Using her eyes, Beth directed her gaze to a drawer beside her bed where the cuff links were. Again, she used her eyes to signify a different coloured paper than her father's gift.

"Pocket put dress."

Jennifer knew Beth had something up her sleeve because she didn't want the gift placed with the other presents under the tree.

The two dressed and went downstairs for a breakfast of strawberries and smoked salmon on toast, all washed down with champagne. Jacques arrived at the table and insisted he must be the one to help Beth eat. This left Jennifer with nothing to do once again. Each time Jacques did something for Beth Jennifer felt more and more redundant. She wanted to tell Jacques to back off, but couldn't say it without knowing whether Beth truly enjoyed his attentions, and she felt she couldn't ask her yet.

Jennifer felt sorry for herself. She had entertained thoughts of quitting her job. She had even gone to the hospital a few days before and asked questions about Jacques. His colleagues had told her he was having his vacation time and wouldn't be back for more than two weeks. She learned he had been an employee at the same hospital for more than three years and yet no one had any bad comments to say about him.

This man sounds perfect. Maybe too perfect.

Over breakfast that morning, she asked, "How long have you worked for the hospital, Jacques?"

"Hmm. Now this is ze question I will have to think about for a moment or two. It's been a few years—perhaps trois?"

"You must enjoy working there."

"Yes, Jennifer. I like ze hospital a lot."

"So, Jacques, how come you spend so much time with Beth? Don't you work full time at the hospital?"

"Zis is my vacation. I have trois more weeks due to me."

"Oh, I see." Knowing he hadn't lied, she stopped asking questions and finished eating breakfast.

Beth and Jacques were interested in no one but each other. When breakfast was over, they left to wander around the Parisian streets together.

In the evening a ball was held in the Great Hall to welcome Christmas morning. The music was gay and light—completely different from Christmas Eves in the workhouse.

Beth's dress shone under the radiant blaze of twenty crystal chandeliers. A Christmas tree glistened and twinkled in the corner next to the band. The whole ambiance of the room was one of kindness, warmth and love. Jacques was overcome with emotion and asked Beth to dance. People sitting at the adjacent tables gasped with horror. Malicious whispers about Jacques began. *Doesn't he know she's sick and can't dance? How cruel to ask a lady in a wheelchair to dance!* To everyone's surprise Beth nodded. Her expression displayed glorious happiness.

Lady Constance looked on with distrust and disapproval. Jacques whisked Beth away in his masculine arms. In seconds, he whirled her around the dance floor. She appeared joyful, and it looked like she was dancing on her own feet as her dress swirled outward to its full width, covering her feet. She caught a glimpse of herself in the mirrors around the hall walls and couldn't believe her eyes. *Look at me. I'm dancing. I'm really dancing!*

"I dance. See, Jacques."

"Yes, you are, my love."

James observed them swirling around the floor and gazing into each other's smiling eyes. They appeared to be so much in love.

"Constance darling. Now I know for sure that Jacques truly cares for

Beth unlike any other man ever has or probably ever will. Look at them."

Drawn to tears by his words, Constance left the room to compose herself in the ladies' restroom.

Ballroom guests who were previously shocked at Jacques's dance request, smiled sweetly at their loving vision. Jennifer watched in astonishment.

At that moment someone tapped her on the shoulder. She jumped with shock and swung her torso around to discover it was Giorgio asking her to dance. Jennifer thought she'd seen the last of him at the elevator. His grinning smirk told her he was only paying attention to her to get what he wanted, which in her opinion was a quick romp in the hay. *How could I be wrong about that? Oh, I'll dance with him anyway. It's time I had a little fun on this holiday.*

Jennifer offered him her hand and Giorgio guided her onto the smooth, polished dance floor. The band played a tango and Giorgio certainly knew how to tango. They danced until her head felt dizzy. Jennifer glanced across the room and glimpsed Beth being twirled. She knew just how she felt because she herself felt gloriously excited by the music, the lights, the gowns and the feeling of being in the arms of a handsome man.

Earlier, on the same night, when Patrick made his way to the ballroom, he met an attractive waitress named Edna from another hotel. The two enjoyed viewing the artwork in the hotel corridors together, so he had been in her company for most of the evening. When there was no more art to see they entered the ballroom and sat at a table. Patrick glanced round the room, looking for Beth.

"She is such a bonnie wee princess. Her sequined dress sparkles and twinkles beneath these lights. It's like she belongs to the stars above."

Edna didn't hear for the dance music.

Beth had a huge grin on her face, looking as happy as a fairytale princess who'd just kissed her very own frog prince. She displayed no outward sign of suspicion or mistrust. Love smouldered in her eyes. Patrick sighed heavily and wished he could dance with his little Beth too. He knew he could never spin her around like Jacques did because of his own gammy leg.

Edna touched Patrick's hand to snap Patrick from his thoughts and down he thumped to Mother Earth. Edna confided in Patrick that she had been married in the past to a nice man. One sad day a letter arrived—he had drowned on a ship manufactured by the same builders of the RMS Titanic.

Patrick didn't know what to say. To lift her spirits he held her hand and changed the topic. "See the wee-yen over yonder?"

"Who? The woman you've been watching?"

"Yes, the wee-yen. The one whose eyes and dress sparkle like the stars in the heavens is ma wee Beth."

"She is your Beth? Is she your daughter?"

"Oh no. Sorry, lassie. I looked after that wee-yen for many years when we lived inside a workhouse in England. Her mother is Lady Constance—the woman wearing the blue dress at that table over yonder. Back then they had fallen upon hard times because her mother would nae give her child up because she was afflicted."

Edna laughed long and hard as she tossed her head backwards. "That young woman is not afflicted, Patrick. Look at her. She's dancing. The afflicted cannot dance."

Patrick detested being called a liar and snarled, "I tell you noo—that wee lassie is afflicted. Look 'ower yonder, Edna." He pointed to the Forsythe table on the far side of the dance floor.

"See that chair with the wheels on it on the other side of the table? That's the wheelchair I made fur her in t' workhouse. Mr. Forsythe just prettied it up a wee bit because she refuses to have a new yen made."

Edna's face contorted into a grimace as if she didn't want to associate herself with people who'd once lived in a workhouse. "You lived in a poorhouse, Patrick? That's where they put all the lazy, good for nothing people. And to think I even liked you...*humph*."

Edna stood up swiftly and kicked her chair backwards to leave. People turned to see what was happening.

Patrick gripped her arm, albeit too firmly. "Calm yerself and sit doon, lassie. Everybody's looking at you. Let me explain a few things tae you afore you go. Ye can nae just run off with nae explanation."

"Well, it is dimly lit this side of the room so no one can see me sitting with a workhouse vagabond. I suppose it wouldn't hurt to hear you out."

Patrick took another swig of Scotch whiskey, leaned back in his chair and clasped his hands behind his head. He liked Edna and didn't want her thinking anything bad about him.

"Firstly, Edna, I'm nae a vagabond. Let me tell ye how it was, lassie. See Lady Constance, the good-looking woman over yonder wearing the royal-blue gown? She is the mother o' my beautiful Beth. Ye see her husband left them when Beth was just a few years old. Because the child was disabled, her own family did nae want her daughter living with them either, and because Lady Constance was headstrong she refused any help for just herself. See, they wanted her tae part with Beth—tae lock her up in a convent somewhere or worse, in an asylum. Lady Constance ended up in a workhouse because of her choice. And it was the best pick, so it was."

"Oh my goodness! That lady lived in a workhouse as well...because of her family, you say? She seems to have breeding. Who are her family?"

"Aye, lass. That woman's a saint so she is. O' aye. She's fiery in all the right ways. Her Aunt Betsy, Lady Elisabeth Witherspoon, was scared o' Beth. Said she was full o' demons. So she would nae have her in her hoose."

"*The* Witherspoons?" Edna had heard about the wealthy Witherspoon family from affluent people in the hotel.

"Now wait a minute, lassie. Maybe I should nae mention any mare about them. You can see they're well off noo. She was born in tae nobility as well, you know." Patrick had taken a few large gulps of whiskey by this time, so felt courageous enough to talk about his own past. "Let me tell ye about me and how I ended up living there. See, my family owned a castle in Scotland—"

"Dear God, Patrick, you were born into a noble family as well?"

"Aye, lassie. A truly noble one. A renegade clan broke in tae our castle and kidnapped me when I was nothing but a bairn, but nae afore they'd tortured and killed my family. I was sold tae a farmer who beat the hell out o' me. Being a headstrong lad, I runs away and ended up working at a manor in the north of England."

"Patrick. I thought you said Scotland?"

"Aye. I hiked down from Scotland to England."

"How old were you, Patrick?"

"I was just a child. One day when I was working at that English manor, I hurt my leg driving a horse and carriage over fast. Stupid it was. I could nae work as their stable boy anymore with a gammy leg. So I was pushed in tae the same workhouse where I met Lady Constance and Beth."

Edna must have at least thought him sincere, even if she may have thought his story sounded farfetched, because she decided to hang around awhile longer to see what else transpired.

Midnight sneaked up on the happy group as the music ended abruptly with a waltz. Jacques wanted to take Beth to her room and carried her toward the elevator.

Lady Constance put a stop to it. "My daughter has had enough excitement this evening and needs to rest. You can see her again tomorrow morning at church, Jacques."

Beth's paranoia returned. She glared at her mother, imagining she wanted to spoil her life. Jennifer put sobbing Beth to bed, insisting that Constance just wanted the best for her. Beth stared at the wall and cried for ten minutes before she slept.

Next morning the first knock on their door was Patrick, arriving to give Beth her Christmas treat, a huge bar of chocolate. She loved chocolate, which was the gift he had given her every year since the first tiny piece he'd found on the workhouse floor that icy morning years before. He placed a small piece onto her waiting tongue and watched her expression as it melted, thick and creamy.

After Christmas breakfast, Jacques arrived to attend church with Beth. She was happy to see him, but at the same time she grew overwhelmed with thoughts of why any man would pay such an interest in her. *What if this man is secretly possessed and planning to hurt me like Mary did?*

No one wished to harm Beth. She'd been distrusting people more and more as each day passed by, even people she'd known for years. Christmas Day or not, Beth's mood shifted to paranoia. Constance rang for the hotel physician.

"This woman needs to calm down," the doctor said.

Beth screamed, "Want Jacques. Want Jacques."

Constance wouldn't allow it because she was already too excited and sent him away.

"I you hate," Beth growled. The excitement of the last few weeks had been too much for her. She felt confused. The only thing she knew for sure was that she must be with Jacques and no one else would do.

A commanding blue spectre looked on, wondering what was coming over Beth, because it couldn't calm her down either. It was as if she didn't notice the blue spectre was even in the room.

James, Lady Constance and Patrick set out for church that morning. Jennifer couldn't go, but left Beth in her room crying. Her continuous screams ripped at Jennifer's nerve ends. It annoyed her so much she gritted her teeth and plugged her ears with cotton wadding.

After the church service, Constance returned and asked Jennifer, "How is my daughter feeling now she's had a couple of hours' rest?"

"Milady, I'm sorry to inform you that Beth has been highly strung with nonstop screaming since you left."

They called the doctor again. He came at once and gave Beth a stronger sedative.

"Her condition appears to have deteriorated. I'm not sure which treatment to give her because, to my knowledge, her type of handicap hasn't been studied. Keep her as quiet as possible and if she becomes more agitated, give one of these three pills with food."

The doctor left.

Jennifer was exhausted and needed to rest. She gave Beth a pill so she could sleep for a while.

Jacques climbed the hotel trellis as Jennifer slept and snuck under the bedcovers beside Beth. Some time had passed and her medication had begun to wear off. She experienced feelings of apprehension as he lay beside her. He did not touch her intimately. He just snuggled up close and slept with her for the rest of the night, hugging as if they were children.

When Jennifer awoke the next morning she was mortified to see Jacques in bed with Beth. Jennifer roared, "Get out, Jacques."

He didn't want someone to involve the police, so he left.

Beth glared at Jennifer, with slits for eyes and an angry purple face.

"Kill you. Me will. Kill." Beth growled.

Jennifer left the room and bumped into Constance in the hallway.

"Milady, Jacques has been here all night. I found him in bed with your daughter this morning."

"He's done what?"

"It's all right now, milady. I've sent him away."

Furious, Constance ran to tell her husband. "James, I do not like what has been happening between Jacques and Beth of late. In order to stop his shenanigans, we must return to England at once. What is going on between them can never bear fruit."

She sucked in a deep breath. "Oh my God, James. What if my daughter is pregnant? How could she birth a child in her condition? I am so livid with him for sleeping with her."

"Constance, I'm confident that Jacques loves Beth. We both saw it on the dance floor. Nevertheless, to appease you we will board the first ship home and not visit Italy this year."

James trundled up the hall to inform Jennifer and Beth that they were returning to England posthaste.

"That is a shame, sir, because I know she would enjoy Italy. And besides, Jacques will not be there."

Jennifer wanted to go to Italy herself and felt disgruntled the trip was ruined because Beth had turned into a spoiled brat.

In order to dress screaming Beth safely, Jennifer sedated her because her whole body thrashed profusely.

"Want me Jacques."

Beth cried nonstop the whole trip home. Her old friend Patrick couldn't even pacify her, although she was somewhat quieter when he was with her.

No one realised that Jacques and Beth had only slept together and that nothing else had happened. Neither of them had a chance to clear up the confusion before being torn from each other's arms.

CHAPTER TWENTY-TWO

Back at the manor, Constance remained deep in thought for hours each day about how far her daughter's intimacy had gone with Jacques. She thought her daughter might be pregnant. Constance began to withdraw from life and became gravely ill, both mentally and physically.

James did his best to understand why his wife was still so concerned about the incident in France. Nothing he said could console her. Her mind drifted into nothingness as she stared at walls, exactly the same way she did in Garlands Asylum.

The depressing atmosphere in the house made Jennifer feel uneasy because she was convinced the family blamed her for everything. She packed her things and left without a word to anyone. It wasn't until lunchtime that a maid realised she'd gone.

James couldn't decide what to do other than find someone else to take over her work. He rang the bell to summon a maid.

"You might already know that Jennifer has left. No one knows why or where she went, but we need help to find a new nurse. I have more commercial business to attend to in two weeks."

"Where will we find someone who is trained at such short notice, sir?"

"Well, I brought you here to ask where Jennifer came from?"

"I think Lady Constance placed an advertisement somewhere. We can't ask her now because her mind has gone again. Oops, I'm sorry for seeming disrespectful, sir. You could enquire at the pub. Meanwhile I'll go and ask Cook. She's been here a long time, so maybe she knows."

The maid raced to the scullery, red-faced, and explained the problem to Cook.

"Until he finds somebody else to care for Beth, one of us will have to step up to the plate," Cook said, looking at the maid. "Who will do it?"

"Don't look at me. I'm far too busy with me housework. What about Gloria? She'll help out."

"She'll have to and that'll be an end to it. Go and fetch her so we can tell her wit's gone on."

In the meantime, James paid a visit to the Anchor Vaults tavern to ask the regulars if they knew how to find a new nurse. The rough, unkempt barman said to James, "Speak with the overweight woman sitting beside that clean-shaven senior man in the corner."

The woman had lank, greasy brown hair and a spotty complexion. Although somewhat repulsed by her appearance, James approached her. "Madam, I am Mr. Forsythe. Why would the barman suggest I speak with you about a nursing position with my family?"

"Because I am an experienced nurse, sir, and he knows I need another job. I've just cleaned the hotel kitchen so please forgive me dirty appearance. I also clean places to take more money home for me dear sick ol' mother."

"Are you really a trained nurse, miss? What is your name?"

"Linda Hobbs is me name, sir. If I don't find a decent paying position soon, then I might end up living in Ginns Workhouse again. Lord only knows what would happen to me dear ol' mother then."

Without asking why she had lived in the workhouse, he replied, "Really, miss. Would you consider working in my household at Forsythe Manor as our nurse? I will pay you handsomely. I'm sure it will be more than sufficient to take care of your dear mother."

Linda accepted without hesitation.

"I can begin work tomorrow evening at seven. Is this time agreeable with you, Mr. Forsythe sir? Oh yes. I will also need time off to take care of me ol' mother each day as well."

"Yes, yes. You may have time off to see to your mother each evening. This is excellent. I shall inform my housekeeper to expect you tomorrow night at seven o'clock sharp. She will collect you at the manor gates to guide you to your quarters."

James stuffed a handful of coins into her hand, relieved he'd found someone and didn't notice the black fleas jumping off her clothing onto the light-coloured pine table.

"Yes, Mr. Forsythe. Thank you kindly," Linda said, gripping the money so tightly it made circular marks in the palm of her dirty, sweaty hand.

Exultant, James left the pub, not knowing he had hired the same Linda Hobbs who, along with Mary Crab, had held séances in Ginns years earlier.

James returned home and enlightened his wife. "I've engaged a new caregiver for your daughter."

Constance didn't give him a sideways glance. Disappointed that she'd said nothing, when he thought she should have been grateful, he left the room and slammed the door.

Beth's door was ajar and she had heard everything. *What do I do now, blue spirit? I can see mother is heading for another nervous breakdown. Her eyes look as if she is not of this world.*

The blue spirit replied, "Stay quiet and remain calm. This situation will resolve itself in time and you will come to no harm."

The following evening Linda Hobbs arrived at the manor, dirt-free. The cook instructed her to wear a uniform when she went to meet her Ladyship in order to make the best possible impression.

Constance didn't ask Linda any questions at all. She welcomed her in a faraway tone, as though she didn't know why Linda was even at the house. "Welcome to my home, Linda. I'm happy to see you and I hope you enjoy your stay here."

Afterward, Gloria introduced Linda to Beth, who felt a little uneasy but was unable to put her finger on what troubled her.

James left for Europe a week later.

When James returned from his business trip a few months later, Constance had regained most of her physical strength. James did his utmost to make her feel happy since she didn't smile anymore. On warm days he invited their friends to garden parties and threw grand balls in the evenings. Over the weeks, nothing pleased Constance.

Although she had appeared oblivious to what was taking place around her, she had been very conscious of things going on. Constance was fully aware that Linda's eyes were on James and that James's eyes were always on Linda. Neither of them knew that Constance had noticed anything.

Linda had given her body to James during a full-blown love affair, which lasted several weeks. When Constance realised her husband had bedded the nurse, her temper let loose. She charged out of the mansion in an electrical fury and went to the stables to order Patrick to get their vehicle ready.

Patrick scowled. *Oh God, what's garn on here now?*

Constance raced to her Aunt Betsy's to explain the depraved things her husband had done with Linda.

"Connie, you must put up with his behaviour. Say nothing. Otherwise he may well accuse you of mania and commit you into Garlands Asylum. Surely you can remember that awful place?"

Constance was beside herself and screamed at her aunt.

"I cannot ignore his actions any longer. I will not suffer humiliation at the hands of any man ever again. I'm leaving him!"

"You're talking like a simpleton, Connie. Look, if you leave him you might end up in the same dire financial situation as the last time when you had to live in the workhouse. If Ginns does not take you back, and sometimes they don't, then you could end up in a whorehouse."

Constance hadn't thought of that. Her face turned paper white and she almost fainted.

"Men! They always have the final say," she declared defiantly. "Unknown to James, I've been stealing his money for more than a year just in case something like this happened again. Auntie, I trust no man. I trust no priest. Beth and I will move to James's summer house in Scotland. He is weak-willed and will loathe the disgrace of a divorce, so this time I win. We needn't let anyone outside the family know I've left him."

Unable to speak, Betsy just sat with her mouth open.

"Auntie. He can tell people that my daughter and I have gone on a long vacation. Then he can live with that floozy nurse, just like nothing scandalous had happened."

"You seem to have it all worked out. Except what if your plan fails?"

"I don't want to broadcast his infidelity. I've been humiliated enough. This is my second marriage and it's happened again. Some of my friends wouldn't understand me leaving him. They might even say his infidelity was my fault. I'm very aware that many of them put up with this sort of behaviour from their own husbands for fear of finding themselves destitute."

"Yes, they would be frightened. They don't have the strong inner stamina you have, Connie. Did you ever tell any of your friends about your previous marriage? Perhaps the Whitehaven gossipers have already put paid to your little secret."

"No, Aunt Betsy. I didn't want any of them to know. If anyone already knows then they did not mention it to me."

Constance drank a glass of port and rested awhile before she returned home.

When she arrived back at Forsythe manor she yelled upstairs to Gloria, "Pack our bags. We are leaving this damn place. I'm taking you and some other staff with us."

Gloria was pleased. "Certainly, milady."

John, the gentle gardener, placed everyone's bags into the car and asked Patrick, "What's going on?"

"We're going on a long trip to Helen Rose Cottage, lad. It's near Ecclefechan in southwest Scotland."

"Why, Pat? That's a long way to drive."

"Nae you mind about that, lad. Besides, it will only take two days to reach it."

Because Patrick snapped his words out, John mentioned nothing else.

The vehicle was slow moving.

"Not me go," rebellious Beth said, fearing they'd end up in calamitous Ginns again, and this time there was five of them to feed. She cried off and on the whole trip.

When they were on the uphill approach to Helen Rose Cottage, Constance noted it was large and not at all undersized like her husband had implied. The cottage lawn badly needed a manicure. A wisteria grew on either side of the doorway and roses of every color under the sun lined a cobbled driveway that was reminiscent of the old roads in Europe.

Constance exited the vehicle first. Patrick placed tearful Beth into her wheelchair and hobbled inside with everyone else following. Inside the dusty entrance hall on the right stood a massive stone fireplace with a carved wooden mantle and a Venus de Milo statuette sitting proudly at its centre. Two sparkling chandeliers adorned the ceiling. Sunlight graced the crystals with its rays, throwing rainbows across the walls. Beth noticed the coloured hues as well. She quietened down and gazed open mouthed at the colourful rainbows strewn throughout the room. Inside each blue shaft of light was the face of a spectral entity that only Beth could see.

A winding staircase with a metal handrail led upstairs to three bathrooms, five bedrooms, two parlours and a dining room, large enough to seat twenty people. The lowest level included a decent sized scullery and servants' quarters. On turning to exit the rear entrance, they found more trees, an attractive pagoda and a small bridge over a fishpond. Beyond that, stables adjoined a three-room cabin. This became Patrick and John's home.

Woodlands grew on three sides of the cottage. On the fourth side they saw an amazing south-facing view of the Solway Frith and the Irish Sea. Helen Rose Cottage would be a serene place to live in peace and in harmony with nature.

Constance grew calmer in just one week. She made a trip to the nearby village with John to find more staff. She hired Minnie to be their cook and Anna as a scullery maid. Gloria was glad that Constance had hired more help because she had more work than she could deal with, especially with looking after Beth.

Weeks later, while Constance was in the hallway admiring a painting, Gloria decided her Ladyship was sufficiently composed to tell her that Linda was not the only woman her husband had bedded back at the manor. Gloria needed to get it all off her chest so her own conscience was clear. It had been troubling her.

"He'd slept with all of us scullery maids. Me, as well. It was either let him 'ave his evil way wiv us and say noffin', madam, or be thrown into the street. Isn't that right, John?" Gloria said, with tears in her eyes. She turned to look at John, who had just sauntered through the back door with Patrick hobbling behind.

"Aye, Miss Gloria, that be true. Anything could have happened if thee had opened thy mouth to anyone at the manor. I think what some of them thar rich men do to the lasses be a wicked, wicked thing."

Patrick nodded in agreement.

Once again Constance's volcanic temper erupted. She kicked the couch, overturned tables and threw the Venus statuette on the mantel into the fire. She looked like she wanted to kill James. She turned to face Gloria, who ducked as if to avoid a slap in the face. Constance's skin colour changed to purple.

Gloria practically fainted with fright seeing Constance's gritted teeth. She dropped to her knees, scared out of her wits, grabbed Constance's skirt hem. "Oh, I beg you, milady. Please don't be angry wiv me. It weren't my fault. I did not enjoy his attentions. We was all forced into it, ma'am, or else. I for one had no place else to go and he knew it."

"Don't touch me, Gloria. Leave this room immediately."

Gloria ran out of the room, leaving the door slightly ajar and heard Constance turn ballistic once more. Gloria peeked through the crack along the door hinges. The room looked like a war zone as Constance threw more vases at the walls and sent a small chair soaring through a window.

She knew Constance had been so sure that her second husband had possessed a little family decency. Gloria suspected the woman felt worse about her broken marriage because she had been proven wrong.

Unable to control the fiendish volcano within her, Constance screamed, "Why can't men be faithful and keep their stick inside their pants?"

With that, Gloria spun on her heals and leaped down the staircase two steps at a time, crying repeatedly, "It's not my fault. It's not my fault!"

Minnie was in the kitchen. When she saw Gloria's tears, she said,

"What the hell has gotten into you?" All of a sudden it seemed to hit her like a landslide. "Aw, damn it. She's told her Ladyship what went on with James and the female servants, didn't she, Gloria?"

Gloria nodded.

"You're a sodding fool for coughing up," Minnie said with a scowl. "You shouldn't have mentioned any of it and let bygones be bygones."

Eventually Gloria stopped crying and the two of them speculated what her Ladyship might do.

"Do you think she will discharge me, Minnie?"

"Christ, Gloria. Why did you have to tell her? You damned idiot. The woman was calmer than she's been for days."

"Oh, finish making supper. I'm going for a walk."

"Get back in here and help me peel these vegetables!"

Gloria paid no mind to Minnie and ran out the back door into the orchard.

Lady Constance didn't eat dinner or utter another sound for the rest of the day. This time the long-term staff was pleased she had gone quiet.

"At least we'll all have a home until she recovers from this episode," Minnie said to Gloria later that evening.

Gloria frowned. "I don't know why I told her. I feel no better for having done it."

Minnie shook her head in dismay.

Two days later a woman dressed in stylish country garb with a yellow parasol strolled up the garden path with news for Constance. Gloria opened the door.

"Hello. I'm Mrs. Anne Farquhar, your neighbour from across the valley, the other side of these woods. I've recently returned from Cumberland and bring Lady Constance news of Whitehaven."

"Please wait in the parlour, madam, while I fetch her Ladyship."

Gloria pointed the way and raced upstairs, apprehensive of the reception she might receive. She knocked on Constance's door and nervously entered.

"Milady. There's a woman here to see you. She said she's your neighbour, Mrs. Anne Farquhar. I put 'er in the parlour, ma'am. She is waiting to tell you news from Whitehaven. I hope it was the right thing to do."

Constance nodded without a word and went downstairs to the parlour. "What news do you have that you feel might be of interest to me, Mrs. Far-Bottom?" Constance said in a snippy tone of voice.

"Thank you for the audience, milady. You might be interested to hear your husband has received visitors, Mr. and Mrs. Bartholomew. My friend in Whitehaven said you knew the couple yourself from a holiday some time back."

"Thank you for going out of your way to pass this information to me. However, the manor isn't my home anymore."

A slight frown came onto Mrs. Farquhar's face and she paused as if not knowing what else to say.

Constance broke the silence. "How far did you have to travel? Would you like some refreshment before you return home?"

"Oh, it's all right, milady. I just live across the valley. I must return home to see to my husband. Thank you all the same for your hospitable invitation." She curtsied and left.

Constance sat in quiet reflection of what the woman had said. After a few moments she realised she didn't want the Bartholomews to hear only James's side of the story. For this reason alone, she gave John enough money to journey to Forsythe Manor with a message, inviting the Bartholomews to visit her at the Scottish summer house. John couldn't drive a car, so he saddled a horse from the stables and galloped away at the animal's top speed.

Two weeks later a carriage arrived at the cottage door and out stepped the Bartholomews, who were welcomed into the front room by Gloria. While drinking a refreshing cup of tea, the couple informed Constance how lonely her husband was and that he was gravely ill.

Edward Bartholomew went on to say, "Your husband asked us to deliver a message to you, to plead for your forgiveness. This is the note." He passed her a slip of paper.

Constance wouldn't hear any of it or even read the note.

"Thank you for your trouble bringing this letter but please do not speak his name to me again."

Margaret Bartholomew sighed watching Constance place the note onto the end table. "Oh, Constance. What has James done that is so bad you cannot forgive him?"

Constance's face turned bright red. She rang a small silver bell on the end table to summon Gloria. "Show my guests to a room upstairs."

Afterwards, Gloria returned to the kitchen, feeling guilty she'd craftily slipped the note into her apron pocket while she was serving tea and scones. She showed it to Minnie as she was preparing dinner. "I thought her Ladyship would destroy it and maybe regret it later."

Minnie stuffed the note in a drawer of the old sideboard beside the scullery door "That letter must be kept safe until her Ladyship is in a quiet mind to read it."

The following morning was sunny with a slight sea breeze. The sky was blue and a pungent scent of flowers floated in the air. Margaret and Constance went for a walk around the fishpond, and when half an hour had passed by, Anna took them tea and cake to eat in the shade of the pagoda.

The two women chatted happily, until Margaret introduced infidelity into the conversation. She gasped when Constance's serenity changed to rage as she picked up stones and threw them hard into the still water as if attempting to smash her own reflection. The rings rippled outward like seismic activity had occurred underground.

Constance roared, "James! I hate you. I hate you!" She held her own hair tightly as if she was about to rip it out.

Margaret moved her chair farther away and remained quiet. Five long minutes later when Constance calmed down, the two women walked back to the house in silence.

Beth had been sitting beside Gloria, looking out of the window when they heard her mother yelling. "What now angry mother? Calm been."

Gloria decided now Beth was a young adult, she had the right to know what had happened. When Gloria finished telling her, Beth frowned while shaking her head."Glo me stay, angry mother. No want near."

"You want to stay here, Beth, to allow your mother's rage to dissipate?"

"Yes dinner here."

Gloria told Constance of Beth's wishes. "Your daughter wants to have her meals in her bedroom today, ma'am, so that you can entertain your guests in private." A white lie but a lie nonetheless.

By this time Constance appeared aloof, as if she didn't care about anything.

Edward and Margaret kept the conversation between them light each day. They daren't mention James's name to Constance for fear she would go into a blind rage again. Eventually, Constance's wrath dissipated and she was glad of their company. The days rolled by until Constance simmered down and was able to talk about James without losing her grip.

"My husband broke my heart when he bedded my daughter's nurse."

Margaret's face flushed bright pink.

Constance carried on speaking. "So I left him. Since we arrived here, my maid has told me that James had bedded many of the manor's female servants."

Edward's face turned morose and appeared shocked. "Milady, I do not want to know any more. My wife's face is red with embarrassment. As for me, well I'm convinced your husband is fully repentant and wishes to make amends...if he can. He is troubled about his actions and would like you to visit him so he can prove his change of heart."

Constance turned her face away from Edward.

The veins in her neck protruded as if they were about to explode so he didn't push the topic again for the rest of the day.

It took many days' worth of conversations to coax her to visit James. One day, while they talked of all the happy times before her husband's behaviour turned sour, Constance said, "Very well, my friends. I will go to visit him, if only to gloat while he wallows in self-pity. We will set off tomorrow. Beth shall remain here."

After a difficult, bumpy journey combined with dreary wet weather, the three friends arrived at Forsythe Manor. When Constance walked inside, she experienced vivid flashbacks of James's infidelity with the servants. It stopped her dead in her tracks. Yet she managed to contain herself and remain calm. Edward took her arm to guide her to the room where James was lying as if someone had turned on a tap and drained the life from him.

James's eyes were sunk deep into his skull. His cheeks lacked so much flesh that his bones were almost protruding through his skin, and his arms were as thin as kindling sticks. He appeared wretched and desolate.

For the first time, Constance felt pity seeing her once-proud husband's life waning. She remembered that she'd wished him dead weeks earlier and felt guilty, thinking her curse had come true.

She left the room to visit the horses and came across a stable hand. "Stableman, why did you stay here when everyone else left?"

"Milady. I stayed to look after the horses. I refused to go near the manor house for a long time."

"And Linda. What of her?"

"You mean the nurse? She left the manor a day or so after you departed for Scotland, milady. He has been alone ever since with neither a cook nor maid. Even the manor gardeners deserted him. Everyone had plainly had enough of your husband's offensive debauchery. The women who left were worried they mightn't get another job if it leaked out about his depraved ways toward them."

"I see. Is there anything else you'd like to tell me?"

"Since the Bartholomews left the manor to visit you in Scotland, milady, I can tell you that your husband has eaten little. He consumes cognac by the barrel load. I figure it's an attempt to numb the constant ache of loneliness."

She thanked him for his openness and kept her thoughts to herself. *So now James doesn't have the strength to open a bottle by himself. He cries like a hurt child, grieving for past losses and for the future loss to come—his life—as it ebbs away like a river surging toward a waterfall. I cannot cope with his snivelling wails. It reminds me of Ginns Workhouse and the asylum.*

Constance dashed away to wander around the grounds in an attempt to find peace.

Discovering James was as unbalanced as she herself had been numerous times came as a bit of a shock to her. She had always known he was weak, or gentle, as some people might prefer to call it. Bad memories of the workhouse and the asylum flooded her mind for hours. *I wish I'd never returned to this miserable manor.*

As evening drew close, her mind was in a total tizzy, not knowing what to do. She sent a message to Father McDougal asking him to pray for her, although she did not invite him to visit.

Sometime later Father McDougal swished through the door like a pompous peacock alone and uninvited. The priest encouraged Constance to give James another chance. She prayed aloud asking God for guidance. When she said, "Amen," Father McDougal spoke.

"Constance, my child. To err is human. The weak are unable to forgive. You are strong and can easily forgive. Have mercy."

She heard his message as though God Himself had spoken it. Consequently, she and Beth moved back into the manor, and so did Gloria, Patrick and John. The Scottish staff, Minnie and Anna, remained at Helen Rose Cottage to take care of it and the gardens in case she needed to return.

Edward and Margaret's cupid work was almost at an end. They helped find more servants for Forsythe Manor and made sure everything was in better order than when they had first arrived.

After a couple of weeks the manor was running smoothly once again, and Constance had managed to store all memories of Linda and James's sexual depravities in the furthest reaches of her mind. She was able to sit with him and nurse him back to health, and once more her heart grew whole.

Even though things were quiet, Beth considered her mother's fiery emotions as a walking time bomb that could explode at the first sign of trouble. However, things went well. The following month Edward and Margaret left for warmer climates, feeling joyful that they'd lent a hand in the couple's reunion.

CHAPTER TWENTY-THREE

All remained peaceful. In 1929 when the first buds of spring arrived. Constance said to the now much stronger James, "I want to become involved with the women's rights movement. I've heard a great deal of work needs to be done."

James had neither qualms nor uncertainties about her decision now he'd gained respect for females after seeing the error of his drunken immoral ways. His heart was finally on the side of women and the rights they deserved. The couple both joined the women's movement to help them in their fight, and fully geared, held meeting after meeting at the manor.

Beth stayed away and confided in Gloria. "Nuts. Not good she. Stress Bad. Crazy this, Glo."

"You'll be fine, Miss Beth, if you can manage to stay out of it all."

Beth often wondered, *will mother go overboard again?*

She was mistaken. Both James and Constance entered a new life together and an adventure based on equality for all.

The years passed rapidly by.

One evening in early summer, Beth enjoyed another moonlight walk with Gloria. Beth fixed her eyes on the romantic full moon and reflected on Jacques. *Hardly a day passes by that I haven't dreamed of you, my Jacques, and our wonderful time together in France. It seems like an eternity away now. Why didn't you follow me? Although we were together for just a short time, I thought you truly loved me. I've missed you so much.*

Just before bedtime Beth gazed through the window and mused once again upon the same hazy rings round the moon she had once looked upon in France with Jacques. Something deep inside of her snapped. She couldn't stand being without him any longer. She typed a letter to Jacques Madeleine at the hospital where they first met in the hopes he still worked there. Beth prayed her missive would find him.

"Mail now Jacques to," Beth said to Gloria.

"It's too late for today's post, miss. The post office is shut. I'll do it first thing in the morning."

Beth couldn't sleep for thinking about the letter finding Jacques.

The next day directly after breakfast, Gloria stole a postage stamp from Constance's desk and wrote the address on the envelope. Beth giggled girlishly as Gloria pulled on her coat. She trundled across the little stone bridge down Primrose lane in the direction of the post office. Late spring blossoms dropped petals all around like pink snow in preparation for the summer berries' arrival.

Gloria watched as the letter was stamped and thrown into the postman's mail sack. On the way home she worried about whether Constance would discover she stole the postage stamp and would discharge her for being a thief. Gloria worried unduly. Her Ladyship, busy with charitable meetings, hadn't noticed one missing.

Weeks turned into months with no word from Jacques. Each night the moon turned paler as it danced around the pink and purple skies of autumn. Beth prayed her letter would find Jacques before winter, before the snows fell, making north England's roads impassable. *Enough time has gone by without you, my beloved Jacques. Mother is always so busy. So what is there for me in life now? Just lonely emptiness. I miss your arms around me.*

About four months after Gloria had mailed Jacques's letter, she spotted a stranger trundling up the driveway after a heavy rainfall, leaving muddy footprints where he'd stepped. She raced downstairs to see who it was, secretly hoping it was Beth's love.

The man introduced himself. "I am Monsieur Jacques Madeleine. I am 'ere from France to see my Beth."

Gloria couldn't believe her ears. "Oh my God. This is indeed a miracle. I'd hoped it was you. Beth will be so pleased to see you after all these years. I know she has missed you so."

"She missed me too? This is good news."

Frantic that his presence would displease Constance, Gloria grabbed Jacques's sleeve and dragged him indoors as fast as she could and sneaked him upstairs. She'd learned from the long-term staff that Constance hated Jacques. They wouldn't say why, just that she didn't want him anywhere near her daughter. This was the reason they'd left Paris in a hurry years before and had never returned there.

Gloria worried about how Constance would react now and felt scared that her Ladyship would discover Jacques was on the property. Gloria's eyes were everywhere, like a spy watching to make sure no one had seen who she'd dragged upstairs.

"Follow me, Jacques." She placed her index finger against her pursed lips, warning him to be quiet. Then she raced him up the last few steps and opened the door to Beth's dimly lit room. With a little push from Gloria, Jacques slipped inside and stood silently in the shadowy area beside the door. At first Beth didn't recognise who was standing there. Jacques paused for a few seconds, unsure what to do and not knowing whose room it was, until Gloria declared, "Beth, I have wonderful news for you. Jacques is here!"

He then stepped forward into the light. Beth noted the same soulful, tender eyes that belonged to the man she'd fallen in love with many years before.

"Jacques my." Unrestricted tears of gladness sprung from her eyes like a fountain. Within seconds, she tilted her head downward, feeling embarrassed of her appearance because she wasn't the pretty young girl Jacques had met in Paris anymore. Now it was autumn 1929 and she was thirty years of age.

"Jacques me now old. Young not."

"Oh, I don't care, my love. I am older too."

He sucked a quivering breath into his lungs in what seemed to be an attempt to hold back his own tears. He sighed. "My dahling. I 'ave never stopped dreaming about you. I still love you more than my own breath."

Beth couldn't believe her ears. *I'm important to someone...to him...to my Jacques!*

He picked her up in his strong arms and whizzed her around and around, the same way as when they had danced on their last evening together in Paris, on Christmas Eve before being wrenched apart.

As they embraced, their auras glowed and melted together in a colourful heavenly embrace. Beth could barely contain her loving excitement. She screeched like an excited child being waltzed around by a parent. *This man, this wonderful man, has travelled all the way from France. For me!*

Something inside her ignited with passion. For the first time since

Paris she felt like a complete, sexy woman. Her stomach throbbed and her heart pounded.

With his eyes full of tears, Jacques returned her to the chair and said in his sexy French accent, "Beth, ma chérie. Your eyes...oh how they still sparkle. I have missed you so much. I went back to ze hotel after ze dance but you had disappeared. I thought I'd lost you forever. No one would tell me where you were or would give me your English address. I remembered you were going to Italy so I went there in search of you. Oh, dahling, I've thought of nothing but you each day. I love you, Beth. You are my soul. Please, please, will you marry me?" He dropped to his knees in front of her and his kneecaps banged down hard on the floor. But he didn't seem to care.

Beth's tear-filled eyes widened. Her heart seemed to stop dead. Then it raced faster as each heartbeat rolled into the other and vibrated as one tuneful note.

Jacques continued, "Beth, my love. I will feel like ze king if you accept my proposal. I want to kiss you a million times each day for ze rest of my life. I never want to spend another moment without you again." He continued to kiss her face until she was breathless.

Beth nodded. "Yes, yes me Jacques."

Gloria gasped with happiness and tears ran down her freckled cheeks.

Beth cried a river of euphoric tears and Jacques dried her tears with his lips.

"You have jest made me ze happiest man in ze world!"

Looking unsure of how Constance would react to their marriage, Gloria whispered, "Congratulations, you two. I'm so happy for you. But, Beth dear, you must listen to me now. Your mother might be annoyed about your pending marriage and put a stop to it. Why don't you both elope to Gretna Green, in Scotland, to marry over the anvil? Patrick and I could make up a story that we're going to Helen Rose Cottage again for a holiday. We can tell your parents you're bored and the break would perk you up. I think that plan might work. They can't do anything once you're married."

Beth laughed and screeched. "Yes!" Her arms and legs thrashed, demonstrating how thrilled she was with Gloria's scheme. Jacques and Beth laughed, cried and embraced all at the same time like a couple of teenage soul mates.

That night at dinner Gloria mentioned the Scottish holiday to Constance and James while Jacques remained upstairs out of sight.

"My wife and I have been rather busy, Gloria. I didn't realize how neglected dear Beth felt." James turned to his wife. "Dearest, a holiday would be a good thing for her."

Constance replied, "All right, Gloria. Prepare everything and Patrick will go with you and Beth."

Gloria packed their bags directly after dinner, but didn't tell Patrick about Jacques until the following morning.

"Look Patrick. Jacques showed up last night."

Patrick's face lit up with disbelief and joy all rolled into one. "Does Constance know?"

"No, and Beth is going to Scotland today to marry Jacques over the anvil. You must not tell a living soul about this plan, all right? Go and pack your bags, because you're coming too."

Patrick laughed nervously and then his laughter turned to tears. "Ma wee lassie has found her love again."

"No, Patrick. He found her from a letter I posted months ago to that French hospital he used to work in. We prayed he was still there."

"Oh, Gloria. I couldn't be happier. Righty-oh! What do I have tae do?"

"You must keep Jacques on the floor of the vehicle until we're ready to leave."

"That's easy. Just bring him over in ten minutes."

Patrick took Beth and their trunks to the car. Gloria sneaked Jacques over to the garage disguised in a cloak, and he lay flat on the car floor until they drove away. Constance and James waved goodbye. When they had travelled some distance, Jacques climbed onto the seat beside Beth.

Their first stop in Scotland was the anvil at Gretna Green. Gloria dressed Beth in a white gown that she'd stolen from Constance's closet and Patrick picked some wildflowers for a bouquet. When the ceremony was over, they continued on to Helen Rose Cottage for their honeymoon.

Patrick was an old romantic. He told the newlyweds to wait outside their room for a few minutes so he could spread flower petals on the floor and their bed. He felt so happy that his wee Beth had found her long lost love. "Beth ma wee-yen, if I die tomorrow then I'll die in joyful contentment."

Six weeks later they returned to Forsythe manor. As Gloria announced Mr. and Mrs. Madeleine, she and Patrick listened for verbal fireworks. Constance's comment floored them both.

"Beth isn't a child anymore. She can do as she pleases."

"I agree. Welcome to the family, Jacques," James said.

"Dad me loves you, mother too me love."

James smiled warmly. "Anything for you, precious angel. Your mother and I just want you to be happy."

Their reactions made Beth wish she'd sent a letter to Jacques sooner.

The newlyweds used the upper floors of the manor as their

temporary matrimonial home until rooms on the ground level were adapted to suit Beth and her husband.

The following year Jacques gave Constance a wonderful surprise. "You will become a grandmother very soon, milady."

She was delighted that a new life was coming into the world, but the actual birth worried her because of her daughter's medical condition.

James hired Dr. Madelany and Dr. Irvine, two notable surgeons, to examine Beth. Both doctors decided a caesarean birth would be the best course of action.

As the foetus grew larger, Beth's breathing was laboured, especially when her baby moved or kicked inside her. She had never imagined how hard it would be to experience seizures as well as a full term pregnancy. Beth spoke about her feelings to Jacques, who also worried about the birth.

"Jacques no again baby."

He pleaded with her to type her exact wishes. "Ma chérie. I wish your words were clearer. Please, you must type your exact thoughts. I do not want to misunderstand you."

Beth typed her message clearly. "Jacques, my love, I don't want any more children. This pregnancy has been hard for me to bear, along with spasms. I hope you are agreeable, darling. I think it's for the best."

Regardless of his personal wishes, Jacques sympathised with his wife and instructed the surgeons to perform sterilization during the caesarean section. As the doctors began to operate, they realised Beth bore two babies. Neither doctor thought much of the blue spirit that emerged during the surgery. Thinking the blue shape was the moon reflecting onto the mirrors, they dismissed it. After they checked the health of both babies and found them to be in the pink, the blue spirit whizzed round the manor singing. Two more blue spirits manifested and joined in the song. Even the doctors noticed. They couldn't explain any of it away, so they ignored the whole incident.

Beth and Jacques named their elder twin girl Connie, after Beth's strong willed mother, and called their other baby Angela, after the angels in heaven.

In 1934, when Angela and Connie had reached three years of age, their grandmother died of consumption. Beth's heart was crushed into a trillion sections, each piece feeling its own individual agony.

The family held a funeral service befitting a queen in Saint Nicholas Church, the same church Constance and James were married in. Her final resting place was to be at the eleventh-century Saint Bees Priory in its tiny walled cemetery. After the public service, the family cortège followed Constance's body on her last journey on earth, from Whitehaven to Saint Bees inside a black hearse pulled by four plumed stallions.

The path that flanked the Beowulf Stone arch had large, uneven rocks protruding from the ground. Yet somehow an aged Patrick, although limping, managed to push Beth safely to her mother's graveside as her family followed behind. Father McDougal held a small family service at the grave. Beth cried so many tears that she couldn't make out anything further than three feet in front of her or even see the blue spectre standing with her for comfort.

The sun broke through the clouds during the prayer recital at the graveside. As it shone onto the ground, they lowered Constance's casket. Another blue light appeared and flickered like a cool fire beside her coffin. Deep inside the light was the figure of a female. All of a sudden, Constance appeared beside it.

A third spirit remained at Beth's side.

Beth sensed the first unknown entity had manifested to guide her mother to a better place. Perhaps it was Constance's own mother. Her heart exploded with love when she glanced at her stepfather because she knew he could see it too, since his eyes were full of so much love.

No, Beth thought, *my incredible mother is not dead. She is alive, inside the blue flame for all eternity.*

It took more than two years before Beth recovered from the loss of her mother. Even with Jacques and her children at her side, she was terribly lonely, like something had hacked her heart from her chest.

In 1937, seventy-three-year-old Patrick departed this life. Beth missed him more than she missed her mother. He had always been there to protect her. Patrick had no living family that anyone knew about, so he was interred in the family plot at Saint Bees Priory beside Lady Constance. The few words on his memorial plaque read, "Here lays Patrick MacCrinan, a Scottish Saint from Ginns."

Meanwhile James Sr. found another nurse to help middle-aged Jacques and Gloria take care of Beth and the children. He took his time to choose her carefully. Mrs. Lillian Canterbury, a jolly, vivacious young senior, was the best fit. As time went by she and Beth became close friends.

One day Lillian went shopping in Whitehaven and she overheard two women talking about one of Beth's earlier nurses, Jennifer Thompson. Lillian told Beth what she'd heard.

Intrigued and still struggling vocally, Beth said, "What? Me tell."

"Well, those two chatterboxes said that Jennifer had gone to the Americas to live in a convent, to study the meaning of life. I don't know how they knew where she had gone. They said they haven't heard anything about her since."

Lillian saw a look of concern growing on Beth's face.

"I'm sure she will be all right, Beth dear."

"No tell stories, Lil more. Missed Jen," Beth said.

"Sorry, dear. I missed the first part of their conversation so there is no more to tell you. Just that she had gone to the Americas to study. I'm sure she'll be fine."

In time, the manor became a pleasant place to live again. Everyone cheerfully went about their business, until there was another sudden death—Beth's stepfather James Forsythe.

Her family was disappearing fast.

It rained hard the day of James's funeral. The graveyard had more than three inches of water floating on the heavy clay soil with nowhere to drain. Although typical for Cumbrian weather, it seldom rained much harder than that day. It was like thousands of angels cried for James's death. Water gushed through the cemetery toward the perimeter walls. It rapidly loosened a few headstones and they fell over.

Jacques would not allow his family to exit the limousine to stand beside James's grave, in case they slipped. He insisted they stay in the vehicle. The limo driver took them as close as he could, and the family embraced inside the car for the whole service. Afterwards, Beth's shrinking family and a few friends returned to the manor to hold a private wake.

No one slept that night.

Three days later a lawyer arrived to read Mr. Forsythe's will. Past discussions with his own children, James Jr. and Martha, had alerted him to the fact that they didn't want the property bequeathed to them. So his stepdaughter Beth received the manor and a half-share of all he owned. Everything else would be shared equally between James Jr. and Martha, who'd left the region directly after the funeral. They planned to live and work in the south.

The manor was quiet without young James and Martha, and without Beth's children, Angela and Connie. They were now young adults who attended Lancaster University.

Jacques lived long enough to see his precious daughters succeed in their chosen professions before he died in 1962. His funeral was a small quiet one at Saint Bees. No one knew who to notify about his death, except to inform the hospital in France where he used to work. Lillian and Beth hoped someone there would inform Jacques's family of his passing, if they knew he had any.

CHAPTER TWENTY-FOUR

Time rolled by amazingly quickly for Beth, while she lived through a haze of emotions and regrets, until she reached the grand old age of 101. Loneliness practically killed her many times, without her family and Jacques by her side.

She always hoped her children would return much more for their holidays, but they never did. Compared to their city life, the manor was a dreary place for them to be. They only returned home on special occasions like Christmas.

On seventh, March, 2000, Lillian popped to the butchers to buy minced beef for supper and overheard two women talking. Apparently, Mrs. Harris, a prominent psychic, planned to return to Whitehaven the following week to search for a retirement property.

Lillian sped home on two wheels, around bends in the roads, to tell Beth the news because she was heavily into anything about the psyche and paranormal. Lillian's news provoked a spasm.

When Beth's seizure drifted away, she typed an invitation to the psychic, requesting her to hold a private sitting at the manor. Animated, Beth fidgeted and fumbled at her typewriter with great enthusiasm. Her typing stick slipped from her mouth many times and flew across to the other side of the room. Poor old Lillian's back and knees ached with having to bend and pick up the stick.

When Beth finished typing she said, "Lil tell no, house. Quiet keep. Take psychic to."

Lillian understood her need for privacy and jumped into her little red car to deliver the letter by hand.

Mrs. Harris arrived at the manor later that afternoon. She and Beth retired to the cheery yellow drawing room. The psychic spoke with a portentous tone. "Milady, you will soon see the reincarnation of your twin sister, Sarah."

Beth's eyes lit up and her legs writhed, declaring her inner glee. "More tell." A spasm followed.

Mrs. Harris called for Lillian who rushed in to make sure Beth didn't hurt herself.

"Will she be all right, nurse?"

"Yes, Mrs. Harris. She'll be fine. Her seizures are normally short lived. Except her last one was strong. Your meeting is taxing her, so you will have to leave now."

Although drained by the seizure, spunky Beth insisted Mrs. Harris should stay. "Finish tell."

"Very well, milady. As long as you feel strong enough."

"Hmm...quick."

"You will see the reincarnation of your twin sister, Sarah, in a few days' time at a past-life meeting in the White Heaven Weekly employees' hall. In this lifetime, your sister Sarah is a columnist and her name is Sally Witherspane."

The old woman, unable to contain her joy, grew so excited she practically fell out of her wheelchair.

Lillian had been watching from the hallway and re-entered the room.

"Beth, you're exerting yourself too much today. Please remember what the doctor told you. You must remain calm."

Beth knew her death was imminent at 101 years of age. She was in constant pain and eager to die because she firmly believed she would rejoin her husband. She said to Mrs. Harris, "Me soon Jacques see?"

The psychic nodded wholeheartedly with a beaming smile on her face, "Yes, milady. You will."

"More?"

No, milady. That is all I know. Lillian thinks you need to rest now. Goodbye."

The psychic walked toward the door to leave. "I can see no other event in Beth's future," she said to Lillian as she passed by, "except attending the past-life meeting soon."

Lillian was in a hurry to put Beth to bed after so many seizures and didn't pay attention to her words. She ushered the psychic outside, while cramming sixty British pounds into her hand as payment for the private session. Once again the psychic tried to tell Lillian the meeting would be

Beth's last day on earth. But it was like talking to a garden post. Lillian just didn't want to hear any of it.

The week passed at a snail's pace for Beth. Lillian was surprised to learn, from a flyer in their mailbox, that there really was a past-life group in town that weekend on twelfth, March. She showed it to Beth. "That psychic is good, eh?"

Beth was so excited she suffered a small spasm.

"I take it you still want to attend then?"

"Yes," Beth said. Her inability to restrain her enthusiasm made her bite her tongue.

After the past-life meeting ended, Lillian spoke to James Jr., who had arrived a day or two earlier with his nieces for holiday. She didn't dare mention that the psychic had already said the previous week that this would happen.

"Her Ladyship has been in an exceedingly emotional state all evening, sir. When we were about to leave the community hall tonight I saw her wink and smile at a young female reporter."

James Jr. shrugged his shoulders. He too was growing old and weary. "Lillian, just put her to bed please. I'm tired. Let's talk about what happened at the meeting tomorrow."

That night Beth slipped into a blissful sleep and did not awaken.

Her obituary, written by Sally Witherspane from the White Heaven Weekly, concluded, "The surviving relatives of the deceased Mrs. Madeleine claim that a strange blue light encompassed their relative's bedroom on the night she died. It remained there until dawn. Her funeral service will be at Saint Bees Priory. Only family flowers at the graveside. All other floral tributes may be donated to the children's ward at West Cumberland Hospital."

The family concealed the rest of the story from the public, for fear of ridicule. It went something like this...

James Jr. and his nieces observed six phantom images holding hands at the centre of a blue light. They were Beth, Constance, James Sr., Jacques and Patrick. No one recognized the sixth figure.

The last glimmer of blue faded at dawn. The hymn that Jennifer used to sing for Beth when she was younger was heard coming from beyond the willow tree.

I sing a song of the saints of God
Patient and brave and true.
Who toiled and fought and lived and died
For the Lord they loved and knew...

Two new maids hired by James Jr. rushed outside to investigate the melody. They returned with pasty faces, reporting they had seen three females and three males strolling together along the garden path by the big old willow tree.

James Jr., almost one hundred years old himself, turned to face the maids. "Who were they?"

"Well, sir," one soft-spoken maid said, "I asked them who they were. They said their names were Lady Constance, James, Beth, Jacques, Patrick and Jennifer."

The old man fell backward into the wingchair behind him, flabbergasted, and his face drained of colour. A parlour maid who had worked at the manor for a few years yelled, "You're lying. Why would you see this vision and not the staff they know?"

The maid looked James Jr. directly in his eyes. "I'm not telling untruths, sir. She will tell you." She pointed to her co-worker, who gave a swift nod in reply.

The maid continued, "And as God is my witness, sir, a dazzling blue light surrounded them." The maid drew a large circle above her head excitedly with her arms. "We could still hear them singing as the six of them...well, sir, they floated upward and became one light, and then it burst into a huge sparkling rainbow. Oh sir, you should have seen it. It was so gloriously blue and bright." She glanced at the window. "Begging your pardon, sir, but if you look outside now you will see it still adorns the sky."

James, his grieving relatives and the other staff moved across to the window to see it themselves. They grew speechless upon seeing the bluest rainbow they had ever seen. The window was open and in the distance a melodious singing echo floated through the air. It sounded like it was saying, "Goodbye. We are happy. We have all found each other again. Jennifer is here too. Sally, mother says she loves you. She loves you all. Jacques and I love you all. Children, look after each other until we meet again. Goodbye, goodbye..."

James Jr. moved away from the window, clearly in awe, and he flopped into the chair beside Beth's typewriter. One of his hands rested on her old desk. He spotted something underneath—a letter typed by Beth and dated seventh, March. Five days before she died.

"Why did this paper suddenly appear here? Surely someone must have seen this. Who put it here?" James Jr. said, shaking the paper. He looked at everyone in the room for a response.

"How strange. I don't know who would have put it there, Uncle," Connie said.

James gleaned from the letter's contents that his sister knew her death was looming. The missive was addressed to Harry Johnson, the new part owner of the White Heaven Weekly, it read as follows.

Dear editor,

I know death is upon me. I want to ask your readers to be considerate of one another. All life must be cherished. Please ask your readers not to call disabled people spastic or other unkind names. We are human beings with feelings. These words hurt us more than if our hearts were impaled on a spear. My name is Beth. I was never spastic, or possessed by a demon, as I've been called throughout my life by both children in the workhouse and adults in our community.

When I was born it was taboo to give birth to a fatherless child, or even keep a disabled child like me. Many of us suffered or died unnecessarily. Innocent children were thrown onto the merciless streets and left to starve. Some malformed children were sold to circuses for amusement. Some were murdered at birth. I've been unable to speak properly throughout my whole life. My muscles always misbehaved, although my mind was active. Then I learned how to use a typewriter. There are few who understand how it feels to be a prisoner inside your own body as I am.

Sometimes I thought God was punishing me for something I had done wrong in a past life. Then one day my life became rich. I found my beloved husband, and when my Jacques died I missed him terribly. However, I knew I'd see him again one day. Past lives and life after death exist. Do not be afraid. We are all placed on earth to do different jobs or to help each other and, most importantly, to grow.

Goodbye. I offer my love to all. Until my next incarnation.

Mrs. Beth Madeleine

(Lady Elisa Witherspoon. 1899-2000)

EPILOGUE

A week after Beth's funeral, Sally Witherspane moved into the manor as instructed by Beth Madeleine. Lillian lived there for another year to assist Sally to fit into her new surroundings. James Jr. and Martha rang her from time to time and visited for short holidays.

Within a few weeks of Sally moving in she had an idea. She needed extra income to cover expensive renovations, so she hired three staff and turned part of the manor into a hotel for wealthy spiritual fanatics. Her new venture became a great success. Sally kept the west wing for herself so she could gaze at the wonderful sunsets across the Solway Frith.

While working together at the newspaper office, Peter Flannigan and Sally became special friends. They wandered around the interior of Saint Nicholas Church and the Holy Trinity Gardens and read the old headstones. Sally discovered the plaque which mentioned the burial of George Washington's grandmother, Mildred Warner Gale, and her slave girl, Jane.

Peter said, "Do you know this old church burned down in 1971, the same year you were born, Sally? I think it was the same month too."

"Wow, Peter. I wonder if there was a spiritual connection involved."

"What, Sally?"

She shook her head while shrugging her shoulders, smiled and said nothing, deciding the answer was for another tale.

When Sally gazed at the chapel's beautiful etched glass doors on gloomy days she glimpsed a blue glow radiating inside. It warmed her soul. She told no one and was unsure if Peter had seen it or not. She didn't care. For now it would be her little secret.

Peter visited Sally at the manor on weekends, and she proudly showed him the Witherspoon paintings. She told him stories about her ancestors, and particularly about Beth and Beth's mother, Lady Constance.

"Strange how things have turned out isn't it, Sally? There you were adopted and didn't know you would inherit all of this." He looked around at the finely carved woodwork. "You must feel so lucky."

"Yes, Peter. I do. I also feel blessed that I took a chance to let you into my life."

Peter blushed.

He wined and dined Sally, escorted her to movies and enjoyed cozy chats with her beside the morning-room fire. After six months he plucked up the courage to pop the question and she said yes. Their marriage ceremony was in the chapel of Saint Nicholas Church. After the wedding, Sally and Peter spent a weeklong honeymoon in Storrs Hall, overlooking Lake Windermere.

While they were away, the foundation stones in Ginns' cellar shook. Because the area didn't suffer from major earthquakes, the townspeople assumed the rumbling was just the old building settling down after it had been turned into a modern store. No one remembered about the demon imprisoned behind the ancient arch in the cellar so long ago, or that whenever a *special* child was conceived it enraged the demon. And now the evil entity grew more incensed than ever before, because it knew that a child would be born at the manor, a stronghold against evil forces because of the blue entities who resided there. And this was why the earth had shaken.

When the newlyweds returned from their honeymoon, Peter moved into the manor with his bride. They continued working at the newspaper's office together, and before two months had passed by, Sally's doctor told her she was pregnant. The expecting parents were ecstatic.

Sally took maternity leave six months into her pregnancy. She continued writing the Witherspoon memoirs to fill her time and titled it *White Heaven Women* after the hall which had reunited her with her half-sister, Beth Madeleine. Sally considered it a fitting name for their family's record.

Peter didn't mind when his wife worked on the Witherspoon memoirs three evenings a week. He loved her no matter what she did. As she wrote, and regardless of the weather, he meandered through the grounds to admire several dancing blue illuminations. Their special blue glow made him feel secure. Peter normally confided in his wife about everything but not about the blue lights. They were his secret.

And Sally didn't tell him that three blue spirits sang lullabies to their unborn baby every day. The unusual lyrics made her wonder if the child she carried was the reincarnation of another soul.

More importantly, whose soul would it be?

Message from the Author

Dear reader:

"Once upon a time..." roughly one hundred years ago (I'm a senior), I lived near Whitehaven, a town in north England. I worked as a home nurse for a woman suffering from Cerebral Palsy. She could hardly speak, but could use foul language like a trouper! It was enough to make your toes curl up, and due to her lack of speech, I didn't try to stop her swearing. She enjoyed listening to short stories I'd written either in the local pub or while I pushed her around in her wheelchair.

This woman inspired me to write a serious novel, and up popped Beth, a woman with the same physical problems. Not happy with just those physical problems, I wanted the setting to be in a different century with long gowns and carriages, and to include reincarnation. Tricky, with little dialogue from one of the main characters.

As Beth's story progressed, her mother and other family members appeared and all of a sudden the story began to write itself. As my creative muse took charge, local historical workhouses and asylums jumped into the fray and from nowhere blue ghosts floated in, threatening to spook my cat. What a mix! And why blue ghosts? How can a new writer include all these things and still write something that is readable?

With Beth's lack of communication and my own inexperience at writing for adults, WHITE HEAVEN WOMEN took countless re-writes. A few years into its creation, I joined a Canadian online writing group where I met Cheryl Kaye Tardif. Members would email work to the group for critique and Cheryl said she liked my story and encouraged me to continue with its creation. Eventually, friends charmed me into submitting to publishers. After a few refusals, I gave up and returned to the drawing board. By this time, Cheryl had begun her own publishing company and suggested she might publish WHITE HEAVEN WOMEN. You know the rest.

Note: Whitehaven residents call their town "White 'eaven," droping the 'h' and pronouncing the 'ea' as in 'egg.' That's somewhat ironic because their sandy beach is black from disused coal mines and there are no white cliffs or rocks.

~ Jessie

About the Author

Jessie B. Tyson was born, raised and educated in Cumbria, England. She has worked in Canada and England as a Community Support Worker, mostly with disabled adults, and she volunteers regularly.

Jessie first began writing children's and fantasy stories, and then moved on to adult readers. She's always enjoys turning her dreams into something readable.

Jessie currently lives in Victoria, BC, with her two kitties and her vivid imagination.

http://jessiebtyson.blogspot.com/
http://www.facebook.com/JessieBTyson
http://twitter.com/JessieBTyson

IMAJIN BOOKS

Quality fiction beyond your wildest dreams

For your next ebook or paperback purchase, please visit:

www.imajinbooks.com

www.twitter.com/imajinbooks

Made in the USA
Charleston, SC
04 December 2016